When the *Honeymoon* Is Over

Holly M. Jewell

AuthorHouse™
1663 Liberty Drive
Bloomington, IN 47403
www.authorhouse.com
Phone: 1-800-839-8640

© *2011 Holly M. Jewell. All rights reserved.*

No part of this book may be reproduced, stored in a retrieval system, or transmitted by any means without the written permission of the author.

First published by AuthorHouse   2/22/2011

ISBN: 978-1-4567-3886-0 (hc)
ISBN: 978-1-4567-3885-3 (e)
ISBN: 978-1-4567-3887-7 (sc)

Library of Congress Control Number: 2011902652

Printed in the United States of America

Any people depicted in stock imagery provided by Thinkstock are models, and such images are being used for illustrative purposes only. Certain stock imagery © Thinkstock.

This book is printed on acid-free paper.

Because of the dynamic nature of the Internet, any web addresses or links contained in this book may have changed since publication and may no longer be valid. The views expressed in this work are solely those of the author and do not necessarily reflect the views of the publisher, and the publisher hereby disclaims any responsibility for them.

Dedicated

To God
From whom my blessings come from
To my Daddy Johnny E. Williams Jewell RIP
To My Mommy and son
Jordan I love you
And
Barron J. Courtney
Thank You

Acknowledgements

I would like to first thank God for giving me a vision and passion for this craft, if it wasn't for the experiences and the times He said no, wait, not yet, this book would be just a dream. Second I want to say thank you to my family. Mommy I love you and thank you for being such a loving, caring, and giving woman, blessed by God to stand when standing became a test of your faith. To my sister Jamie my best friend, I will pass that math class and get my degree if it kills me lol. To my son Jordan I love you and I couldn't ask for a better child keep making me proud, also to my nephews Dez and Derilyn keep doing what you do best get it done and to my brother in law Derilyn how about those Saints!

I would like to give special thanks to my friends who stood by me during the most difficult time in my life; the passing of my Father Johnny E. Williams Jewell, to Fay, Punkin, Lashonda, and Linda I couldn't ask for a better group of friends you guys are simply the best! To Dee thanks for all the Taco Bell trips and to Christina thank you for the coupons to McDonalds love those free frappe. I certainly can't forget my sister in law Djuna when I started this journey to the Dallas area I needed a place to lay my head, you opened your doors and for that I will forever be grateful. I would also like to say thanks to Joe for getting the glitches out of my computer during this process and to Allen thank you for checking my car before I hit the 20 heading southeast to the boot.

To my friend Donnie you are in fact a wonderful assistant thank you for everything you do and to my models Rochell, Nessa, Terrance, Romie and Malcolm you are simply the best thank you guys and just maybe we will make it to Essence! On that note I would like to thank L & G photography for your beautiful work of art. Last but not least thank you to my Facebook family and friends for your love and support God bless.

Chapter 1- -Kelly Jackson

Dear Kelly:

I can't do this anymore I'm tired and I know you are too, I'm asking you to move off post when you get the chance. I don't love you anymore I don't know why I just don't. I know you will be hurt, but I can't help that. I'm sorry, but I can't pretend any longer.

God Bless you,

Ethan

I drop the letter and immediately found myself doubling over from emotional pain. My heart never felt so much anxiety I fall to the floor; and grab my chest feeling my heart pumping fast and furious, I felt like everything I worked so hard for was in vain. Screaming out to God as loud as my voice box would allow I yell.

"My husband said he doesn't love me anymore, why God why? I have prayed, I have tried to be a good wife, I did what I was supposed to do why are you doing this to me what have I done so wrong?" My face was red, eyes were puffy, I cried for hours.

Not knowing what to say I sat there in shock for hours at a time. I didn't eat, drink, nor did I pick up the phone for two days, my family and friends came by to see me I didn't answer the door. I never felt so hurt and betrayed in all my life. It was like someone has taken a knife and cut out my very soul, as well as my heart. This jackass had the nerve to leave me a note on the coffee table, who does that?

"How dare he do this to me?" Those were the first soft spoken words I said out loud since I screamed out to God two days ago. I slowly climb out of bed and look in the mirror, only to find myself looking a hot mess, my hair was all over my head, eyes were puffy, and spirit crushed. I had to get it together and soon, it was only two weeks before the Christmas holidays. What a way to spend Christmas, looking for a place to stay. I had to speak to the almighty because I didn't know what else to do. I fall to my knees and press my face against the carpet on the floor.

"Lord, I ask that you please forgive me of my sins and I'm asking you to give me strength to make it through this hard time, this is your servant's prayer Amen."

I felt an uplift of divine power while rising from my knees. I took a shower, put on a pair of sweats, pulled my hair up in a ponytail, grabbed my black Guess hand bag and keys and headed to my husband's unit. The moment I pulled in the driveway to park my car my heart skips a beat; I collect my emotions and take one last look in my rear view mirror. I step out the car with confidence and a diva attitude as I slowly make my move towards the office door sporting my Guess shades to hide my original pain.

"Hello Captain Moore, how are you today?"

"I'm doing just fine madam and you?"

"I'm okay is my husband in?"

He looked at me with pity in his eyes I could tell his buddies knew what was going on. "Yes he's in his office you need me to get him for you?"

"No, I got this I need to see him now."

"Madam you're welcome to go right ahead."

At this point I didn't give a damn if I was welcomed or not

When the Honeymoon Is Over

because I was mad as hell I walked through the doors as if I owned the place feeling like crap but looking like Tyra Banks stepping into a photo shoot. I hold my hand bag on my left arm and my shades continue to cover my pain. I sashay down the hall as I pass the handsome soldier boys as they watch my light brown thick thighs 5'9 frame make way closer to my husband's office door. I take a deep breath and knock softly as my heart pounds loudly due to the anxiety attack that I felt invading my space, but I struggled to remain calm.

"Come in"

I walked in, his back was turned he was talking on the phone. He had no idea it was me standing there listening to his sorry ass.

"Baby, I'll see you tonight alright got to go someone just stepped in, love you."

He turned around only to see me standing there with my hands on my hips as I play it cool, his bright eyes turned dark and cold. He cleared his throat.

"Oh, Hello Kelly"

He acted unconcern and that really hurt, but at that very moment I became a stronger woman, and for the first time, I saw him for the demon he really is. I didn't say a word, I was too mad to say anything for a second or two. He couldn't look me in the face; he started shuffling papers on his desk trying to look busy.

"Well Lieutenant Ethan James Jackson I just wanted to say thank you for the note that was really noble."

"Look Kelly what else was I suppose to do?"

"Well I don't expect you to do anything!"

"We'll leave!"

I took one hard breath as I walked closer to his desk and position myself on one leg pointing my finger dead in his face, the same face that once captured my heart while placing my other hand on my hip and said firmly.

"First Let me tell you something, I can't believe how you're acting towards me, when all I have ever done was love you and treat you with respect and this is what I get!"

"I'm Sorry_"

"Yes Ethan, for the past two years you been sorry brotha. I tell you this much you have lost the best thing that has happened to you baby believe that!"

I walked out of his office and slammed the door. The soldiers standing outside looked and whispered to one another trying to look busy while peeping behind papers and trying to find out what was really going on. I walked out of that building with a new attitude and a much needed break of this mess, but the pain I felt was nothing I could describe and he would never know how much he truly hurt me.

I hand over eight hundred dollars for my deposit on a one-bed room condo in Alexandria, Louisiana just minutes from the airport where I work. I needed to be strong. At least that's what I keep telling myself; it's all in the attitude. I walked around checking out my new spot. I liked the area; it was really nice and quiet. I ran into one of my new neighbors, he had on a fitted baseball cap turned backwards with an A on it and some green sweats and T shirt, carrying a black Nike gym bag.

"Hello Miss Lady my name is Cory."

He extended his hand to greet me with a hand shake and smile I accepted.

"Hello, Kelly is my name."

He offered a wide grin looking like a damn chess cat peeping in a sea food store.

"I live next door to you."

"That's nice to know."

"Well if you need anything just let me know."

I looked at the handsome man and tried to ignore his outer

beauty. Then suddenly that's when it hit me who he was I snapped my fingers trying to collect my thoughts.

"You look like someone I know, I can't place your face, but I've seen you somewhere before."

"People tell me that all the time."

He winks his eye.

"Oh my no you're that super model Cory Washington!"

He blushes humbly.

"Yes, I am."

"I can't believe you're my neighbor, I read that article on you in Essence Bachelor Edition wow."

"Well I am and if you need anything here is my number call me I want to welcome you to the area."

I blushed as I took his card.

"Thank you."

I was overwhelmed as I walked into my new condo. It had a beautiful open floor plan with a fireplace, pass through bar, crown molding, trey ceilings, and a walk in California closet. The huge bathroom had a spa tub and separate shower but the best feature was the balcony. It over looked the small city and from the third floor, I could see downtown from where I was and I stepped out on it allowing the wind to kiss my face and the sun light to hit my skin, thinking with tears in my eyes I have to love me now and learning to love me was quite a difficult task but I had no other choice since my honeymoon was over.

Chapter 2 - - Jada Knight

I try to live what you call a drama free lifestyle. I'm a mom to a six-month-old daughter name Jordan, and a loving wife of six years to the most carefree spirit filled man name Byron Knight, who is in fact a wonderful father and husband not to mention, he's very easy on the eyes.

My Husband is a very hard worker, At times I think he works too hard, but with him working as hard as he does give me the option to stay at home, but my choice is to work because I was taught that every woman needs a sense of who she is outside of marriage. My checks goes to the bank and every now and then I treat myself to the finer things in life because we're blessed to have such a beautiful life and I give God thanks every day for the type of man I have and for our daughter He blessed us with.

Byron owns a custom paint and body shop just four blocks from our home in Pineville Louisiana not only that, he has a desktop publishing business on the side. He tells me all the time that a man is not a man if he can't take care of his family so he pays all the bills and make sure were ok financially putting money aside for our child's education and rainy days is a must, this is what I love about my husband but sometimes I think it's our blessing and our curse.

I put the key in the door with my daughter Jordan on my hip; I walk in the house put the diaper bag down and go over to the answering machine to check my messages. The first message was from my mother.

"Hey sweetie this is mom, I need to know what time are you bringing Jordan over tomorrow?"

The next message was from my best friend Madison.

"Hey girl what's up? I know your anniversary is this week and I know you have big plans so just give me a short ring when you get in all-right."

I place Jordan down on the floor to let her crawl around while I listen to my next message.

"Hey baby when I get home I need to talk to you about this weekend."

I find myself getting a lump in my throat. He's a good man no doubt about that, but his ass knows how to get under my skin at times.

"I know he's not going to back out of this now!"

I pull off my stilettos and slide into my fun Mickey Mouse house slippers, then walk in the kitchen, and pull out some chicken to bake, I turn around and look into the pantry and grab a box of macaroni and cheese alone with some sweet peas. Jordan crawls over to me and pulls herself up by my leg I bend down to pick her up.

"Mommy wasn't paying any attention to you."

I give her a kiss on the forehead and put her in her bouncing chair so she can kick and bounce till she gets tired. I really had to get out of my work clothes so I decided to go into our bedroom and really get comfortable putting on my big Old Navy tee shirt and sweat pants, so I could really throw down. I walk back into my beautiful open floor plan kitchen and start dinner, while doing so I decided to call Madison back on speaker phone; she picks up on the third ring.

"Hello"

"Hi girl this J what's up?"

When the Honeymoon Is Over

"Hey, Jada how is the family and my God daughter?"

"Jordan is fine and Byron is well_ he's ok."

"You sound a little down what's wrong?"

"Nothing just tired; long day at work is all."

"Honey this is Madison you talking to remember."

"I know, I think Byron is going to cancel our plans again this weekend."

"Aw sweetie I'm sorry, but look on the bright side_"

"What bright side? I'm tired of looking on the bright side I want time alone with my husband."

"I understand."

"Madison, I get tired of playing the good wife I want to be bad with my man sometimes. He works all the time he never have time for me, no sex in about three weeks."

"Honey I didn't know."

"I try to smile and understand and I know he's good to us, but this has got to come to an end. He works twelve-hour days at the shop and when he's off, one of those days he's doing something with his friends. I don't mind, but I want some time alone, I don't know how much more of this crap I can take for real."

"Tell him how you feel; you two have a good relationship"

"I've told him, it's about work and paying bills, which is all right with me I can't complain about that but I need more."

"Honey, men say were never satisfied."

Madison starts to laugh trying to get me to laugh as well.

"Girl don't, play I'm not in the mood."

"I was only trying to be funny."

"I know I'm just so mad."

"How often do you tell him you're mad?"

"Huh?"

"How often do you tell him you're mad?"

"Well I don't like to make waves we have a good marriage."

"Not if you don't tell the man what's on your mind you don't."

"What are you talking about?"

"I know I don't have a man, but that's by choice, but I know how to deal with the brothas trust me. What I'm saying, if you don't let him know what it is you're feeling then you're lying to yourself sista."

"But he's good to us."

"Girl let me break it down to you, for you to understand where it is I'm coming from. He is supposed to be good to you and Jordan; you're his family why shouldn't he be? So often we get caught up with a man who don't do anything right and when he does something right we can't handle it and we don't want to make waves. You better stop being a jelly fish and get a damn back bone girlfriend."

"I guess."

"Guess some hell Jada you're a strong black woman and you need to stop acting like you don't have a say so in this marriage. Byron is a good decent man and we all know by the size of your wedding ring that the man love you ok. But when you signed that contract with him that didn't mean you lose yourself in the mist of the marriage, you play a major part in this too girl."

"You made your point you're so deep."

"It gets deeper, he is doing nothing unusual Jada, you need to let him know how you feel, to me that's not making waves baby that's telling your man that you're not happy with some things he chooses to do. You need him emotional as well as spiritual and you really need to connect with him sexually. You're married so you have that right. Your body wants to have sex and you're not pleased with that being absent from your life."

"I never looked at it that way."

"Honey, I'm serious you need to be heard too. I often see so many of my young sistas settle for less then what they deserve, when something good come in their direction they have no idea how to act because their use to being treated like hookers off the streets, we have to know that were mothers of this earth."

"You are indeed a deep sista with some heavy words to lay on the brothas and sistas."

"Honey, I know my calling it's time you know too. I'm happy that you have a good marriage and I also want to see you get the things you need from your husband. Byron is a decent man like I said before and I see nothing wrong with encouraging him to continue to be, but you need something too that's all I'm saying."

"Thank you girl I needed that pep talk I just might sit down and talk with him tonight."

"You do that because we all need to share what's on our minds."

"I know exactly what you mean."

"Well honey I have class in about an hour maybe we can get together soon."

"I'll like that I haven't seen you in over three months we need to do that real soon okay and give Colin a kiss for me."

"All right will do maybe I'll make that drive to Pineville and see what's up with ya."

"Ok smooches"

"Smooches back at ya."

We both hung up I looked at Jordan and saw that she fell asleep in her chair; she looked so cute and peaceful. Funny how children can get into so much all day long, but the moment they fall asleep they look so peaceful. I left her in the chair asleep while I finish dinner. The phone rings I push the speakerphone button.

"Hello"

"Hello Jada how are you?"

"I'm fine Kobe how you doing?"

"I'm chillen, is Byron in?"

"Nope, he's out he should be home in another hour would you like for me to have him call you when he gets home."

"No I'll catch him later."

"All right, how's your family?"

"They fine"

"That's good, I will tell Byron you called."

"Alright"

Kobe and Byron have been friends since high school when Kobe got married Byron was his best man. Kobe seems to be a really nice guy but that Keisha is a piece of work. Once Kobe and Keisha had a major disagreement and to defuse the situation he decided to blow it off by coming over to our house for a while and cool off. Just so happen Madison was over and we decided to play a game of spades. It was a war between the men and the women the game lasted until 2:00am and would have continued if the doorbell hadn't interrupted. Byron got up from the table to answer the door with me in tow there stood Keisha in her slippers and robe asking if Kobe was here. She heard another female's voice and pushed Byron out of the way and into the house uninvited she enters loud and ghetto that is. She wasn't trying to hear anything we were saying she thought that she caught Kobe in a hellish act of some kind. To her sad surprise she saw Madison standing there with a smirk smile on her face and Keisha rolled her eyes to the heavens because Madison was Kobe's first cousin. Feeling dumb and out of place she just turned around and headed towards the front door with Kobe in tow. He continues to apologize for that night.

Curled up in bed reading a book by my favorite author I wait for my man to walk through the door. I look over at the clock to see that it's already 10:00pm. I pick up the phone to dial his number to see where he could be. Suddenly I hear the front door open, and put the phone down and place the book on my lap. I Pull off my reading glasses and wait for him to enter the room. I hear him heat up the microwave and cut on the TV and change it to ESPN. Finally he decided to walk down the hall and into our bedroom flashing his sexy smile, showing off his polished super white teeth.

"Hey honey" I speak first.

"Hi baby how was your day?"

"Fine, I thought you would be home earlier so we could catch a movie or something."

The 6/4 brotha pulls off his shirt showing off his diamond cut body and jet black skin.

"Baby I'm sorry I had to finish this car I been doing for about a week. I promised this guy I would have it ready by 6:00 Friday evening."

I smile at my hazel eye honey and forgive him for being late.

"Well, okay what's up for this weekend?"

"Oh yeah about this weekend we can't go I'm sorry."

"Sorry baby I been looking forward to this all month and now you're saying we can't go!"

Byron sits on the side of the bed as he rub his hands over his tightly neat dreads trying not to look at me as I sit there with tears in my eyes. He later leans over to kiss me on my poked out lips.

"I was looking forward to this too, but I have to work I have some publishing to do for this couple that's having a wedding in three weeks and they need me to have some place cards and some other last minute things ready for them by Monday."

"You promised me that this weekend was our weekend Byron!"

"Jada honey I know, but we can use the money."

"Okay Byron do what you do."

Byron knew he messed up he didn't say a word he just looked at me as the tears flow from my eyes he hated the fact that I was upset with him but he had to meet some deadlines and maybe I needed to be a better understanding wife and be grateful to have a man that works.

"Honey, I thought the idea of having your own business was that you run it, you don't let it run you?"

"I know, but sometimes I have to put in long hours so that we can live in this house, drive those luxury SUV's_"

"I get what you saying you don't have to explain."

I was furious with this man right now because he simply didn't get where I was coming from and now that our honeymoon stage of our marriage has taken a U turn I had to do something to get to my happy place again.

Chapter 3 - - Madison Courtney

I'm currently a student at Grambling State University in Louisiana with a full time job working for American Airlines. I have a thirteen-year-old son who keeps me on my toes, with his basketball games and school projects. Being a single mom isn't easy but loving Collin Jr. is. Before Jr. Came alone I represented Oakland California, home of the Oakland A's and the Raiders. I'm a graduate of Oakland High School and from there went into the Air Force.

My last duty station was in Shreveport, La. where I decided to stay for a while. That's where I met Collin Pane; at the time he was a student at Grambling State studying to become a lawyer, two years in our relationship is when I carelessly got pregnant with our love child. Collin graduated from college when Jr. was six months old. He later asked me to marry him. I gave it some serious thought but wasn't sure that's what I wanted to do just yet. Because I hadn't finished school I didn't want to rush into marriage and I certainly didn't want to marry him because we had a baby. Collin later moved to south Louisiana where he accepted a job there. I decided to go back to school and work on my degree after Collin Jr. turned ten. While revamping my life, I needed some me time and much needed space to clear my head and do my thing. Having a child was certainly not in my plans, but having a man who wanted me for me and not because I had his baby would not be the idea relationship I was going to settle for. Now don't get me wrong Collin is truly an amazing man but I have to say being the strong black woman I am, I can make a life for myself and my child, being open minded because I know that Collin is in fact a good father to our love child.

Finally I make it home from a long day and walk into my house to find the music sky high.

"Collin Jr. where are you? I know you hear me boy!"

I yell and scream over the sounds of Nelly bumping in my ear. I walk over to the stereo and turn it down.

"Jr., come here!"

Racing out of his room and up the hall to meet me in the living room with the cordless phone in his hand, he smiles and looks up at me with those big brown eyes and long eyelashes and hair all over his head.

"Mom I didn't_"

"I don't want to hear it, why was this radio turned up so loud?"

"Momma, I'm sorry."

"Collin, I heard the music while sitting in my car with my radio on now that was loud!"

"I know mom I'm sorry okay."

"Yeah, yeah whatever, and what's with that head of yours?"

I grab him by the hair and pull him towards me giving him a hug.

"Well, you said you were going to twist my hair this week so I took it down."

"I see, it's so long and thick, and who is on the phone?"

"Oh I almost forgot hello Deshay you still there?"

"Boy, get off the phone right now so we can go over home work."

"Come on Mah just ten more minutes please!"

"Ten and no longer you hear me?"

"Yes"

He went to his room to finish his conversation. I walk down the hall and into my room to take a bath. As I pull off my clothes I hear a knock at the door. I pull the plush terry cloth towel up around me.

"Yes Jr. what do you need son?"

"Momma, daddy's on the phone and he wants to speak to you."

I open the door slightly and grab the phone. I go over to my queen size bed with my big plush terry cloth towel wrapped around my curvy frame I answer with a soft tone in my voice.

"Hello"

"Hey what's up?"

"What's up with you?"

"Nothing I was just thinking about you and Jr."

"Really that's nice I was just thinking about the tub."

"That sounds good to me can I join you?"

"Honey, I think you know the answer to that question." we both chuckle,

"I know I was just having some fun. I have to talk with you about something seriously."

I slowly walk into the bathroom with the phone to my ear listening to what Collin had to say, sitting on the side of the tub pouring bubble bath into my water.

"Madison, can you hear me?"

"Yes, I'm listening my bath water is running I apologize, I just got home and I need this relaxation time."

"Do you need me to call you back?"

"No, I'm listening"

I pull off the towel and slide my body down into the tub with the phone to my ear.

"Talk to me daddy."

We both laugh, suddenly Collin got silent.

"What's up I know it's something you need to holla at me about what's up black man?"

"Well, it's Jackie."

"What about her you got her pregnant?"

"No she's not having a baby I'm careful about things like that."

"So what's going on?"

"Well you know we been dating for two years now and this weekend I have plans to ask her to marry me and I would like Jr. to come and be with us if that's alright with you?"

My heart stood still. Trying not to stumble over my words I said,

"Well Collin congratulations. I'm happy for you."

I found myself a little jealous, but I knew in my heart that Collin was not the man for me, I have always been tight with him, and Jackie was never a problem and Jr. really liked her, but what made this so different, I couldn't understand where these feelings were coming from.

"Thank you I couldn't ask for a better baby mamma."

We both laugh, but this time I really wanted to cry, but I had to be that strong black woman inside and out.

"Well I don't have a problem with Collin coming this weekend as a matter of fact I was going to ask you what was on your date book because some friends of mine were getting together and doing some stuff this weekend."

"Well, I see it all worked out just fine, I will be in on Friday to pick him up."

"That's fine with me."

"I haven't said anything to him about it yet so if you don't_"

"Collin you don't have to worry about me baby you're secret is safe."

"You have a good night."

"You too thanks for calling."

"It's all good!"

"I will see you on Friday."

"Bye my little May Flower."

"Good bye Collin."

Collin was a rare breed; in fact that's what made me fall in love with him in the first place. Jackie was a wonderful woman, the reason why I approved of her, was the fact that she treated our son well. Now these feelings I'm experiencing is something new, and I'm not digging them because my eyes are filled with water and my heart is sadden because of these turn of events. I don't understand but I have to accept the choices I made and suppress these feelings of regret and take this charge and do my time like a woman, and move forward because I knew this day was coming I just didn't know it would be today.

Chapter 4 - - Kobe Richard

I consider myself a hard working twenty nine year old brotha who wants nothing but the best for my family. I've been married to my high school sweetheart for nine years, we were happy at least three of those years, after that it's been hell every since. We share a beautiful daughter name Shayla; she's everything to me and most importantly, she's the common dominator that keeps this family together. Don't get me wrong I love my wife but Keisha keeps her horns out every chance she get, to work on my damn nerves. I say she get a thrill out of making my life pure hell. We split up at least twice a year. She would always say things will change but they seem to get worse each time. I'm tired and stressed to a point of no return and don't know how much more I can take.

"Good morning."

I look at my wife waking up after a long night of battle once again.

"Good morning."

I place my arms around her as we lay next to one another.

"Do you remember my boy Jalen?"

"Yeah, what about him I don't really care to be honest?"

I try to ignore her negative comment as usual and be civil because she is who she is.

"Well he and his girlfriend moved here from Atlanta Georgia about a year ago and he has finally opened his night club called the Black Onyx and opening night is this weekend."

"Ok and what!"

Keisha and I both sit up in the bed.

"I was wondering if you would like to go out with me and we can__"

"No!"

I rub my chin taking a deep breath trying to stay calm.

"Why?"

Keisha looks over at me and rolls her eyes.

"Simply because I said so, you know I can't stand you're simple minded friends." I get out of bed and look down at Keisha finding myself getting frustrated with this conversation real quick.

"Why all my friends have to be simple minded what about your_ Oh I forgot you really don't have any friends only that nosey sister Eve and not to mention your mom the man hater?"

"Look don't start with me today about my family and I won't start with you about your no good family."

"Why my family have to be all that!"

"Well sweetheart that sister of yours is no good and she really makes me plum sick to my stomach!"

"Look, Brenda has nothing to do with this alright"

"You started with me so I will be the one to finish it up partner."

I can't seem to talk with this woman so I walk into the bathroom I don't know why I even try to communicate with that demon. It's always a battle and I'm quite sick of it. I reach into the shower and cut the water on. Shortly after, Keisha walks in and picks up her toothbrush and begins to brush with a mouth full of toothpaste and says.

"What are you doing today?"

I look at her shaking my head trying not to say something crazy.

"I told you last night that I was going to check out some buildings so I can open my store."

She spits out her toothpaste.

"You are going to look for a building?"

I take a hard breath because this woman was getting on my damn nerves for real.

"Yes, that's what I said."

"You don't have to get stupid with me I just asked."

"Well you already knew that!"

"Look Kobe I just asked alright!"

I turn around to get into the shower. She pulls off her clothes and jumps in.

"Hey you"

She taps me on the back while I wash my face with soap.

"What?"

"I want to do something this weekend with you?"

I find my blood pressure raising this bipolar chick is crazy.

"I asked you did you want to go out to the club with me."

"I don't want to do that maybe we can go and see a movie."

" Keisha, why is it when I want to go and do something with you, you never want to do it, but when you want to do something I'm suppose to drop everything and do what you want to do?"

"It's not that I'm not a club person."

"Whatever Keisha I don't have time to argue with you."

I finished my shower and got out before I went off on this woman. I then grabbed a towel out of the closet to dry off as I walk into the bedroom closet to find something to put on. I found an old pair of faded 501's and a t-shirt. Keisha walks in behind me and grabs a black skirt and blue blouse. She looks over at me and smiles. I was too pissed off to return the smile I thought maybe she's loosing it. One minute she's the loving wife and the next she's the hellcat.

"Well Shayla and I are going to the mall today so if you need us call me on my cell." I stopped lacing up my shoes and shot her an incredulous look.

"You know Brenda called last night."

"What about her? She has nothing to do with me taking Shayla out."

"Girl, don't act stupid with me you know Brenda planned this day with Shayla about a week ago."

"I forgot well she and I are going out so she has to plan another time."

"Why don't you plan another day with Shayla?"

Keisha's eyes went tight and her lips pressed together.

"Why I have to make plans with my own daughter. I said that she's not going with Brenda and that's that!"

"Look, whatever problem you have with my sister that's between you and her, this doesn't have anything to do with little Shay alright!"

"I told you Shayla and I are going to the mall I'm not going to say it again."

My face turned blood red at this point my eyes squinted together and my lips went into a knot.

"You know I'm just about tired of you and the way you handle things in this house hold. You need to stop acting foolish and be my wife and set an example for our daughter."

She folds her arms shifting her weight from one foot to the next and rolled her eyes as she begins to yell.

"Foolish who are you calling a fool_"

"See there you go putting words in my mouth I didn't say, never mind woman I have to go you go in there and tell your daughter she's not going with her aunt today I just won't do it I told Shayla last night that she was still going to the circus but you do what you want to do."

"Look brotha no one told you to go out and get you a girlfriend and tear this house apart you did that!"

I balled my fist hitting the wall in anger.

"You know what Keisha you bring Jewel up to me again__ I told you I met her when you and I were not together it was almost a year_ hell maybe it was a year but the real reason_ never mind_"

"Just say it!"

"What you want me to say?"

"Daddy!"

Shayla stood there wiping her eyes I turned around to see my innocent daughter trying to play it cool as I walk towards her.

"Hey honey what you doing?"

"Did Aunt Brenda call yet? I can't wait to go to the circus she promised we can sit close so we won't miss a thing!"

Keisha walked toward her.

"Well honey mommy is going to take you shopping today wouldn't you like that better than going to the circus?"

Shayla looks over at me with big tears forming in her eyes. I couldn't stand the look she was giving me so I walked over and kiss her on the forehead.

"Well baby girl you go get what you're going to wear and I will call Aunt Brenda and see what time she wants me to drop you off at her house alright."

Shayla smiles and hugs me.

"I still can spend the night huh daddy?"

"Well baby we will see what Brenda has to say about it okay now you go get your stuff together."

She went skipping down the hall towards her room. I turn around and look at Keisha. She wasn't pleased at what she just witnessed.

"You know what I can't stand you, you make me sick you bastard!"

My eyes filled with water; her words cut like a knife I wanted to know how long I have before I go over the edge, how can a woman who once praised me with her words of I love now curse me with the same tongue. My heart felt pain but my love for my daughter allows me to remain.

Chapter 5- - Cory Washington

*I*t was already 5:00 a.m. the alarm clock goes off, I roll over, jump out of bed, walk to the bathroom to drain the main vain.
I wash my hands and face, brush my teeth and pop back in the bedroom and throw on a pair of sweats so I can hit the gym.

Being a super model was not as easy as it looked. I had to travel, keep in shape, and study lines for scripts. While earning my degree in Business Management I met an agent name Kimberly, we became friends and started working together. She saw something in me I didn't see in myself. I never thought about modeling until Kim enter my life saying how good I look in front of a camera. I later decided to take some acting classes to further my career. Eight years later here I am doing something most people dream about. The only thing that was missing was the woman that truly had my rib.

I had relationships, which of course didn't work to my liking. Either I meet women who had no direction or women who didn't have a clue if it was handed to them on a sliver platter. Finally I found misses right, Latisha Moss, the woman of my dreams the woman I wanted to spend the rest of my life with but there was only one problem, she was already married. When I first met Latisha she didn't bother telling me that she was married and a year in our relationship I found out that the woman I been spending most of my time with was a liar and a cheat, one because she didn't tell me she was married, and two I had to find out from her husband who gave me a call one night.

I was mad as hell to know the woman I was in love with and wanted to make my wife was already hitched, she had me twisted and messed up for real. When I found this crap out I broke it off for about a month. She told me she was getting out of the marriage because it was over and she didn't want to tell me because she didn't want to lose the best thing that has ever happened to her and my foolish heart bought the damn story and waited like a fool, not to mention a brotha was good to her ass. Three years later I still wanted to know what was taking so long. Next thing you know Tisha was not coming around as much and she made excuses and so on. Of course I was growing tired of the lies so I decided to pay her a visit without calling and there he was out in the yard planting flowers with her ass. Didn't look like a marriage that was breaking up to me. I didn't bother getting out of the car. I drove around for an hour or two thinking about the time wasted with her. I felt like a fool and didn't want to have anything to do with the whore after that, hell I worked very hard to stay out of the media and she played me like a violin.

I decided to move down south to get away from Tisha and start over, so six months later and a new life down south became my world. Since the move I talked with her twice but the relationship was defiantly not the same and never will be. At least I was near my mother and sister who always supported me, sometimes family is all you have.

"Hello"

"Hello Cory, this Olivia what are you doing?"

"I was watching TV just came in from the gym what's up with you?"

"Nothing, I was wondering if I could come over later and maybe we can make it a blockbuster night."

"Well I guess we can huddle up I'll be back early let's say around 9:00 alright."

"That's cool I'll bring popcorn."

"Yeah you do that baby, and I will have some of your favorite wine on ice."

"Sounds good to me good bye Cory"

"Bye baby."

Olivia's an independent beauty consultant with Mary Kay cosmetics. She just made director in the company and was doing well for herself. That's what I liked about her, she didn't ask for anything but my time. I've only been dating her for about one month since I moved to Alexandria. I liked spending time with the beauty queen but wasn't ready for a relationship. My mind and heart belonged to a woman that was not right for me and I knew in order to get self together I had some soul searching to do and only God above could help me out of this one.

Chapter 6- - Jalen Napoleon

*M*oving to Central Louisiana was a decision my girlfriend of seven years and I decided to do. Atlanta Georgia was our home for more than five years, although we love living in the dirty south, we wanted to bring some new flavor to the Alexandria area, that's when we decided to open a night spot called The Black Onyx. It's been a long time coming and finally I see the results manifesting.

I consider myself a blessed man to have such a supportive woman by my side Reagan McQueen didn't hesitate to make this move with me and so I decided to do a little something special to let her know how much I love and appreciate her. I bought her a house in Charles Park community, a well respected neighborhood in the heart of Alexandria not to mention just ten minutes away from the club.

Now, don't get me wrong Reagan is not just a woman along for the ride she's smart, talented, and the head coach for Louisiana College women's basketball team. She's also beautiful, fine, and all that, I wouldn't have it any other way. Beauty and brains is the new trend for men like me. I can't have a dumb flaky woman, not happening here. I'm truly proud of her and the accomplishment she's made. She's only been the head coach in Rebel City better known as Pineville Louisiana for only a year. Since her transition her girls is the best in the state and two of her players were drafted to play for the WNBA. When she's not on the road working she worked hard at home being the best at whatever she did from making love to me, to being an Iron Chef and keeping a clean house. You can say a brother is truly blessed with the best woman ever no drama, no nagging, no stress, what more can a man ask for.

"Honey breakfast is on the table."

"Thanks baby." I sit down and give thanks for my food.

"What are your plans for the day?" I ask while chewing on my hash browns.

"I don't have plans to do anything until tonight oh; I might go to the mall and pick me out a nice out fit to wear. I saw this dress designed by Dolce and Gabbana I liked with the back out and it fits me like a glove I think that's my freakym dress." We both chuckle," Well I tell you what, I really don't want anyone to see my goods as long as it's tasteful, I don't care." Reagan raised her eyebrow.

"Brotha let me tell you something I have too much class to walk around like a hoochie mamma."

"Mah, I know I was only joking please keep your thong on okay!

You know I talked with my boy Kobe he said he was coming to the club tonight and he might bring his wife."

"You're talking about the guy you play ball with every other Sunday?"

"Yes that's my boy."

"Well that's nice, I was thinking about planning a dinner party so we can get together and have a game night, couples only like what we use to do in Atlanta."

"Well let me know when you want to do that maybe we can do it on a Sunday."

"That sounds like a nice idea we can start planning for it next month."

"We, I don't think so baby you came up with the idea so you finish it just let me know and I will be sure to show up."

"Jalen you need to stop!"

"Honey I'm only kidding well I have to jet I have an interview with a girl who I hear is a real good bartender so I will see you later alright." I reach over and kiss Ragan on the lips.

"Thank you for the breakfast it was really good baby." She smiles and says.

"Thanks negro"

"Hey man what's up with ya?" Byron shook my hand and greeted me with a smile.

"Man work and more work you know how it is bra."

"Yeah it's been a while and now I'm doing my thing I know tonight is going to be packed with women from all over that's what's up."

"Man I hear you but you have a fine woman that's going to be all up and through this joint I went to the game last Saturday and Reagan was doing her thang as head coach."

"Ninja you better keep your eyes on that woman of yours, Miss Jada, now she's a five star chick."

"Yeah my wife is a beautiful lady and I love her couldn't ask for a better woman but you know I still have eyes that look but I don't touch not allowed."

Byron was my nigga and he loved his family but sometimes his eyes would get him in a world of trouble. He watched this butter cream skin tone female sashay towards the bar where we sit as she makes her way from the ladies room. I have to admit the 5'9 thick madam had swagger that would make a blind man see. Her hair was shiny and black shoulder length and bounced when she walk like in one of those black hair commercials, and those legs and hips scream baby maker the closer she got the sweeter her smell Bath and Body Works had put in overtime on that sexy sista.

"Man who is that dime piece?"

"Vicky, my new bartender"

"Oh really the sista has it going on, so she can mix drinks huh?"

"Yeah man and I heard she's good at it too."

"Well I know where I'll be hanging out tonight!"

"Man you crazy Jada will kill your behind you better get real."

"I'm just kidding" Vicky walks over to where we were sitting.

"Well Jalen is that all you needed from me today?"

"Yes that's it I will see you at six right?"

"Sho you right" She winked at me and smiled at Byron. I said,

"I almost forgot this is my friend Byron and he will be with us tonight so hook him up!"

" Anything you say, nice meeting you Byron and make sure you come see me tonight and I will serve you Vicky's Power Punch it's a drink unlike any other you tasted trust me it goes down smooth but the results are nice so don't let the smooth taste fool you."

"Oh really I'll holla at ya then sista." She grabbed her bag and walked towards the door.

"Man you have something on your hands that sista ain't no joke."

"I know that's why I hired her she's from New York and the sista from what I hear is all that and then some when it comes to her drink mix for real. She's well known in Atlanta and Miami she's also a DJ from time to time and she knows a lot of people."

"Sounds like you're impressed with Miss Vicky."

"I am but this is business man, just business."

Chapter 7 - - Kelly

I walked every morning when I didn't have a flight so I could stay in shape and keep my mind right. Frost was on the ground but the sun was rising slowly, it was going to be a beautiful day. I was off for the next three days so all I wanted to do was relax and read a book and maybe do a little shopping for my new home. Just getting back from my three-mile walk I climb up the stairs where my condo was only to find an envelope taped on the door with my name on it in big bold red letters. I couldn't put my keys in the door fast enough after snatching the note off. Walking into the house I sit on the couch to read the note.

> *Dear Kelly:*
>
> *I don't want you to contact Ethan anymore he do not want you so you need to get it together. I have him and you want him and he wants me. He will contact you by paper only I just thought you needed to know this.*
>
> *Sign,*
>
> *I got your man!*

Piss to a new level my eyes drew tight my blood pressure was out of control I was hurt but more pissed then hurt. Why is this hooker writing me a letter and how did she know where I lived. I haven't contacted Ethan since last week when he called me and wanted to have dinner and discuss getting back together. Of course I let him say what he had to say but I'm not trying to hear his fictitious stories. I folded the letter up and placed it back in the envelope. I then heard a knock at the door; I went to the door and screamed.

"Who is it?"

"It's me Cory is it a bad time?" I opened the door and asked with an attitude.

"What do you need?"

"Nothing, did I catch you at a bad time?"

"Yes you did."

"Well I want to apologize I'll come back another time." I slammed the door in his face. I then thought about what I did and realize it wasn't his fault. He was really a friendly guy I quickly opened the door to find him walking into his apartment.

"Wait Cory" He slowly turns around and looks at me waiting for me to say something.

"I owe you an apology please come in and have a seat I need someone to talk to."

He smiled and said "You're not going to pull a gun on a brotha? Better yet you're not going to slice me up and have my head and ass in the freezer for all the neighbors to smell a week from now is you?" We both laughed.

"No I won't do any of that stuff I'm just a little upset right now and you came up and_"

"Hey you don't have to explain I been there too."

"I bet you have!"

"What you trying to say men don't hurt?"

"No I'm not saying that, all I'm saying is__ well I don't know what I'm saying." I broke down in front of him a stranger something I'm not accustom to doing. He places his hand on my back and starts to comfort me.

"What's the matter?" Cory says as he wipes a tear from my eye.

"I just got this note on my door and it's from my soon to be ex husbands girlfriend."

When the Honeymoon Is Over

"Why is she contacting you?"

"I really couldn't tell you because I really don't know."

"Well don't cry you want to sit down." We both walk over to the couch. Cory didn't know what to do. He put his right arm around me and pulled me close to him.

"You know what?" I didn't say a word but cry silently, as I begin to listen to Cory's voice of reason.

"I been hurt too so I know what it is you're feeling." I looked up with red eyes and tears rolling down my cheeks.

"Really you, you seem like you can have any woman you want."

"And you can have any man you want because Kelly you are indeed a beautiful woman and I have to admit you caught my eye the day I met you that's the reason why I gave you my number." I blushed knowing he was just being nice.

"I guess you right I don't seem to have any problems getting a man's attention."

"Woman you fine and if you're husband can't see that then he's the fool. I don't know what went on between the two of you but I do know this, things get better as time moves on." I looked at Cory through teary eyes and said,

"I wish it would hurry up because I feel like someone died."

"I told you I know the feeling you just have to work through the pain."

"And how do you do that?"

"Do something you like. Read something positive travel with friends." I worked up a smiled.

"I travel on my job."

"Really what is it you do?"

"I'm a flight attendant."

"Well I know you fly for free so when you're not working just go and get out there."

"I think I will thank you."

"You're a sweet lady."

"How you know?" My sad face changed into a pleasant smile.

"I know because I can see it all over you sista you have that special something about ya."

"Oh that's nice to know I'm glad someone think so."

"Tell me something."

"What?"

"What did you come over here for in the first place?"

"I just saw you walk into your house and I noticed you like to walk for exercise when you are home and I wanted to know if you wanted to work out with me at this new gym that I go to on Jackson St. called The Six Pak."

"Really"

"Yeah I like working out and I get out by 5:30am every morning. I wanted to invite you it's really a nice place."

"Sure we can start tomorrow morning."

"Cool well I have to go and get ready."

"Do you mind if I ask ready for what?"

"I have a photo shoot today at 12:00 then I have to come home and pack for a trip to Tennessee on Monday."

"What's in Tennessee?"

"I go visit the children at St Jude hospital and speak to them and I give money to some of the families and make a donation to the hospital."

"That's really nice what made you decide to do that?"

"Well it's a long story but I will make it short I had a best friend in high school his name was Mathew and he found out he had cancer in his stomach I watched him suffer from that and I made him a promise when I grow up I will make a difference in someone's life by giving to a cancer foundation for children. So I keep my promise I also visit with his mom and send her money every year." I smiled as I looked at the floor.

"I'm sorry about your friend."

"Its okay he made peace with God so I know he is asleep and resting in the Lord."

"Well that's really nice to know." Cory stood up and walked towards the door.

"Well I have to go you have a good day sweetie."

"You too thanks for dropping by," I close the door and think to myself what a gentleman.

Chapter 8 - - Jada

"Hello Mr. Sinclair I was just_"

"You don't have to explain I understand I do the same thing when it's a pretty day outside."

I smiled and started to pick through some papers on my desk. After getting caught day dreaming out the window looking at a couple downstairs in the parking lot hugging and kissing. Thinking about how Byron and I use to do the same I missed his arms around me and the long talks we would have well after midnight, I often wonder why things have to change.

"I was wondering would you like to have lunch with me."

I blushed because Cole Sinclair was a sight to be seen, his body was cut like a diamond, and his skin was like dark chocolate dipped in caramel the perfect ten. When he walks into the building all the women pause he didn't act like a man with handsome features he was friendly and down to earth that's what made him that much more attractive.

"I guess I can go to lunch I have to go to the bathroom and I will be ready in five Mr. Sinclair"

"Please, call me Cole I rather you call me by my first name Mrs. Knight."

I couldn't help but flash a genuine grin from one coast to the next.

"You can call me Jada since we're going to be on first name basis."

I then sashay into the bathroom down the hall to check my makeup It's been a while since I been on a lunch date. Well, this wasn't really a date he asked and I accepted besides I can pretend for an hour this man is mine for the asking besides, I'm hungry. I take the comb out of my purse and fix my hair. I then grab my lip-gloss and go over my thick lips. Two of my nosey co-workers walk in and see me sprucing up one of the ladies said,

"Hey you have a hot lunch date?"

"I'm going out but it's not a date." The other woman said,

"Well I hope you two have fun." They both giggle to themselves.

"What do you mean?"

"Girl we heard Cole say he was taking you to lunch."

"Ok he's taking me to lunch but that's it I'm married."

I then throw up my four caret diamond in their ugly ass faces.

"Honey we messing with you, Cole is a gentleman and he's really nice, but he's single and it surprises me that he has no woman I wonder if he's gay?" I roll my eyes into the heavens.

"Ladies I have to go and about him being gay what he does is none of our business." They both stop smiling and rolled their eyes. I put my gloss back in my purse and walked out the door. When I stepped out of the bathroom I met Cole in the hall talking to another co-worker.

"Would you like to join us for lunch?" The young man said as he looked at me walking up the hall dressed in my black Donna Karen pants suit

"No man you do your thing I ain't even mad at ya." Cole looked at him and then hit him with a blow up fist pound and said,

"It's not like that but it's all good." I walked over to Cole.

"You ready?"

"Yep, what would you like to eat lady?"

"I have a taste for a T Bone."

"T Bone it is, you like Copeland's?"

"Yes I love it I'm hungry too."

"So am I"

"It's been a while since I been out to eat." Cole looked at me with those droopy bedroom eyes of his and smiled.

"So it's been awhile I'm glad you enjoyed yourself."

"Me too I have to tell my husband we need to go out more."

"You should do that?"

"I will because I have to say again I enjoyed myself thank you for inviting me."

"I enjoyed the company."

I smiled as I noticed that my boss was staring at me I immediately looked away because for that moment I felt guilty.

"Well I think we been here long enough we have some work to do."

"I agree Jada let's bounce."

We both left tips for the waitress and he paid for the meal. We walk out to the parking lot to his black and gold Escalade.

"Cole may I ask you something personal?"

"As long as it's not too personal I'm a private person and I don't let too many people into my business."

"We'll never mind."

"I don't mind you asking me anything I just wanted you to know that I don't get into other folks business and I don't want them in mine."

"I just wanted to know if you had a girlfriend."

"No, I don't have a girlfriend anything else you want to know?" I start to smile from ear to ear.

"What are you smiling about over there?"

"Well I was thinking about my friend Madison and she's really a nice person and I would like for you to meet her maybe we could do like, a double date."

He offered me a genuine smiled and such a sexy smile at that he had perfectly white teeth that glowed against that deep dark chocolate smooth skin of his putting me in the mind of Lance Gross.

"I don't mean any harm but so many people try setting me up with their friends, and family it rarely works out too well and I'm really not into that, I like choosing my own woman."

"Say no more I understand." I looked out the window as we drove down the street.

After riding for about ten minutes in pure silence Cole reached over and touched my hand and asked,

"What are you thinking about?" I never looked at him just out the window. "Nothing" I felt him looking over at me.

"I know you're over there thinking about something Jada you can't fool me." I glanced over at him and said softly.

"I love my husband." He smiled as he pulls up in the parking lot of the store.

"I'm sure you do lady I guess you wouldn't marry someone you didn't love."

"I guess you're right all I'm saying is that_ we'll never mind."

"No say what you feel."

"I really don't feel right telling you things so personal besides you said you don't get too personal."

"Hey I'm human and if I like you then I will share but I have to feel people out Miss Jada."

See this man is so sexy and the way he said my name right there just made me feel all soft in side. A woman likes the attention from a man, especially when he is fine and smooth like this man.

"I know but you're my boss and I need to keep my personal life to myself."

"Well I guess you're right but since I like you I will offer you my free counseling sessions whenever you want to vent."

"One day I just may take you up on that."

He offers me a smile as he backs his Escalade up in his parking spot. I notice the two women I saw in the bathroom were standing outside smoking their New Ports, they watch us step out of Cole's truck as we walk by Cole speak as he opens the door for me what a perfect gentleman. He says to them in a kind low tone voice,

"Ladies"

They smile back and watch his tight butt as he walks by. I look and give them a fake smile as they rolled their eyes and continue to fill their lungs with smoke. When Cole wasn't looking I looked back and licked out my tongue. They laughed and mumble how silly I was. Of course I didn't care what they think I was there for a paycheck and that was it.

Chapter 9 - - Madison

I fixed my hair in a bun while looking in the mirror. I been crying all week and I know I had to get it together before Collin gets there to pick up Jr. I don't know where these feelings were coming from. I love Collin for being a good father and he was a wonderful man in my life but I had issues that only God could fix.

I've always been strong in mind, spirit and body. I certainly didn't take any wooden nickels and trust too many people. I couldn't let this brotha know what it was I was feeling on the inside. I had my chance and of course I blew it and let him go, so I have to live with that decision for the rest of my life. Now is certainly not the time to throw a pity party, I had less than an hour to get the red out of my eyes and put on a happy face. There was a knock on the bedroom door.

"Jr. that's you?"

"Yes momma, daddy is here to pick me up."

"Baby I will be there in just a moment."

I took one last look in the mirror and checked my face for any blemishes or signs of unhappiness. I then came out of my room, dressed in Polo Jeans and sweatshirt wearing glasses so he couldn't see my eyes. Walking in the living room there sat Collin with Jackie. My heart fell to the floor I wasn't expecting her to be with him. I had to put on my fake smile and pretend I was in Hollywood up for the most supporting actress award.

"Hi how are you?"

Jackie stood up to greet me with a hug.

"Honey I'm fine, been working and busy trying to get my business off the ground." I wanted to scream but I just pretended I was happy and looked over at Collin.

"Well that's wonderful would you two like something to drink?"

Collin winked his eye at me.

"No thanks were going to get Jr. and go because we have so much to do."

I tried not to show any emotion I didn't want to show how hurt I really was. This was so hard for me to do. Jr. came into the room with his bags packed and hair in a ponytail. Jackie grabbed Collin's car keys.

"Jr. you want to go and put you're things in the car."

"Sure Miss Jackie why not" she smiled.

"Well we will be out in the car honey, Madison it's always a pleasure seeing you." I forced a smiled at the beautiful 5'11 former basketball player and said,

"It's always a pleasure, take care."

"Momma I will be back on Sunday alright." I gave him an approving look with tears in my eyes and gave him a hug.

"By sweetie you do what daddy and Miss Jackie tells you ok."

"Momma what's wrong? You have been looking sad all week."

Collin looked at me as I denied it all.

"No honey momma is just tired that's all I need a break from school and work that's it. You go and have a good time with your daddy okay and don't worry about me."

"Ok just do me a favor and get out and have some fun alright!"

"Will do baby."

"Jr I will twist you're hair when we get to my house this afternoon alright."

"That's cool"

They both walked out the front door talking and giggling about the things they were going to do this weekend. Collin stood there looking at me knowing there was something wrong. I try not to make eye contact with him. He reaches for my hand and pulls me close to him, embracing me like he did when we were dating. He slowly bends down to kiss my lips. My heart was racing to a new speed. It's been so long since any man held me so tight and the one man I loved was about to make the biggest move of his life and there was nothing I could do about it but let it go. He offered his tongue and we kissed for over 5 minutes. Collin stopped and looked at me.

"You know I still love you." I smiled as I held his hand and place it over my heart.

"Me too but you have someone who loves you out there waiting for you in the car and she's a beautiful woman and she's going to make a wonderful wife may God bless you two."

"Thanks so much." He looked into my teary eyes and rubs the side of my face.

"I will always love you."

"Roger that Collin."

He wipes his eyes, as he head towards the door. I walk slowly behind him and watch my son and the man that should have been my husband drive off in his black BMW. Waving and smiling and blowing the horn I see my son blowing kisses at me from the back window. I laugh and wave and blow one back at him until I could no longer see the car. I walk back in the house and embrace the emptiness. I pick up the phone because I felt I have grieved enough and it was time for me to get out and live a little so I pick up the phone to call my best friend.

"Hey Jada what's up?"

"I have a free weekend and I was wondering_,"

"Say no more, Jordan is at my moms and Byron's friend has opened a really nice club so we can go and check it out alright!"

"Well I'll see you in a couple of hours."

⁂

There was the black sign that flashed the sign The Black Onyx, the parking lot was full you could hear the music from cars and the people were waiting in line to get inside the club. There were security guards directing traffic. Finally I found a parking spot.

"Girl I look alright?" I say while looking in the mirror putting on some lip-gloss.

"Honey don't you know we still got it going on were Divas I thought you knew." We both giggle. A brotha passed by the car looking, Jada pointed and said to me with excitement in her voice,

"See I told you and we haven't even stepped out the car yet."

"Girl I know it's been so long since I been out to a club I don't know how to act."

"Yes you do just be yourself it will be alright."

I opened the car door and stepped out with my backless Black Salsa dress and red stilettos. My hair was pulled up in a ponytail with the curls hanging down. Jada had on a red Tank top and black low rider jeans her hair was whipped with curls everywhere. We were indeed ready to get our party on. Walking up to the line Jada pulls out her VIP passes and taps me on the shoulder.

"Come on we don't have to pay." My eyes got bright.

"Let's go then" As we walk through the crowd of people the men paused; one man looked at Jada and saw her wedding ring.

"Baby is you happily married or what?" She smiled at the comment.

"I'm happy thank you." We giggled as we make our way through the crowd of people. One guy grabbed my hand.

"Would you like to dance with me?" I smiled and said loudly because the music was bumping the warehouse.

When the Honeymoon Is Over

"Not right now holla at me later." The brown skin brotha smiled and said politely

"I will find you alright." I smiled at the toothless man trying to be polite.

"Not if I don't find you first." He let go of my hand and I caught up with Jada sitting at a bar table in the corner. I sit down and check out the room. I smile at a young man sitting at the table with his buddies next to ours. I look at my friend and say,

"Girl there is some fine brothas in this place tonight!" Jada spots a man sitting at the bar. Their eyes met he smiles and waves, she smiled back.

"Who are you waving at?" I ask as I look around then I see a brotha walking towards our table.

"Who is that?"

"That's my boss."

"Honey your boss is fine."

"And single girl."

"No he isn't"

Cole was dressed in a pair of black slacks, a polo shirt and blue vest. Rocking a pair of gold hoop earrings, his head was shaved clean and smelled wonderful. You could smell him coming with that Joop cologne a mile away.

"Hello ladies" He shook Jada's hand first and gave her a kiss on the cheek.

"What brings you out tonight?"

"I decided to get out the house with a couple of my frat brothers."

"Well that's nice I would like for you to meet my friend Madison." He shakes my hand and also gives me a kiss on the cheek.

"How are you tonight?"

"I'm fine thank you."

"What would you ladies like to drink?" We look at one another and Jada speaks first.

"Well, I will have a Strawberry daiquiri."

"Ok and you?"

"Well I'll have the same thank you."

"I'll be right back ladies." He moves his way through the crowd of people as I watch.

"How do you get a boss like that?"

"Honey ain't he cute?"

"He's not cute girlfriend he's fine as wine and with a face that goes alone with it.

"Now that's a bonus I have to say."

"I know what you mean sista."

"I wanted you two to meet because I think you guys would make a cute couple." My eyes grew tight I haven't had a man in a while I wouldn't know how to act.

"Honey, you know I don't do fix ups they hardly ever work."

"Girl please you need to get off the tough girl role play and live a little."

"Who says I'm not living now."

"Madison Courtney, how long have we been friends?"

"Forever it seems."

"Well I think I know you well enough!" I laughed as I watch Cole bring the drinks to the table.

"Here you go ladies, anything else I can get you?" Jada looked at Cole and smiled.

"No but you're welcome to have a seat."

"I can do better than that you just save a brotha a dance or two I'm going back over to the bar and get my drink on with my buddies I just wanted you to have a drink on me." Jada tilts her glass up to Cole.

"Thanks for the buzz." He smiles.

When the Honeymoon Is Over

"You ladies have a good time on me and if you want more to drink just have Charlene my waitress put it on my tab alright."

I was impressed with this man. You can't get a man to buy you two apple pies from Mickey D's these days. We both looked at one another and said "OK" Cole walked through the crowd and to the bar where he was sitting.

"Girl he's like that at work. Just nice" I looked at Jada as she talked about her boss. She had a glow in her eyes.

"Honey you like this man."

"No he's my boss and I just think he's a nice man."

"Jada he likes you too I can see it."

"No he doesn't he's a gentleman besides he knows I'm a married woman." I take a sip of my drink.

"You can fool some of the people some of the time but you can't fool Madison Courtney none of the time!"

"Whatever, I saw the way he looked at you."

"Jada he only spoke to me I checked the brotha out and he is interested in Jada Knight alright now they're playing my song and I think I'm going to get up and shake my thong!"

I got up, headed to the dance floor and there I was shaking what my mamma gave me all by myself. Jada sits at the table sipping on her drink thinking about what I said. Was this true or not? Cole has been nothing but a gentleman towards her. Walking towards the table Jada looks up and sees Kobe smiling at her.

"What you doing out and about tonight?" She smiles.

"For the same reason why you're out and about"

"You're here alone?"

"Nope Madison's here with me." He looks around to see if he could spot his cousin in the crowd.

"I don't see her, the floor is packed."

"I know I did spot her a few minutes ago."

"Have a seat."

"I guess I can pull up a chair." He reaches for the chair next to him and sits down and watch the people on the dance floor shack it fast.

"Where is Byron?" Jada looked confused.

"You know what I really don't know where he is tonight. I told him I was coming out but I guess he decided to stay at home since I was hooking up with Madison tonight."

"I talked with him earlier but he didn't say what he was going to do."

"Well what made you come out tonight?"

"I needed to get out and express myself you know what I mean?"

"No but I understand."

"Keisha didn't like it but she will be alright too."

"I feel ya." The room was about to slow down the pace the lights changed and a slow jam popped on. I walked up to the table and grabbed my drink. My face was full of beaded sweat.

"Hi Kobe what's up?"

"I'm just chillen and you?"

"Me too, Keisha let you out the house tonight huh?"

"I don't mean any harm but Keisha doesn't rule this nigga and don't you forget that!"

"Ok I hear ya."

I looked at my friend as she sipped her drink and winked her eye. Kobe spotted Jalen coming across the room. He walks up with Ragan on his side.

"Hello people what's up?" Kobe gave his friend some dap and kissed Ragan's hand.

"How are you?"

"I'm Fine and you?"

"I'm cool as a cucumber." She smiles and greets everyone else.

"Is everyone enjoying themselves?" Jada and I nod our heads. I look around the camp and say,

When the Honeymoon Is Over

"Girl it's some fine men in the place to be tonight." Ragan smiles as she looks at Jalen up and down.

"And I have the finest one right here."

"I hear you sista." Reagan offers me a genuine smile and wink.

"Well we were just checking out our VIP's to see if things were ok you all continue to enjoy yourselves alright. Jada you tell that husband of yours he could have come out tonight but its all- good." She smiles and continues to sip on her drink.

"I will be sure to tell him I saw you two tonight." Reagan waves and they walk off greeting others in the crowd. I look at my cousin for about two minutes and shake my head.

"What?" Kobe frowns as he drinks his beer.

"I was just wondering how you do it."

"How I do what?"

"Never mind Kobe you getting all crazy on me."

"Well I want to know what you're talking about girl."

"You know what I'm talking about. Keisha"

"What about my wife?" He sounded irritated.

"Kobe how is Aunt Dorothy and Uncle William?"

"There're fine."

"I'm going by Brenda's house tomorrow maybe I will swing by and see the rest of the family."

"Were having a BQ tomorrow so come by."

"Shayla will be there huh?"

"Yes, why you ask?"

"Well I just wanted to see her I missed her the last time."

"Let's not talk about last time alright."

I knew my cousin was mad and needed a break from all his stress I could see it in his face but I also needed a break from my mixed feelings I was having as well.

Chapter 10 - - Kobe

Shayla and I were sitting at the breakfast table eating while I read the paper.

"Daddy, may I ask you a personal question?"

I take a sip of my milk and put the paper down giving my daughter the attention she deserved, looking like her mother but God I hope she don't be a beast like her ass. Shayla sometimes act as if she was here before at times she was concerned about things a nine year old shouldn't be concerned with but I guess that's how little girls are I suppose.

"Yes baby girl,"

"Are you and mommy mad at each other?"

"Why you say that baby?"

"Well I heard her tell you last night to sleep on the couch."

"Well you don't worry about that okay."

"Well daddy I don't want you to leave again okay." I stop sipping on my milk and look at my daughter and smile.

"Daddy is not going anywhere and don't worry about your mom and me were going to be just fine I promise alright."

"Well if you leave again promise me that you will take me with you I don't care where we go as long as you take me with you."

My heart felt like lead after knowing my daughter's concern about Keisha and me. I am trying to be a good husband and loving father to my child and Keisha's ways make a black man want to holla for real. My child's innocence eyes told me she was dead serious about this. The doorbell rings, I look at my watch only to see it was already ten. I was wondering who that could be at this hour. I go and open the door and there stood my sister. Dressed in her Burberry jacket and hat to match, she always had a thing for labels and fashion.

"Good morning big brother, are you going to let me in or what?

"Hey Brenda what's up come in." Shayla runs to the door.

"Hi Aunt Brenda what's up?"

"Nothing cutie I came by to see you and your daddy to make sure you guys was ok."

Brenda stood 5'5 with a thick frame looking like a mini me, she was only two shades darker than me; she had beautiful silky straight hair that danced with the wind and she had the attitude to match her loving personality, if I have to say it myself we had a beautiful looking family, my parents did well. What Keisha didn't like was the fact I was super close to my sister and nothing and nobody was coming between blood.

"Well black man can I sit down for a spell these shoes are cute but they are killing my feet?"

"I guess have a seat."

I never understood why my sister and women in general have to dress to impress wearing shoes and clothes they don't feel comfortable in that's crazy to me give me a pair of jeans and a T shirt and a brother is cool with that. Now don't get me wrong I love to dress and smell good but I will never be uncomfortable not a chance.

"Shayla I brought you something."

"What is it?"

"Well you have to close your eyes and hold your hands out."

She did just that, as Brenda pulled out a beautiful black doll from Toy World, placing it in Shayla's hands.

"Can I open my eyes now?"

"Yes, sweetie you can."

"Ooh Aunt Brenda we saw this doll in the mall thank you so much."

"Honey you're welcome I also bought her some clothes so you have five outfits to start out with put it in your room okay."

Shayla was so excited she started running to the back with her new doll to tell her mom what she got from Aunt Brenda.

"You have that little girl spoiled rotten you know that."

"I know that's my only niece so you know I have to do something."

"So how are you?"

"I'm okay."

"Are you really okay?"

"Why you ask that?"

"Shayla called me the other day and said that you were unhappy."

"She did what?"

"Well don't get mad at the child but you need to get it together Kobe."

"I am"

"Well did you find a building yet for your shop?"

"Yeah, I think its coming together I have a lot of things to do before that happens."

"If you need any help at all just let me know."

"Thanks"

Walking up the hall Keisha enters the living room and sits on the love seat across from Brenda and me. She didn't say a word as she folds her arms and cross her legs the air suddenly got real thick you could cut the tension with a knife.

"Hi Keisha how are you?" Keisha looks at me and rolls her eyes.

"I'm fine"

Brenda clears her throat as she stands up.

"Well I'm about to go Kobe call me later okay."

"What are you rushing off for?"

"Well I have some things that need to be done don't forget about the BQ, mom and dad said they will start at 2:00." Brenda reaches for me and gives me a hug.

"You know I love you call me if you need me okay."

"I will Shayla and I will be over that way later."

"Do that I will see you later."

Brenda walks out the door. I sit back on the couch and turn on the TV Keisha rolls her eyes.

"What?"

"I didn't say a word."

"You don't have to say a word your actions speak loud enough."

"Why is that hooker coming over here this time of morning?"

"First of all my sister is not a hooker and if you know you don't like her why bother to come into the living room and sit in her face!"

"This is my living room and I sit where I want to sit."

"Keisha I don't understand you sometimes you can be a_"

"What? Say it!" I slam the remote down on the table.

"You know what I'm tired of this day in and day out you're getting on my damn nerves!"

"Well how do you think I feel?"

"I really don't know how you feel and as of right now I don't give a damn."

Keisha stands up and starts to scream at me as if I was a child.

"You can get out of my house right now!"

"Look Keisha if it wasn't for me girl you wouldn't live in this

When the Honeymoon Is Over

over priced apartment so you just shut the hell up! I'm tired of you and your nasty ass ways. I work hard daily, so you can have things, so my daughter can have what she need, and all you seem to do is nag and complain about everything, and everybody so if you want to leave, do it and leave my daughter here!"

Keisha eyes started to fill with water she didn't say a word she stormed to the back and slammed the door. Shayla ran to the front to see what was going on.

"Daddy, what's the matter?"

I sit there with my head in my hands on the couch with tears in my eyes. Shayla walks up to me and comforts me by rubbing my back.

"It's going to be alright daddy."

I didn't say a word I was too shame, my ten year old daughter had to give me comfort. I should be doing that for her this woman made me feel like a punk in my own house and in front of my damn daughter I was just simply fed up with all of it.

Shayla and I drove up to my parent's house the cars were lined up on the street. People were standing and watching as I parked the car. My cousins were standing on the curb talking and listening to music. My daughter and I got out of the Honda, Shayla ran to the house to see her grandparents and I greeted my cousin Marcus.

"What's up nigga?" We gave each other a boy hug and a fist pound.

"Man I'm just trying to stay clean. I can't get myself into anymore trouble you heard me."

Marcus had been in and out of trouble most of his life. He was known for taking a charge that didn't belong to him. He was a good kid but ran with bad company. That was the only life he knew.

"Well man I hear you so how long you been out?"

"It's been a month and I'm not going back. Lisa won't have anything else to do with me."

"Lisa that's the older lady you were living with before you got locked down right?"

"Yeah man I love that woman she stuck by my side until I got out that's what I don't understand. When I went by to see her she just flipped the script telling me some bull about I wish you well. I didn't want to hear all that I wanted to pick up where we left off you know."

"Well you have to understand what you put that woman through when you were out."

"I know but I changed man really I have."

"She doesn't know that she don't want to get hurt and so you have to understand that."

"Man I got a job and everything."

"Marcus didn't you get another girl pregnant while you were with her?" He puts his head down and slaps his hands together.

"I know I did that but those tack heads don't mean anything to me."

"I tell you what, all you can do now is, keep trying and let your actions speak for ya man."

"I here you"

I gave my cousin another fist pound and walked towards the house. Madison was on the front porch playing with Shayla and her dolls.

"Hey what's up?"

"What's up with you a grown woman playing with dolls?"

"Look I always like dolls ok you're never too grown to play with dolls brotha." She laughs as she combs Barbie's hair."

"I don't know about you women sometimes." I walk in the house where my dad and mom sit in the living room.

"What's up old man?" William sits there looking at me knowing something was wrong.

"Where's your wife?"

"She's at home she might be over later."

Knowing that was a damn lie when it rolled off my tongue I hope that trifling man hater stay wherever she is, at this point I don't care where she is or who she is with I wish like hell another man would just take that she devil off my hands.

"Honey did you get something to eat?"

"Not yet ma,"

"Well you better get something to eat and if Keisha doesn't come you take her a plate alright."

"Alright"

"Shayla didn't want anything just yet but you fix her a plate when she gets hungry."

"Ok"

"Boy what's wrong with you?" William asked.

"Nothing just tired I guess."

"Alright son I'm not going into all this with you right now."

Brenda walks in the room and sits on dads lap.

"Say Pop you coming outside to play volley ball? Marcus and a few of his boys are setting up the net now so we can show up and show out!"

"I guess I have to show them how we old school brothers do it."

Brenda and I looked at one another and burst into laughter.

"May I ask what so funny child?"

"Pop please you don't have any kind of game man."

"You wanna bet don't let me show you up out there with your friends and cousins watching."

We all laugh and mumble with one another. Madison and Shayla walk in the room.

"What are you all talking about in here?"

"Pop said he will show us up on the volley ball court."

Madison looks at her uncle and smiles.

"My sweet uncle has skills that will kill."

"Girl that was so corny where you come up with such corny stuff to say?"

"Shut up country."

"Proud to be country thank you very much I'm corn fed and proud of it!"

"Yeah right Kobe" Brenda pops up and says.

"Last one to the volley ball court is a rotten egg."

William jumps up and runs out the door. Dorothy starts to laugh uncontrollable at her husband alone with Madison, Brenda and myself. I said laughing,

"No he didn't just run up out of here like that!"

"Yes Uncle Buck did that!" Madison replied.

Chapter 11 - - Cory

It was well after midnight when Olivia and I finished watching a movie on DVD. I had to get some sleep for an early morning photo shoot for GQ magazine. I certainly didn't want to look tired and drained in my frames so I tried to make my move on getting Olivia out the door without hurting her feelings. I've already been stressed and I needed time alone to get my mind right. I always enjoyed time with Olivia but just wasn't feeling what she was trying to put out. She just wasn't the chocolate to my sundae but I wouldn't dare share that information with her because I did of course like her.

"Well Olivia I want to thank you for coming by." She looked at me and smiled trying not to show any emotion, I knew she had planned to spend the night.

"I enjoyed myself and I really don't want this night to end."

"Neither do I but you know how it is."

"Cory honey I don't mean any harm but you always has so much to do. Why can't you just relax sometimes?"

"I don't have time that's all."

"Well you need to relax. So let me give you a back massage ok." I smiled at the gesture and pull off my T-shirt.

"I want you to lie down on the floor so I can get to your back."

I get up and lay on the floor as she comforts me. She reaches in her purse and pulls out a bottle of baby oil. It was almost as if she planned this whole thing.

As she rubs my back she reaches over and grabs the remote to cut on the stereo and takes in the sounds of Aaliah's beautiful voice.

"Cory you need to relax and let whatever have you so tensed up go baby." She rubs my back and down my legs.

I close my eyes as I feel her warm hands massage my back and legs. It's been awhile since a woman has taken the time to do something for me, not wanting anything in return for a change. I then find myself in deep thought; Olivia starts to move into second gear and kisses me on the back of my neck. My manhood hardens and I roll over and return the favor as I quietly whisper her name. Olivia body was taken over by lust of the flesh, which was not a good move for a woman who didn't know what my next move would be.

Olivia asks, "What's wrong?" Laying there with the covers wrapped around my waist and hands behind my head.

"Nothing just thinking that's all." Olivia moves closer to me as she lays her head in my chest. I never moved I just looked at her and back to the ceiling.

"You seem as if you are in deep thought about something."

"I said nothing!"

Olivia raised her head up and shot me a concern look trying not to get upset I knew I hurt her feelings but I was feeling guilty and didn't know what else to do because now this friendship has moved into a new beginning and this is not where I wanted it to be.

"Okay would you like for me to fix you something to eat?"

"Olivia, I would like for you to just lay there and say nothing just stay still."

Looking confused she placed her head back in my chest trying to understand where it was I was going with this. Olivia was beautiful and intelligent but she just didn't have it. The sex was on point but it just takes more than someone kissing and sucking on me to make me feel anything more. She cared about me and wanted nothing more than to hook me in and she didn't want to make waves so she was submissive. To me that was unattractive and it didn't look good on such a beautiful black woman.

"I can lay with you all day long."

"I could and I would like to but we have to get up I have a photo shoot in a couple of hours and I'm meeting my boys for a game later so I guess I will call you tonight." Olivia didn't show her frustration but I knew she was disappointed but through all that she remained cool.

"Let's get up and take a shower because I have some things I have to do anyway maybe we can get together next week sometime." I smiled at how smooth this was going no drama and all that other stuff.

"Let's get together next week baby that's a good idea and treats and eats on me this time alright." She smiled and got up buck necked and ran to the bathroom to turn on the shower. Hurting Olivia was the last thing I planned to do she was really a nice woman not to mention she was super fine and a freak but something was missing and that was the chemistry that needed to be present.

I walked in the park it was truly a lovely day the birds were singing the sky was blue and there were one or two cirrus clouds that circled the sky but not a sign of rain for miles Kobe and Jalen showed up with their sweats on ready to get started of course Byron was late as always.

"What's up?" Kobe answered, "Man nothing much what's up with Byron where he at?" Jalen says as he rubs his hands over his dreads.

"Man you know that nig is always late it never fails."

"Maybe Jada is giving him the run around today you know she was out at the club night before last." I bounce the ball,

"We can start without him." They walk over to the court where a couple of guys were playing. So they wanted to start a game. Byron came running down the walkway.

"I know yawl ninjas weren't going to start without me?" Kobe looked at him and shook his head.

"Wrong answer man we were about to get started without your ass!"

"Well the man is here."

The park was full and it was the place to be on Sunday's women and men on bikes people showing off their clean cars, music was bumping in the air and half necked honey's everywhere .Martin Luther King Park was just a beautiful park and when these fools were not fighting it was just a cool place to hang out.

The game went on for hours, so by the end of the third game the sun was about to set and the crowd was about to down size, it was time to go and enjoy the rest of the evening with the family and get ready to start planning for blue Monday.

"Man ain't that your wife?" I ask, Byron looked around and saw that it was Jada, Jordan and Madison walking towards the court. He stopped with the ball and started walking towards her. Kobe sits on the bench by the court and with me alongside him.

"Man who is that woman with Jada?"

"That's Madison my cousin."

"Your cousin, tell me it ain't so?"

"Yeah my cousin fool what part of that you not understanding."

"Man you too ugly to have a cousin that fine."

"Man our whole family is full of good looks I don't know what

When the Honeymoon Is Over

you talking bout fool." I shake my head and smile as I watch Madison get closer.

"Man her body is tight she must have painted on those Jeans."

"Man shut up, I don't look at my cousin like that she's like my sister. Were closer since she moved down south, she's from California."

"California that's very interesting"

"Yeah, ain't that's where you're from?"

"Yes the west coast baby that's where it's at."

Madison walks over to Kobe and Cory. She hit's Kobe in the arm playfully.

"What's up cousin?"

"Nothing I thought you were gone home."

"I'm on my way I thought I would drop Jada and Jordan off here to be with her hubby."

"Man I know you going to introduce me to this lovely lady?"

"Oh Madison this is Cory."

She offers me a smile and gives me a handshake.

"Cory, you look so familiar."

"I said the same thing about you?"

"Kobe tells me that you're from California."

"Yes I am."

"I lived in the Bay Area most of my life."

Her eyes widen and she begins to smile.

"Me too_"

"What school did you attend?"

"Oakland High School_"

"No, you kidding, I went to Oakland High too!"

"Is your name Madison Courtney?"

"Yes"

"I'm Cory Washington." Madison heart stopped for a brief second as she screamed. "Cory it's been so long since I've seen you!" They both hugged. Kobe eyes widen as he see the two strangers embrace.

"Damn what's up with that?" Kobe grins from ear to ear showing off the grill in his mouth.

Madison was excited as she calls Jada over and tells her the news about Cory and her.

"Girl you will not believe what I'm about to tell you." Jada smiles as she passes Jordan to her daddy they all stand in a circle talking with one another.

"What? Tell me because I'm on need to know basis here."

"I use to date this man back in the day when we were in High school and here we are three thousand miles, a long way from home, year's later standing in a park down south." They all laugh at how Madison expresses herself.

"I cannot believe this Cory how have you been? Are you married or what?"

"No I'm not married but I'm dating and working hard."

"I have seen you in magazines and a couple of movies I'm so thrilled to know you're doing alright for yourself."

"Well what are you doing Miss Air Force?"

"You remember?"

"How can I forget, I thought I was never going to see your face again."

"Now if this isn't a small world."

"Don't I know it?"

"Madison you look good girl, better then high school."

"Well thank you, I think."

"You're looking good yourself." I couldn't stop smiling

"Can I get your number maybe we can get together and chat sometimes?"

"Well you can walk me to my car because I have to get ready

to go back north so I can meet my son his daddy is bringing him back home today."

"Oh really you have a son?"

"Yes he's my only child."

"Well are you married?"

"No single and happy."

I laugh at the comment but deep down was hoping to change all that and give her something to do.

"Madison you always been happy so are you seeing anyone special?"

"No I'm really single my son keeps me pretty busy. Between basketball games and dances at school I don't have much time for anything else. I'm out of the military and so I go to school it's taking forever to get this degree but it's soon to come."

"I can't believe we are here talking with one another."

"How are your sister and mother?"

"There here in Louisiana I have to take you by to see them. I know they will be surprise to see your face." Madison reaches out to give me another hug.

"Cory it's always a pleasure to meet up with old friends maybe we can do something together in the near future."

I didn't want to let her go. She at one time in my life was very dear to me. She was with me during the time my father died in a tragic car accident on his way to one of my basketball games. Madison gave me comfort and peace. I would forever be grateful to her.

"I have to get with you real soon okay." She reaches in her car to get her blackberry out to enter his number.

"I'll get your number when you call me!"

I couldn't stop smiling because all these years this woman still makes me weak in the damn knees simply by her beautiful presence. I help her in the car by closing the door she turns on the engine and lets the window down. She sees Jada and Byron walking up.

"Oh I thought you were coming to say bye but I see you get with this Negro and forget about a sista I see how you gone act."

"No it's not that honey you know a sista loves you!"

"I understand you have a safe trip and be strong my sista!" Madison rises up a black power fist, smiles and waves at her friend as she yells out the window.

"Remember to keep it real people peace and blesses to you all." Cory yells at her and says,

"I will call you as soon as you call my phone." Kobe looks and says,

"So you use to date my cousin?" I walk to his car with Kobe in tow.

"Yep and she was something special she's sweet man."

"I've already figured that much out because you're focused on that phone, I hope you don't lose it because you might have a heart attack or something!"

"Man, seriously that's one woman I plan to wait by the phone for I will guard this with my life for real that woman looks good and I'm going to make sure I give her a call as soon as she text or call me.

Chapter 12 - - Jalen

Reagan *enjoys her quiet* time reading her book by one of her favorite author's. She looked absolutely relaxed not to mention gorgeous in her silk blue pajamas. Although I'm not a fan of the scarf around the head she made that scarf look fierce. I'm proud to say she's my woman that supports whatever I do; she's my personal cheerleader and a beautiful black woman at that. She's drama free, smart as a whip, what man wouldn't want all that. I walked in the house to find her curled on the couch with her New Orleans Saints blanket across her legs.

"Baby I'm home." Looking over the corners of her book she yells.

"I'm in the living room."

I start pulling off my shirt walk in the living room and flop on the couch next to Reagan.

"What's up with you?" She greets me with a smile.

"Nothing just sitting here reading."

"I figured that much out!" We both chuckle,

"You need to come over here and give poppa a kiss."

Reagan looked at me and started to laugh.

"What's so funny?"

I shot her a dumb founded look. Reagan then pulls me by my dreads and said.

"Come here baby give me a kiss."

We kissed well over five minutes.

"Now that's a welcome home kiss ma." She smiles and says,

"Yeah poppy that's what I'm talking bout!"

Reagan sits back and picks up her book and starts to read again.

"Are you coming to the club with me tonight?"

"Baby I'm really tired you go ahead and do your thing alright."

"Well I wasn't going to stay all night I was just going for a couple of hours to make sure everything's okay you know its karaoke Monday."

"Oh really, now that's going to be fun!"

"I started to do it on Fridays but I'm going to do it on Mondays and Thursdays it's going to be off the chain. I just bought the equipment today and tested it this afternoon so I been busy all day."

"What kind of music do you have?"

"I have some old school, R and B, and hip hop. I think it's going to go over well. I will soon have a live broad cast every Saturday night; I also set up something with the radio station so that I can get them to do a little something, something for the club. It's all coming together."

"I am so proud of you Poppy."

"Thank you for having my back."

"You got that baby!"

I get up and walk into the kitchen to grab a bite to eat before I had to jet out again.

"Honey we have any lunch meat?"

Reagan puts her book down and walks in the kitchen. She then grabs the handle of the microwave and pulls out a dinner plate with greens, yams, corn bread and fried chicken.

"Now do you still want a sandwich baby?"

When the Honeymoon Is Over

"I'm sorry I didn't know you cooked?"

"Honey when have you known me not to cook?"

"Reagan, I didn't smell anything so I__"

Putting the plate on the table alone with a paper towel she grabs me around the waist and kissed me on the neck.

"I love you Jalen and don't you ever forget that!"

"Alright I won't I sit down and begin to clean my plate. Reagan of course goes back into her comfort zone and finishes her book.

※

Stepping out of the shower I grab my towel and start to dry off, reaching over to grab my silk boxers I walk into our bedroom trying not to wake Reagan up. I crawl into bed putting my arm around her waist as I grab the remote to get my sleep number right because Ragan always change my number when she make up the bed, it was 4:00 am. She rolls over and looks at the clock letting out a disapproving moan.

"Hey baby"

"Hi sweetie the club was hot tonight!"

"Really" she gives me an incredulous look with her piercing eyes.

"Yeah we had a good turn out about hundred people showed up and it was good."

Turning over Reagan tries to find a comfortable spot in the bed not trying to blow this out the water but inside she was furious I felt it because she knew the club closes at one during the week and two on Friday, Saturday, and Sunday.

"Baby you not mad with me huh?"

"Not at all sugar just go to sleep I have to get up at 6:00."

"Alright I'll see you in the morning wake me up I'm going to meet Cory at the gym at 7:00 he said he was going to get there a little late tomorrow so I'm going to catch him there at that time."

"Ok now just go to sleep, good night!"

"Goodnight baby." I reach over and give her a kiss on the cheek. She rolls over and snug's under me as usual, it's amazing even when she's upset with me she still shows me love what man wouldn't want a woman like that.

I was tired; last night was too much for me. I had to get home and take a nap before going to the club. Having my own club was more work then I planned, I enjoyed the people but still needed some time alone with Reagan. She didn't say much to me about the late hours I keep, but how much can one woman take. I love Reagan; she was almost too good to be true.

Finally I reach our house blowing hard; I kneel over and catch what was left of my breath from the jog home from the gym. This was my fifth day in a row, I made a promise to myself that I will keep in shape and work on that six-pack I been trying to get for a year now! Cory helps me out by being there to support and push a brotha to success. I'm just tired and worn out because I just wasn't use to being up so early after being out all night. I stumble in the house and found Regan sitting in the kitchen reading the newspaper and drinking a cup of Hazel Nut coffee.

"Hi baby how was your work out?"

Blowing, trying to catch my breath Reagan smiles and laughs to herself.

"What you smiling about over there."

"Oh nothing"

"You were laughing at me huh?"

"No baby I will never do that!"

"Well your man is going to be fine soon."

"Honey you already fine to me with that smooth black skin and your beautiful white teeth what more can a woman ask for."

I stand up right there and start to flex my muscles.

"So you think your man fine huh?" She smiles.

"Yes I do, you're great like Tony the Tiger"

I grab a bottle of water out of the fridge.

"Thank you for the vote of confidence."

She stands up and grabs me around my neck to give me a hug.

"Baby I would love you if you looked like ET, I would love you if you was blind cripple and crazy, I would love you if you had one eye in the center of your__"

"Stop_ you know you're not telling the truth so just hold up."

"I was just trying to prove a point you my man and I love you and I have your back one hundred percent."

I kiss her on the lips.

"I have your back too baby."

Just getting home from basketball practice Reagan runs a tub full of water and baby bath to end her day in a relax environment lighting candles around her garden tub she pulls her hair up in a bun and rumbles through her CD's and stumble on Luther V. Smiling from ear to ear Reagan remise the countless hours of how her and Jalen would make love to the sounds of his voice bumping through their speakers. She pops the CD in and slides into the soaker tub humming alone with the music as she relaxes.

An hour has passed and Reagan's skin was beginning to wrinkle. She stands up and rinses herself off looking over at the clock it was already 10:00pm time to watch her show Martin. She grabs a towel and turns on the TV as she dries herself off. She puts on her black silk gown and climbs into her King size bed and gets focused on her show. As she watches the show and get into it the phone rings.

"Now who could this be?" She asks herself as she checks the caller ID box it said unknown caller she picks up.

"Hello"

"Hello baby how are you doing in Louisiana?"

"Hi, mom I'm doing well how you?"

"I'm doing just fine honey."

"Where is daddy?"

"He's playing cards with your brother and Katie."

"Really, they are doing alright I suppose?"

"Your brother asks Katie to marry him yesterday."

"Really mom that's nice."

Reagan was happy for her brother because he and Katie had been dating for about two years and she was already part of the family as far as she was concerned.

"Reagan, honey when are you coming home to visit us?"

"Momma I really don't know but I will soon okay."

"How's Jalen?"

"He's doing fine."

"Your brother wants to speak to you."

"Hey baby sis what's up?"

"Hi Todd what's going on?"

"Katie and I are planning an engagement party next month you coming right?"

"I will do my best to be there."

"That's what I'm talking about my sister got my back!"

"Always"

"Where's my brother in law?"

"You mean Jalen?"

When the Honeymoon Is Over

"Yeah silly what's with you I always called him brother in law, what that fool did something to you?"

"No it's ok."

"Well why you sound like you down?"

"I'm not down Todd I'm just tired I had basketball practice today and getting ready for some things that's it."

"Reagan I know you but I will let you slide with that alright."

"Whatever"

"Whatever nothing I know my sister and you sound as if you're not happy."

"I'm happy you should see our house it's beautiful and I just love the neighborhood its lovely."

"Katie and I are going to ride down one weekend and check things out alone with ma and pop."

"You guys need to do that!"

"We will talk about that soon, Katie wants to holla at ya."

"Hello Reagan"

"Hi Katie what's up girl? Congratulations you hooked the playa huh?"

"Yeah he finally asks a sista to jump the broom."

"I hear ya you have any plans dates just yet?"

"Well were looking at next spring so you know I want you in the wedding."

"I'm there you know."

"I saw Braxtine at The Underground about a week ago were going to lunch tomorrow."

"That's good I wish I was there, I miss the ATL for real but living here in Alexandria is not all that bad, the cost of living is not too bad and where I live is really a nice area."

"Todd said we were going to ride out that way I never been to Louisiana."

"Well it's alright I like coaching my ladies team and there are interesting people here."

"I bet well honey I'm going to let you speak to pop."

"Hey baby girl what's popping?"

"Pop what's popping, you been looking at videos again and trying to be hip."

"Little girl I'm the king of hip I teach these youngsters how to be hip you heard me."

"Daddy you so crazy what will ma do with you?"

"She can't handle me baby girl I have to slow up so she can catch up?"

"I hear you pop."

"So what's up with Jalen he opened that club yet?"

"Yes sir he did and it's really a nice spot to hang out for the old school and young"

"Well I have to check it out baby girl when we come out that way. So are you going to try and come to your brother's party?"

"Yep I wouldn't miss it for the world."

"Well you tell Jalen to come too."

"I will"

"Your mother wants to holla back at you I love you."

"I love you too Pop you take it easy and don't give ma a hard time you hear me."

"Sure thing baby love you."

"Well daughter I just wanted to say bye and I love you sweetie you take care and tell Jalen hello for me alright."

"I will ma you take care and I love you all so much."

"Bye"

They hung up the phone Reagan was happy for her brother. She wanted nothing less than to see him and Katie happy. Todd was a good man and Katie was a sweet woman and they complement one another so well. Todd wanted Katie to move in his house with him about a year ago but Katie told him not unless I have a ring on my finger and papers at the courthouse saying I belong there. Todd wasn't too happy about that but he respected her decision, at the time he wasn't ready to marry her. Katie stood her ground and now her and Todd are about to get married. Reagan started to get sad because Katie and her brother only been together two years and they were getting married and her and Jalen been together seven and not once has he mentioned marriage now what's wrong with that picture.

Chapter 13 - Kelly

I had planned to meet with Ethan at eight o'clock I wanted nothing more than to get out of this mess. I love my husband but enough was enough. I was sick of his lies and mental abuse. The doorbell rings and I take a final look in the mirror to make sure my hair and makeup was in place. I slowly walk to the door as my heart makes her debut from silent to a loud pounding sound within seconds; I had to calm down as I take a hard breath.

"Who is it?"

"It's Cory"

I open the door and stand there offering him my sexiest smile, practicing my most fierce look that I learned from Americas Next top Model.

"Wow"

"Wow, is that a good wow or a bad wow?"

"It's a you look sexy wow."

I have to admit I felt great because Cory and I worked out together every chance we get and my low rider jeans were hugging my curves and Sean John tank was squeezing my love handles nicely, I had to admit I felt tasteful and sexy.

"I am grateful."

"Where are you going if you don't mind me asking?"

"I'm not going anywhere my ex husband is coming and were going to discuss some things."

"Well I hope things work out when he sees you in this get up that fool ain't going nowhere believe that!"

"Oh yeah he's going because I will not take his abuse anymore and to top it off I'm going to give him his rings back tonight!"

"Oh really,"

"Yes really, Ethan has played me for the last time. I may love him but I'm stronger then people give me credit for."

"Well little mama do your thing."

As Cory makes his exit out my door there steps a half white brotha dressed in a Nike wind suit and matching baseball fitted cap coming up the stairs with flowers in his hands. Cory thought to himself you got to be kidding me. He knew this was Ethan because he first looked lost, and second he just looks as if he was ready to do one of Keith Sweat numbers and beg. Ethan watched Cory as he left my apartment. He looked like a lion ready to attack, but at the same time trying to control his emotions and remain cool.

I found that to be quite interesting but I really didn't give a damn. When Cory passes by the stranger he didn't smile nor did he pay any attention on how Ethan was looking him up and down. I stood there with the look of surprise upon my face because it's been a while since I seen this so called Godly man I called my soul mate. I had to admit the man was looking good but I couldn't let that cloud my good judgment on how this monster treated me, besides I made up my mind to kick him to the curb.

"Hey baby how you doing?"

"I'm doing just fine come in and have a seat."

"Would you like something to drink?"

Ethan takes in the new pad checking out the art on the wall and the scent of Febreze candles that invaded his nostrils. He makes his way to my new Ashley plush sectional couch and get comfortable. Dinner was on the stove cooked just in case his sorry ass wanted to eat a little something.

"I really like your place it's really nice, here is something extra to add to your plant collection."

"Thank you."

I took in the scent of the beautiful white roses and placed them in my new crystal vase I bought in San Francisco a month ago. Buying flowers was nothing new, this brotha had a plan and little did he know I wasn't trying to hear what he had to say all I wanted was out of this game I was going to checkmate his sorry ass.

"I had been thinking about you a lot lately."

"Well to be honest with you baby I haven't thought about you too much."

Those fiery darts hit him straight in the heart.

"Well I guess you can say I deserve that."

"You have no idea what you deserve but I forgive you."

He smiles as he tries to get close to my lips and give me a kiss. But I wasn't having it I place my manicure hand up to meet his lips.

"Honey look I said I forgive you but I will never forget. All the lies all the women oh and the note you don't know why but you just don't love me anymore nigga please."

"Look Kelly I can't say it enough I am sorry and I have prayed about this and I want our marriage to work out because I been wrong and yes I have done some foul stuff to you and I'm sorry and I would like another chance to prove I can be a man and the husband that you been praying for."

I stand up and walk to the kitchen.

"Would you like something to eat? I prepared rice and gravy, chicken and yams."

Ethan looked at me and smiled with pain in his eyes thinking this was going to be harder then he thought.

"You have some soul food going on here huh."

"Yep, I needed to eat and so I cooked."

"I guess I can grab a bite just fix me a big hardy plate like you did back in the day when we first got married."

I turned towards the stove where he couldn't see the expression upon my face. I roll my eyes up to the ceiling and crossed them as I looked in the cabinet to find him a plate.

"Have you talked with your mom lately?"

"I haven't talked with my mother in over a month."

I turn around and place the chicken on his plate.

"You mean to tell me you haven't talked with your mom in over a month."

"Well she's been on me about you lately and I wasn't trying to hear all that!"

"You something,"

"What you mean by that statement?"

"What I mean is that you act as if you have something against women it's something personal with you."

"Why you say that?"

"Well you act as if women have no rights and if you can't control them then you have no need for them that's all I'm saying!"

He looked, as he turned a shade darker feeling a little bit agitated at the comment.

"Look I have changed and I had time to change if only you give me another chance to prove that I have."

Placing the plate down before him trying to be calm and not slap the hell out of his no good for nothing behind I say,

"Would you like something to drink besides water man?"

He shot me a look like he didn't know who I was anymore, yeah I changed a great bit not just the jeans I wear but my attitude was new, the once soft spoken lady from the south had an edge that spoke louder than any voice box .

"Whatever you have I will be glad to drink."

I look in the fridge and pull out a bottle of Coke and grab some ice out the freezer and begin to pour it into his glass.

"Thank you."

"You welcome."

When the Honeymoon Is Over

I fix my plate and sit down beside him.

"It's always a pleasure being in your company."

I look at him and smiled as I pull a piece of chicken off the fork. I didn't say a word for about five minutes.

"May I ask you a question?"

"Why now?"

"What you mean?"

"Let me break it down to ya why are you so concern about us now when you had three years to get this thing right?"

He shifted his weight feeling the spotlight was on him. He then gets up and puts his plate in the sink and start to draw some water so he could wash the dishes.

"You don't have to do that you haven't washed dishes before so there's no need for it now!"

"Kelly, why are you making this hard for me woman I still love you?"

"Why have you made this hard for me? Why are you here and why do you think I should just pack up and make it easy for you? All I've done was love you, treat you kind, and all you ever done was put me down, call me fat, call me out of my name, and let's not forget treating me as if I was your hooker off the street. Oh and the women you had in the streets that you allowed to disrespect me and you sweetheart did nothing to correct or check her big mouth, low life, wide face ass !"

Ethan stood in the living room looking at the flowers he gave me an hour ago. He pulled one out and got down upon one knee though tear filled eyes he looks up at me.

"Baby I'm sorry."

He looked pathetic I rolled my eyes as I watched my husband who I believed was really earning his Grammy for the best performance of the year.

"Ethan damn all that, what I wanted and needed from you was love then and now all I want from you is a divorce."

Still on one knee looking sad and dismantled Ethan got up and placed the flower back with the group and grabbed his keys as he took one last look at his soon to be ex wife.

" I am so sorry you feel what you feel and I want to say I'm sorry for breaking you the way I did I was wrong_"

"Save the drama for your momma."

"You don't have to be like that the bible says_"

"Negro don't you dare come up in mine trying to preach and teach now. We started out praying but when times got hard where did you go while I sat there night after night praying for you to come home to me! Where were you when I begged you to work things out! Where were you when I set up an appointment with our pastor and you said you didn't want him in our business? But you can get up in the choir and sing like you was so holy, man don't come up in here and try and tell me how I should act you better pull that drama on someone who gives a damn."

"Ok Kelly you feel that way so be it alright!"

I grab his rings and place the carat diamond and gold band in his hands.

"What you don't want your rings I gave this to you."

"Baby you can have those rings I have no need and not only the rings I will be giving you your name back as well."

Ethan picked up his keys off the coffee table and took a long hard breath because he felt defeated crushed and destroyed. I had to checkmate his ass this round but my heart was still feeling love for this fool!

Chapter 14 - - Jada

I was tired and sleepy from being up all night with my daughter who just would not allow sleep to find her. KFC had to make the meal for my family tonight. Fridays are always busy at work and coming home to be a mother, wife, and housekeeper was all a part of my daily thing I enjoyed most of the time, but today was different. I walk into the living room to find my husband asleep on the couch, it was somewhat unusual.

"Byron"

I shake him awake as he rolls over only to start talking in his sleep about some cows and horses. I look at him and laugh, wondering what that was all about, I try poking him in the head with my fingernail.

"Wake up!"

He slowly comes to as I stand there with Jordan in my arms dressed in a blue pantsuit I wore to work, he looks at me up and down rubbing his eyes as he tries to focus.

"Baby where you going?"

"Are you high have you been smoking something?"

"NO!"

"I just got home from work and picked up Jordan from the day care to come home and find you asleep on the couch what's up with that?"

I put Jordan down and sit beside him as I pick up the remote and flip through the channels he start to sit up beside me and begins to yawn.

"Guess I was just tired, I came home for lunch and the rest is history."

I pat him on the leg and make eyes at Jordan who makes her way to the floor so she could crawl around and get into things.

"Honey you work all the time we need to just get away and do something as husband and wife."

Byron wipes his mouth.

"Baby I know you want to get away and all that but you have to understand that I have to work extra hard so we don't have to struggle."

"Honey I know but what profits a man who gains the whole world and losses his family over it as well as his soul!"

"Look Jada I don't need to be preached to today. Baby I work hard trying to pay the bills and all that! You know I have my___"

"Forget it Byron I know you have your own business and all that but even God rested on the Sabbath day!"

I got up from my seated position, took my child so I could clean her up. I rolled my eyes as I walk down the hall. Byron picks up the remote and starts to flip through the channels. Meanwhile I was in Jordan's room changing her diaper. My eyes filled with tears I didn't know what to do. It seems as if I was living in vain with this man I married, damn the house and the SUV and anything else that resemble stuff that keeps the loving part of our marriage in this shambled mess.

We have been living in this house like sister and brother for the past three weeks. He's too tired to touch me and when I go and buy something new the nigga don't even look my way his overworked ass is too tired to notice.

I was being taken for granted and I try not to break down and start thinking crazy thoughts like infidelity and stuff that I know wasn't happening, or was it? The devil is always busy plotting to destroy a marriage because if he can destroy a marriage he can destroy the church. I was not about to let that happen not to my family I work so hard to keep together!

"Hello Cole how you feel today?"

"I'm fine and you?"

"I can't complain it makes no sense to."

"Well that's a good thought; you seem to be in a good mood today."

"You know what I am in a good mood I made a decision when I woke up this morning that I wasn't going to let anything or anybody steal my joy today because God gave it to me and I will not allow the devil to take it away no matter how hard he tries!"

"I hear you sista preach."

"Jada you look as if a heavy load has been lifted off of you." Cole said smiling.

"It has, I learned that if I can't change the world I can't allow it to change who I am."

"You have a point there I have some struggles of my own and so I know what you mean!"

"Oh really, what's that all about?"

I had a look of surprise on my face because he never really talk about anything personal.

"Everyone has something they're struggling with so you're not alone I promise you that."

"I know but sometimes I feel as if I'm alone and I don't have anyone that can relate to what it is I'm going through."

"You know sometimes I feel the same, Jada I think there are times in our lives we feel like that but my grandmother always told me God is a mighty God and there's nothing too hard, too big or small for him to work out!"

"My grandmother use to tell me that too, you think we have the same grandmother?"

I walk in the house only to find my husband and daughter on the couch asleep, trying not to wake them up I tip in the bedroom to find the camera to catch a Kodak moment. I snap three pictures I love my family more than life itself. They are indeed the reason why I breathe. I walk upstairs to the bedroom and slip off my suit and put on a pair of sweats and tee shirt I pick up the phone to dial Madison who I haven't talked with since we went out a couple weeks ago. The answering machine comes on and I begin to leave a message.

"Hey stranger what's ___"

"Jada what's up girl?"

Madison picks up.

"I was beginning to wonder about you."

"Honey between school and work and going to Collin's basketball games I been swamp."

"I hear you honey it's been something here too."

"Cory and I been talking we been having fun!"

"You know it's about time you take timeout for yourself."

"I know it's been a while since I had fun like this. I can't remember the last time I had someone in my life other then my child."

"Girl doesn't it feel good."

"Yes it does. I have something to share with you."

"What is it?"

"You know the weekend I came up to visit?"

"Yes, didn't we have fun? We need to do that again."

"Yes, and soon but anyway that was the weekend Collin Jr. went down south to visit with his father. That was the weekend

Collin Sr. asked Jackie to marry him and he wanted Collin to be there when he asked her."

"Well how do you feel?"

"Honey I'm okay with that I'm happy for them, Jackie said she had been waiting for him to ask her for about a year now."

"I'm going to ask you again how do you feel about that?"

"I told you I'm okay with it."

"Madison I know how you feel about Collin and you know how he feels about you."

"Jada that's my past and I'm going to leave it there alright!"

Madison sits down on the bed as she holds back the tears that were beginning to form in the corner of her eyes.

"Ok Madison if you say so."

"It's okay Jr. Like Jackie and she treat him as if he is her child as well, I think we're going to have a beautiful blended family relationship."

Jada smiles knowing her friend was hurting but wouldn't dare tell her because she's this strong black woman that can't and will not be broken.

"As long as everyone is happy I guess that's all that matters love."

"Collin and Jackie will be just fine and Jackie loves him a lot. She told me she couldn't understand why I wouldn't marry him. I told her it just wasn't my time and Collin is a wonderful man."

"Madison you know what you doing?"

"What do you mean by that?"

"Well I think you're afraid of being in a relationship you don't let anyone get too close when they get close you run or you push them away and why is that?"

"I don't know what you talking about."

"Oh yeah you know what I'm talking about."

"To be honest with you I don't, I just have things I need to do and being in a relationship is not one of them besides I have a son and I don't want him to see me with this and that man!"

"Madison when is the last time you been with a man?"

Madison twirls in her hair as she finds herself getting frustrated.

"I give up because I haven't been with anyone in about two years."

"That's my point you can't let anyone get too close to Miss strong black woman. Forget all that for a minute ok and live a little do that for me."

She couldn't believe her friend read her like an open book and she knew deep down she was telling the truth.

"I guess I can have some fun Cory is sweet and I enjoy his company but remember were only friends nothing more, nothing less, and I'm enjoying that right now."

"You don't know what God's plan is for your life you just hold on because change is coming you just stand still and listen to the voice of God."

"Oh look at you talking Bishop Jada Knight what's going on with you?"

"Oh nothing I just have some new things going on that's all."

"I can tell I need to pay you a visit and see what the deal is yo."

"You do that and I will chat with you real soon."

"Alright Collin Jr. and I may be that way soon love you."

"I love you too you just remember what I said!"

"Don't worry I'll be happy"

Chapter 15 - - Madison

I was fit to be tired trying to study for test, and not to mention work was most defiantly stressing me out, I was in need of a break from both. The only thing I enjoyed the most was my son's basketball games, in which he had one in three hours so I had at least two of those three to rest and of course as soon as I closed my eyes the phone starts to call all the single ladies.

"Hello"

"Hey baby, what it do?"

"Hi Collin what's up?"

"I'm good I'm calling for Jr. is he there?"

"No he's at school he has a game tonight."

"Oh okay, he stayed after school."

"Yes, I can have him call you when we come home tonight."

"I will be there in less than an hour I'm calling from my cell I promised Jr. I would be at his game tonight."

"So you and Jackie, are you guys staying in town tonight?"

"No I'm alone Jackie had something to do I told her I would be back tomorrow I'm staying at the Hampton Inn tonight I would like for Jr. to stay with me?"

"I suppose he can, but that little rascal didn't mention to me that you were coming."

"I apologize if this is an inconvenience to you; to be honest I didn't know if I was going to make it."

"No, its okay we might go to Alexandria tomorrow."

"Oh okay well maybe after the game all three of us can go out to eat on me."

"I guess we can do that."

"Madison I'll be there in about 45 minutes ok."

"Be careful I will see you when you get here."

"Bye"

"Bye."

I was ready as I was going to be, my hair was pulled up in a ponytail makeup done and smelling like Prada, I didn't know what to expect the doorbell rings. I take one last look in the mirror to make sure there were no flaws in my skin I checked my nose for particles. I walk slowly to the door so it didn't seem as if I was too excited about seeing him. I slowly open the door and there he stood looking handsome as he could be with his baseball cap slapped backwards on his head wearing his black Sean John windbreakers jogging suit and Michael Jordan Nike air tennis smelling like Usher.

"Hello Madison." I stood there for at least a minute before saying anything my stomach had a thousand butterflies dancing around.

"Come on in we have at least an hour before game time."

"You look nice as always."

"Thank you."

"Have a seat; would you like to have something to drink?"

"Yes, please"

I make my way into the kitchen and grab a bottle of coke.

"Would you like crushed ice or regular?"

"Crushed is fine I need something cold."

I need something cold myself because what I'm feeling right now is unholy. I nervously walk over to him and hand him a glass of ice and a bottle of coke.

"Thank you."

"You're welcome"

He smiles as he takes a sip of his Coke pouring the rest into his glass not taking his eyes off me making me nervous as hell.

"You sure can make a good glass of coke."

"You're so crazy."

"I know but seriously how you been doing?"

"Why you ask?"

"Because I want to know that's all I haven't seen you since we dropped Jr off about a month ago."

"I been working and going to school you know me I have a lot on my plate these days."

"I hear you, Jackie's been running me crazy with this wedding stuff I just want to show up in a tux that's it she can run around and do whatever for the wedding but I really don't have the time you know."

"I understand"

"Do you really?"

"Yes Collin I understand your point and I also understand where she's coming from. I am a woman."

"I know that better than anyone!"

"Shut up crazy!"

"I understand but she have to go this and that place and the wedding is a year off I really don't get it."

"I don't expect you to because you're a man."

"What you mean by that?"

"First of all it takes a year to plan a wedding silly and second you will never understand the work that goes into planning something that big."

"Oh tell me something, she can just give me a time and I'll be there."

"You think like most men and that's ok."

"Well I just want Jackie to be happy that's all."

"You really love her huh?"

"Yes I do she's supportive and she's her own woman that's what I like most about her." I hide my jealously with a smile.

"That's important being your own woman doing your thing and not forgetting who you are."

"That's true but also you become as one in the spirit."

"I believe that because that's bible but also you have a brain and you can think for yourself, you don't have to have a man to think for you."

"Madison what I love about you is that you are your own woman but at the same time it's like you're afraid to let anyone get too close."

"Why you say that?"

"Its true girl you need some of that foul ground broken up."

"Collin you know nothing about me and ____"

"I'm not trying to get you upset, but may I ask you one question?" Rolling my eyes I suddenly get defensive folding my arms trying not to make eye contact,

"What's that?"

"What's the real reason why you didn't want to marry me?"

I nearly went into heart failure when that question popped up.

"Real talk, I was afraid."

"Afraid of what Madison, Me loving you too much, girl you and Collin Jr mean the world to me and I still love you but I respect your decision."

"I really wanted the same but___"

"There is no but, Madison when you said no to my proposal I thought I was going to blow a main vain in my heart. Baby I tried to keep my swagger in check but my damn heart was crushed and real talk you're the only woman I ever shed a damn tear over."

"Collin I didn't know that."

"You didn't know a lot of things, I cried for a long time after that. Now let me be real with you and I don't ever want to hear this again. I still love you and always will love you and I know you feel the same towards me. I felt it in the last kiss we shared, in which that will never happen again."

My eyes soften and tears started to roll down my face as I leaned into Collin's chest and he comforted me.

"I am so sorry for hurting you." He rubs my back.

"It's okay I just want you to heal from your broken wounds because you are such a beautiful woman and you deserve so much more. Just let someone into your world and give them a chance that's all."

"Daddy thanks for coming to the game!"

"So you know I wouldn't have missed this for the world."

"I know did you see me hit those three points at the end of the fourth quarter that won the game!"

I smiled, as I place my arms around my son.

"Honey everybody saw the shot that saved your team a loss."

"I'm so proud of you."

"Thanks daddy I'm going over here to talk with some of my friends is that alright?"

"You go and meet us at your daddy's car in ten minutes."

"Ok ma I'll be right there."

"What are we going to do with him?"

"I don't know but I know the boy has skills he inherited that from me."

"Whatever."

"Ms. Courtney"

I turned around and looked at the tall light completed man that greets me with a smile and hand shake.

"Your son played a wonderful game tonight."

"Thank you coach McGee?"

"I been working with Collin and he have some serious skills and I would love to work with him in my summer program at basketball camp in Dallas."

"This is Collin's father Collin Sr. and maybe we can talk about that soon."

They shake hands.

"It's nice to meet you."

"You as well, I see you been teaching my son how to be a team player."

"Well I teach them all how to play like a team and make decisions that best make the team look good."

"Well it was really nice to meet you I do have plans of coming back to see you guys play Shreveport."

"You do that! We have a game next week so you come back I know Ms. Courtney will be here."

"I live in South Louisiana but I will make it my business to come back."

"Well I have to go and talk with some more parents and head home you take it easy and drive safe."

"I will coach."

"He's such a nice man and I like the way he work with Collin."

"He was looking at you sista."

"Please, I can't help that I got it like that!"

Chapter 16 - - Kobe

Brenda and I were out on the balcony looking at Shayla on the playground with all the other kids. The weather was nice considering it was mid January and 88 degrees. Keisha was at her part time job and I have God to thank for that. Shayla and I often have a pleasant time when Keisha is away from home since she has become a major pain in my ass. I decided to get my hair wash and braided today since the wicked witch of the South was away for a few hours. Brenda braided my hair every two weeks and today was just a perfect day to have her come over she was finishing up my last three braids.

"Your hair is really cute."

"We'll look at me I'm a handsome dude." I rub my chin and shoot my sister a wide grin.

"Negro please you wish you looked half as good as I do with your calf head ass."

"All the women want a brotha like me I'm a playa I thought you knew."

"Ok playa I'm not going to go there with you."

Marcus pulls up in the parking lot bumping his music with the trunk rattling the sounds tearing up his frame if you ask me with all that damn noise.

"Look at Marcus, his car is tight."

"I see I guess he's doing alright the last time I talked with him was at mom and dad's BQ at the house."

"What's up ninja?"

Marcus looks around and throws up a peace sign as he walks towards me. His hair was in a blow out Afro, sporting his blue and white Nike wind suit and tennis to match. Marcus makes his way up the stairs as he passes a couple of ladies watching his smooth swag, he nods and make eye contact.

"How you beautiful fine women doing today?"

They giggle and watch him pass and said among themselves.

"Fine if you bring your fine ass back our way."

He heard the comment and said,

"I'll holla back at yawl lata." He walks in the apartment and to the balcony where his cousins wait.

"What it do?"

"Man what you doing in this part of town?"

"I'm chillen man." Marcus looked happy he couldn't stop smiling.

"What's up with you why are you standing there smiling looking like an old chess cat?" Brenda said while finishing my last braid.

"Baby I just feel good I had a job interview to go off shore and the man called me Friday and said I had the job. I passed my drug test and I tell you it felt good to walk up in that clinic and know I was going to pass that test." Brenda offered a smile.

"See I knew you could do it that's what's up."

"Not only that my homeboys that I freestyle with said this dude from Baton Rouge wants to get us in the studio next weekend. My boy T knows a dude down south that have some hook ups and so they heard our demo and said they wanted to invest in us!"

"Man what a break!" I give my cousin some dap.

"See life can offer you some good stuff if you just do what's right."

"Yeah man but I had to learn the hard way. My mom's is so

happy right now, when I told her I passed the drug test for the off shore job she burst into tears. Moms have been through a lot cuz."

"Honey you can do anything you put your mind to, believe that!"

"Well Marcus, you tried talking to Lisa again?" I interrupt.

"Yeah man she was really happy about the job I told her I was going to take care of her and her son with the money I bring in."

"So you two are back together."

"Nope not really she said that she wants to know if I'm going to really keep the job and stay focused on my future before she takes a chance."

Brenda comments. "Do you blame her ninja you wasn't no good before you got locked down you kelp that girl upset and she was really good to your black ass!"

"I love Lisa and I'm going to do right by her this time because I know she is the only one that will have my back when I'm down yo."

"Man I feel what you saying you do your thing and stay focused."

"Brenda will you do my hair tonight?"

"What time Marcus because my man is coming over tonight?"

"Can you do it around seven?"

"Yeah I can swing that just call me and I'll hook you up, now Marcus don't have me waiting for you."

"Come on Brenda have I ever done that to you?"

"Ninja please you did it two weeks ago!"

"Alright I did that!" He laughs.

"But I had something to do baby girl forgive me if I don't come I will call you. Better yet here is my cell holla at me." Brenda snatches the paper out of his hand and places it in her pocket. Shayla races in the house and onto the balcony in tears Brenda grabs her.

"What's wrong baby?"

"Mommy slapped me and told me to get home now because I wasn't supposed to be out alone but I was right there on the playground I told her you and daddy were on the porch and she yelled at me anyway."

"Honey stop crying okay go in the house and wash your face aunt Brenda is going to take care of this alright give me a hug."

I was already downstairs yelling as Keisha stands beside her car. Brenda races down stairs Marcus in tow.

"Keisha!"

I try to stop my sister from saying anything by holding her arm.

"Be quiet." Marcus watches alone with all the neighbors.

"No I'm not going to be quiet because my niece is up there crying because you hit her in the face for no reason at all clowning her in front of her friends all you had to do Keisha was tell her to go in the house but you have such an attitude that won't end you have to show your natural butt."

"Look girl you stay out of my business and get a man of your own and a family of your own and leave my family alone!"

Brenda snatched away from me as I just give up and walk upstairs to make sure my daughter was not seeing this drama fest.

"You act as if I want my brother yes I love him more then you can imagine but he's my brother and that little girl in there I love her as if she's my own child!"

"I wouldn't care if___"

"Ladies let's take this in the house people are watching." Marcus said calmly.

"I don't care, this heffa is crazy and everyone knows it. She has thrown all his clothes into the street before and then begs for him to work things out and his dumb___"

"Brenda, Keisha is not worth it okay." Marcus grabs his cousin and walks back towards the apartment building.

"I don't know where you're going because you're not welcome in my house."

"If you must know I'm going to get my things and I'm out of here I don't want to be in your house!"

"Get your stuff and don't come back! And Marcus you don't bring your thuggish ass back either!"

"Look little mamma I was coming to holla at Kobe not you baby girl but if you don't want me at your house bitch you only have to tell me once."

Keisha walks back to her car as she pulls out some bags and hopes they leave before she could get to the door. Brenda was upset Marcus talks as they walk in the house.

"I can't believe that girl, she's an angry bitch."

"She is so stupid Kobe need to get rid of her for real!" I sit on the couch with my head in my hands I am so tired of the drama its damn if I do and damn if I don't.

"Look Brenda I don't need to hear this right now!"

"Kobe if you weren't my brother I would have put a whipping on that girl for real!"

"I know just holla at me later I'll be by your house okay!"

"Alright I love you."

"Man I'll see you later alright."

"Alright dog, and congratulations again on the job"

Keisha walks in with the bags in her hands.

"Tramp you ain't out my house yet?" I stand up and yell my blood pressure rise to a new level.

"Keisha that's enough I'm tired of you calling my sister out of her name!"

"I can care less who she is that's a tramp and she will forever be a tramp in my book now get the hell out of my house!" Brenda looked at Shayla standing there with tears in her eyes as she watches her mom walk in the kitchen with the bags she was carrying.

"Honey, give Aunt Brenda a hug." Brenda reaches for her niece.

"Can I go with you Aunt Brenda?" She whispers

"Maybe your daddy can bring you over later ok I will have ice cream waiting for you alright!"

"Ok I love you."

Brenda winks at her brother as she and Marcus heads towards the door.

"Man you hold it down dude and keep your head up."

He extends his hand up in a black power fist. I manage to laugh as they walk out the door. After doing so I turn and look at Keisha.

"Keisha, may I ask you a question."

She sits on the couch as if nothing was wrong crossing her fat legs.

"What is it?" I couldn't stand the sight of her she has gotten ugly over the year not in looks but in her attitude.

"Why did you hit Shayla in the face?"

"I always told her if you weren't outside or I wasn't out there she was not to come out!"

"Didn't she tell you I was getting my hair done and I was watching her?"

"Kobe I didn't see you and no she didn't say that she said that you were upstairs."

"You act as if I don't have any sense at times, you know as well as I do, I'm not going to let anything happen to Shay."

"I didn't know I will talk to her later I was just upset and it got all out of hand with your sister and cousin all in mine."

"Brenda was upset about you hitting Shay that's all."

"I don't care what she was upset about she needs to stay out of my business."

I rub my head trying not to slap the hell out of her trifling ass.

Chapter 17 - - Kobe

It's been five days and Keisha and I haven't really talked with one another, Shayla had been over to Keisha's, mother's house for three of those days.

"Good morning."

Keisha says in a low tone voice trying to wave the white flag by sitting next to me on the love seat in the corner of our living room. I been sleeping on the couch since the day she slapped our daughter.

"Morning Keisha"

I decide to get up and walk towards the bathroom. Keisha walks into the kitchen as she puts on a pot of coffee. I was wondering what move she was going to make next; she knew I had a bad taste in my mouth after her show the other day. It certainly didn't take a rocket scientist to figure out I've had enough of her foolishness. After brushing my teeth and washing my face I walk into the kitchen and make my presence known by sitting at the table with my hands folded together.

"Honey we need to talk."

I bit my bottom lip and said nothing as I give her this disapproval look.

"Did you hear me?"

I stare out the window in deep thought wondering how the hell I find myself in such a mess of a marriage.

"Kobe I'm sorry for everything. We can't keep walking around this house not saying anything to one another tell me what you thinking at least!"

"I have to get ready to go to work after I get off I'm going to pay a deposit on this building I saw down Macarthur Dr. it's a really good location for my shop."

"That's nice but did you hear anything I said."

"Yes I heard you but like I say I have to go to work."

"Can you just call in so we can work on us today?"

"Keisha we have bills to pay, and I can't just call in and I'm tired of working on us to be honest with you."

I know she was trying not to get mad and so she just sucked that up and smiled, but I knew it was only a matter of time before the horns would come out again.

"I understand." Looking unconcern I asked,

"Do you really understand?"

"I understand trust me."

I get up slowly from my seated position and walk up to Keisha and give her a kiss on the cheek.

"Thanks for having our daughter."

She blinks, trying not to show any emotion which was very hard to do considering the situation at hand. Keisha knew this was the beginning of the end she never experienced such coldness in my eyes and the resentment in my heart. I was about to check mate her ass and she knew it. I make my way to the door not looking back I hear Keisha crying I felt like doing the same but decided against that because it was just too much. I have always done what she asked of me, this time was different. The phone rings Keisha picks up trying not to sound like she had been crying.

"Hello"

"Hello honey how is everything?"

"Mrs. Dorothy I'm not doing well at all today."

"What's wrong you feeling bad?"

When the Honeymoon Is Over

"I'm feeling bad and worse I don't think Kobe loves me anymore."

She starts to cry out of control. Dorothy didn't know what to say to her daughter in law because it's been so bad between them for so long and she tried to stay out of her children's business but felt Keisha's pain at that moment.

"Honey stop crying where is Shayla? She really doesn't need to see you like that. "She's at my mom's house she's been over there for a couple of days."

"Well you need to get yourself together."

"I know, I need my husband back and I want it like it was in high school."

"Honey, let me tell you something and this is between you and me. You have to get yourself together first. I know my son has tried working things out with you, and I also know how you treat him."

"Ms. Dorothy___"

"Hush and allow me to finish, you guys have been married going on ten years you have a beautiful and smart daughter who knows what's going on between you two."

"But Ms___"

"Didn't I say hush?"

"Yes but I want you to know that it's not all my fault."

"I didn't say one time that it was your fault Keisha, Kobe has his ways too. But you have to learn how to trust him and love him without all the nagging you do. No man

Likes all that nagging especially when he is doing all he can do to make his marriage work."

"I know I been a little out of hand lately."

"Lately, honey you been out of control for years and my son and no one else son is going to put up with it you understand me?"

"Yes, I understand you perfect. Are you mad with me Mrs. Dorothy?"

Dorothy takes a hard breath.

"Honey, I'm not mad with you today but there are days you made me so angry I wanted to come over there and give you a butt whipping your momma never gave you because of the way you would talk to my child no mother wants their child to be mistreated or hurt."

"Well he's not your child anymore he's my husband."

"See this is the reason why I never say anything to you because of your mouth."

"I'm sorry but it seems as if the family is always on my case."

"Well allow me to tell you this; he will always be my child, and as far as being your husband_ well that's a horse of a different color."

"What you mean?"

"You know exactly what I mean you're a smart girl, use your brain."

Dorothy found herself getting a little upset because she was tired of how Keisha was acting towards the family and how she would belittle her son for no reason.

"Well I know what you're saying but you don't live here to know what goes on behind my doors."

"Honey look I'm not saying Kobe Richard is a saint but if he's not treating you right I don't expect you to take no stuff off him. He is still a man and I don't stand behind him when he is doing wrong. I've always encouraged my son to work on his marriage regardless of what you think!"

"I understand what you saying and I love Kobe very much."

"Keisha, do you really love him?"

"Why you ask that question?"

"The reason why I ask because it's been in my spirit that you really don't love him you don't want to be alone or don't want to see him happy."

"Why would you say something like that Mrs. Dorothy that hurts my feelings."

"Well baby put your feelings on hold for a second and think about what I'm telling you. You two have been unhappy for a long time and it seem as if you're just going through the motions and you go out of your way to make Kobe angry and it seem as if you have control over my sons mind. Now if you don't love him don't play with him like you do."

Keisha puts the phone down to her side because Dorothy has struck a nerve.

"Look I have to go now you have a good day."

"You just remember this conversation was between you and me."

"Yes I will remember that!"

Keisha slammed the phone down mad as hell. Dorothy didn't seem as friendly as usual she seem to be tired of her as well. Keisha started to cry all over again.

I walk through the door after a long day, it was ten o'clock and I was worn out from work. The She Devil was on the couch.

"Hi how was your day today?"

"Long" I didn't offer a smile and I certainly wasn't too happy about her sitting on my bed.

"Well why are you so late getting home?"

"Look woman don't start with me!"

"I just asked a question that's all."

I pull off my shirt and headed to the shower when Shayla heard me and opened her door and yelled.

"Hi daddy"

"Hi butterfly"

I smiled and greeted my daughter with a hug.

"I had fun today; Mommy and I went to the mall and bought some new dresses and shoes you want to see."

"Yeah show daddy what you got!" I saw the look in my daughter's eyes and couldn't tell her I was tired and was not interested in her dress or shoes. Keisha walks in the room and helps her pull out the two dresses she had bought for church.

"I thought this was really cute they were on sale."

She held up the blue and white color dress and the other dress was black and white. Her shoes were black with a wide hill.

"Daddy I love my shoes don't you?"

I smile in agreement.

"Honey they are very nice."

"Daddy please will you come to church with us Saturday?"

Keisha's a Seventh Day Adventist and it's been a while since we went to church and I couldn't remember the last time we went together.

"Daddy will think about it okay baby."

"Ok daddy just whatever you want to do I won't be mad if you don't but mommy would like for you to go with us as a family." I looked at my daughter and knew that this wasn't her idea and I gave her a kiss on the cheek.

"Baby it's time for you to go to bed daddy will see you in the morning okay."

"Ok daddy good night I love you."

"Daddy loves you too."

I walk out the door and down the hall. Keisha was still in the room with our daughter tucking her in as she told her.

"Honey you wasn't suppose to tell him I wanted him to go you was supposed to tell him you wanted him to go."

"Mommy what's wrong, why don't you want daddy to go to church with us?"

"Never mind Shayla good night baby love you and mommy is very sorry about the other day you forgive me?"

"Mommy I love you and I forgive you but you need to stop making daddy mad ok." Keisha eyes filled with tears her daughter

When the Honeymoon Is Over

was too smart for her own good and she knew exactly what was going on and she wanted to make things right for a change.

"Mommy is going to make things okay believe me."

Shayla yawns and turns over. Keisha pulls the covers up and tucks them under her mattress and kisses her on the cheek. She pulls the door shut and walks into the bedroom and sits on the bed while I take my shower. She flips through the channels as she waits patiently for me to finish up. Ten minutes later she hears the water stop, steam enters the bedroom first when I open the bathroom door as I walk out with my blue boxers and tee shirt on. I walk towards the bedroom door. Keisha sits up trying to make herself comfortable on the pillow she was laying on.

"Wait I want you to come get in the bed."

"Good night baby I'm going to sleep on the couch."

"Please Kobe come to bed I'm tired of this game I'm lonely without you in here I can't sleep."

I turn and look at her with cold dark eyes because I wasn't trying to hear all that.

"Baby I'm sorry but this isn't working out for us."

"I want it to and I want things to change as of today."

"I want it to change, but it's always the same old thing and I can't handle this anymore it's time we know that this is not working out!"

"Whatever Kobe, You must have been out seeing Jewel that's why you late and that's why you want to sleep on the couch."

I walk out without saying a word and to the couch I went Keisha threw a shoe at the door missing my head by inches the woman was just crazy and I don't do crazy.

Chapter 18 - - Cory

After I leave the gym I have plans to meet with Madison and her son. The state fair was going on and I promised Collin I would take him. While I put on my sweat pants and shirt, I decided to pop in Usher's new CD. I make my way to the kitchen to fix a protein shake before my workout. The phone rings I look at the caller ID to see who was calling at five am. I hope like hell it wasn't my agent telling me to come in because I needed today, besides I looked forward to seeing Madison's beautiful face. The caller ID said it was out of area. I grab the phone and answer in my nonchalant tone.

"Hello"

Speaking just above a whisper the caller says,

"Hello, Cory"

"Who's speaking?"

"I'm sorry I didn't get a chance to call you back a couple of weeks ago I had something going on with me and I had to handle my business. I place the phone at my side for a moment. I feel my heart pounding thinking at any moment it will jump right out of my chest.

"Latisha, okay it's all good lady I'm cool."

"Cory things haven't been okay since you and I split up and I just had to see if things would work out between my husband and me."

I really wasn't trying to hear this crap now I'm trying to move forward.

"Look I understand we don't have to keep going through this I told you that it's all gravy in the Navy all good in the hood." We both share a weak laugh.

"I know I just miss you so much and I want to know when I can come to Louisiana to see you."

"Now Tisha I don't think that would be wise, besides you have a husband and I'm busy working baby I can't do this right now."

"To be honest with you Cory__"

I interject with a mild force.

"I'm not being mean or anything I'm just trying to move on with my life I felt those three years I spent with you were not only a waste but you broke your promise so why should I trust what you say? Do you realize Tisha that you lied in the beginning of our relationship? I forgave you but then you said that it was over then you went back so you made your bed now lie in it. Now if you think that I'm bitter no, I don't fault you, I fault myself for falling for the okee-doke."

"Look Cory Please don't go off on me I'm sorry, I am I never meant to hurt you, certainly, I didn't lie to you about how I felt, you meant the world to me and still do. I love you with all my being that's true I don't know how to express what it is I'm feeling at this very moment_"

"Look you don't have to and I certainly don't have the time to listen now, I will not and I cannot lie to you about what it is I'm feeling because it's only been a couple of months and sexing you a while back was a huge mistake lady but I still love you in case you're wondering but I have moved on.

"Cory I guess I have to respect that but can we be friends at least?"

"I rather not because we need to get pass all this."

"Ok I accept that I guess I have to, well I thought I would get a chance to see you because my cousin in Baton Rouge is getting married this February and I will be flying there on the fourth to

When the Honeymoon Is Over

help her I will be there for two weeks so I just thought to ask so if you change your mind let me know all right."

"Yeah, sure I will let you know good bye Tisha."

"Bye Cory, have a good day Okay."

"Sure see ya."

I hang up the phone and realize that it was already six o'clock I missed my secession with my trainer this call threw me way off and I have to pay for a training I missed damn.

I run in the apartment two hours later and start the shower so I could get ready for my day with Madison and Collin. But I can't seem to get Latisha off my mind I know I had to move on because she just wasn't the one.

After my shower I take a look in the closet to see what I was going to sport for the day. My walk in closet was neat and clean my shoes were on the shelf, shirts were on the right side and jeans and pants were on the left. I pull out a pair of starch down True Religion Jeans and sweatshirt it was a little cool so I decided to wear my black Polo boots.

Madison turns the radio on to listen to bad Boy J Jigger, her favorite radio personality

"Hey people this is J Jigger doing it in your ear were about to set it off up in this joint. In just minuets I will be pulling the name of the grand prizewinner of the Fantastic Voyage Cruise with our very own morning man the hardest workingman on the radio Tom J

"How are you doing Tom?"

"Oh Jigger I'm doing just fine can't wait to draw this name so we can see who the grand prizewinner is, were about to set sail for the seas this coming June12[th] I look forward to the cruise it's still some months off but it gets better each year. We have on this year's cruise Frankie Beverly and Maze, Boys to Men, Gladys Knight, Little Richard, The Soul Child, Kelly Price, and more were going to have one big party. This is not only a party for us to have a good time it's to help our black college students stay in school. So people if you want to do this to help black students book the cruise and the money made from this cruise will go to the black college fund as you know J Jigger we need to educate our people."

"I hear you Tom I agree with you I plan to be on the cruise. I look forward to this myself it's for seven days right?"

"Right Jigger we will have so much food and fun not to mention the Captain's Ball and dinner so ladies break out your dancing shoes and men come in your swagger suites and let's get this party jumping."

"Well here is the big moment we all been waiting for; the lucky winner of the Tom Joiner fantastic voyage cruise is Ms. Madison Courtney of Ruston La. If you're listening Madison please give us a call here at the station congratulations once again Madison Courtney of Ruston you are indeed our lucky winner of the Fantastic Voyage Cruise. You and a friend will fly to Port Canaveral FL. You will spend one paid night at the Hilton suite hotel and the next evening you will set sail. Madison if you're listening please call us here at the radio station."

Madison couldn't believe that she had won she screamed "I can't believe I won this cruise I can't believe this!"

Collin hears his mom scream so he comes running in her room where she was sitting on the bed with her cordless phone in her hand trying to think of the number she was so excited about winning this cruise she forgot the number to the radio station.

"What is it why are you screaming?"

"Well, son your mom just won a cruise." As she dances around the room listening to the radio as they play "I look good" Collin starts to jig with his mom.

"Mom you won a cruise?"

"Yes, I won you know I never win anything I went to Dillard's in the mall one day and put my name down in a drawing and now I'm going on a cruise."

"That's great mom I'm happy for you now who are you going to take?"

Madison never really thought about that. She was just happy she was going and she had five months to plan.

"I really don't know yet?"

"I know you can take Cory he is so nice to you and you two like being around one another so why not?"

"You have a point I have to see but right now I have to call the radio station do you know the number?"

"Yeah it's 800 447-9799 do you need me to call for you?"

"No son I got this under control you go get your clothes together." Madison then starts to dial the number when her phone begins to ring.

"Hello."

"Well hello to you. You sound happy."

"Who is this?"

"Oh you don't remember your baby daddy?"

"Hi Collin I didn't recognize your voice how are you?"

"I'm fine and you?"

"I'm doing just fine"

"I can hear that, what I'm calling for is to see if Collin could come down next month to go to a Saints function with me."

"I see"

"I will come and pick him up that Thursday can he get out of school for two days?"

"Well I have to think about that because I don't like for him to miss school can you come that Thursday evening maybe then he will only miss one day of school. Now when is the game?"

"Sunday afternoon it's not a game it's a function they are having I will send him back on the plane that Sunday night after the function so he can be back for school that Monday morning."

"Well I have no problem with that as long as he wants to go he can."

"Is he there?"

"Yes he's here let me get him alright." Madison then walk down the hall to see where her son was he stood in his closet checking out the clothes he wanted to wear to the fair.

She handed him the phone.

"Who is this?"

"Look boy just answer the phone and stop asking all these questions."

Madison hands him the phone and walks into the kitchen. After a few seconds Jr walks into the kitchen where his mom was cooking breakfast.

"Here mom daddy wants to speak to you?" She grabs the phone and kisses him on the cheek.

"Now you go and take your bath while I finish cooking so we can be ready when our ride gets here."

"Sure thing momma" Collin runs in the back while his mom put the phone to her ear.

"Hello"

"Yes, it's me, check this out Collin tells me that you're going to the fair today with a male friend anyone I know?"

"Boy you're so nosey"

"Well I know it's been a while since you had someone. Busy with school and work all the time I was beginning to wonder about you."

"In case you're wondering baby boy I still have it."

"Well I saw that the last time I laid eyes on you. Your butt had it going on it was a lot of junk in that trunk girl!"

"You're crazy you need to quit."

"Well baby girl I have to jet you take care alright."

"You do the same." Maybe now she can give the radio station a

When the Honeymoon Is Over

call. As Madison dials the number she then hears. "102Jamz how may I help you today?"

"Yes, maybe you can, this is Madison Courtney and I won the trip!" With excitement in her voice she let out a soft scream.

"Okay Madison I was beginning to wonder if you wanted to go on the voyage congratulations girl what are your plans for this trip like who are you going to take?" "Well I have a friend I would like to take with me but I really don't know his schedule I will be there no matter what!"

"We'll tell me something what's your favorite radio station?"

"102 Jamz of course is the station I keep it locked on!"

"Thank you Madison for calling I have all your information on this card and I would like to take this time to confirm it and you will have your plane tickets in the mail alone with your Sea Pass you go girl I will also be on this cruise so I look forward to seeing you on the ship. Madison you take care and keep it locked on 102 Jamz you heard me."

"I look forward to this cruise and I will be sure to hook up with you on the boat thanks J Jigger." Madison placed the phone down on the charger she then let's out a huge scream. "I'm going on a cruise and it's going to be off the chain!"

Finally I was dressed, smelling good and looking fresh; I grab my I phone off the charger and begin to look around to make sure I didn't leave anything behind. I walk out the door to the parking lot to get in my classic Impala SS. Before I could get the key in the door I hear someone blowing their car horn. Olivia drives up in her brand new Pink Cadillac sporting her Prada shades and red lipstick looking good I must say. Her hair was cut into a fashionable Mohawk; makeup was flawless and always well dressed and ready for business. The Mary Kay businesswomen always look the part. She rolls her window down as she pull up beside me.

"Hey you, what's your story and why haven't I heard from

you?" I give Olivia a sly grin because I really didn't have an answer as I move closer to her new car leaning into the window.

"I been busy and what's with you?"

Olivia frowns as she speaks.

"I have left you messages and still haven't heard from you. I had been worried about you." I open the door to get in Olivia's car I speak to a couple of guys that was passing by. "What's up?" They look back and holla "What's up dawg haven't seen you in a minute."

"Need to get off lock son and holla at us for real." The tall light skin brotha speaks as he throws up a peace sign.

"I hear you I will catch up with yawl later holla at me alright?"

"Okay son."

Olivia looks over her shades at me not saying a word not smiling. I look back at her smiling.

"What, why are you looking at me like that Olivia what have I done now?"

"You don't know?"

"No I don't!"

"Well I don't know if I can take this anymore Cory I really like you, but you always seem so distant and I'm just tired of it."

"Olivia where is this coming from, you acting like I'm your man or something."

"Oh were not a couple huh?"

"I told you I wasn't ready for all that you said you were cool with that." Olivia eyes watered but she refuses to let a tear fall from her face gripping her steering wheel tighter.

"Well Cory I thought you were different from all the other men out there, but you're a jackass just like everyone else."

"Olivia I'm_"

"Save it Cory save the drama for your momma alright get the hell out of my car I don't need you."

"Listen to me Olivia please!"

"What is it?"

"When we started seeing one another I told you that I wasn't ready for anything real serious. You said you didn't have time for a relationship anyway and that you were building your business in Mary Kay. I really thought you meant that."

"Cory you are so shallow, when we slept together and started spending time with one another I just thought that_"

"Wait! You thought wrong and I apologize if I mislead you."

"Cory I'm sorry too because I have to tell you that I'm a damn good woman who is in business for herself that's going places in her life and I don't need you."

"Olivia you are a very beautiful woman and you have done well for yourself I'm sorry you feel the way you do towards me because if given a chance I can be a really good friend to you. I'm just not ready to settle down I told you that my last relationship went due south and I have to sort things out." Olivia gets emotional for a moment.

"You see Cory this is so difficult for me because a good brotha is so hard to find and it just take one woman to screw it all up for the ones who are real. I certainly wish you well, but I have to get gone before I start to scream all up in here."

I get out of the car and stand there as Olivia drive off starting from zero to sixty in a matter of seconds I never seen a Cadillac roll that quickly in a matter of minutes.

Chapter 19 - -Jalen

Getting together on Sundays was the normal setting for us to play ball in the park but this Sunday was different. We decided to make our way to Kobe's apartment complex and set up shop on the asphalt on his court there. Byron and Cory were against Kobe and I, they were winning by four points and we needed to get our asses in line if we were going to win this game. Byron made a slam dunk past Kobe and I have to say I was a little upset but it was only a game so I let it go, as for Kobe he took things a little more serious than I expected him to and push Byron to the ground.

"Man what the hell's wrong with you? It's only a damn game no need to get so serious." Byron tries to understand that this was unlike Kobe to get mad about anything.

"Look man I'm sorry I have some things on my mind and I took it out on you and for that I apologize." Kobe reaches for Byron's hand to pull him off the ground.

"Man you're my dog you know this right but next time you pull some shit like that I'm going to kick your ass and for that I won't apologize!"

They all laugh as they go and sit down at a picnic table grabbing their water bottles.

"Man those are some fine asses walking there." Cory looks at Byron as he wipes the sweat off his face with his towel.

"Man please Madison is all of that and then some! Not only is she fine she's smart." Byron looks at Cory strangely. "Man sounds to me that you're in love with this woman now what's up with that?"

"Not a thing and no I'm not in love don't you know love don't love nobody!" Kobe gets up off the ground and start bouncing the basketball.

"Hey let's play another round." Jalen look at Kobe and waves him off.

"Man let's call it a night on this balling what's with you?" Still bouncing the ball and chewing his gum like it was the last piece he will ever have.

"Nothing I haven't played in a while and I just want to play that's all."

Jalen yells. "Man please you got some crap with you, were your boys you can come out and tell us what's going on."

Kobe stops bouncing the ball and chewing his gum

"Look you niggas can't help me, hell I can't help my damn self it's really messed up how things are going." They all stare at Kobe as he breaks down for a second.

"I'm tired of Keisha she has turned into a witch from hell I can't do a damn thing right in her eyes and I really don't want to be there to tell you the truth I'm only there for Shayla even my daughter knows deep down there is something wrong. Hell it's written all over our faces when we speak to one another and I've grown tired of it."

Cory then speaks "Look man I know you're hurting and for some reason women don't think we hurt but hell, to be honest with you we hurt worse because we're scared to love and let someone love us because when Tisha did that bogus bullshit she did, that hurt like hell and I can't seem to get pass all that and be the girl's friend at least."

Byron places his hand under his chin as he speaks.

"Look we have to make the best out of a bad situation you know. Kobe you have a daughter and to be honest with you man your doing the right thing by staying because you have a family so suck it up and be a real man. As you can see I look at honeys but I'm not going to leave Jada for anyone, bump all what you heard man!"

Jalen then stands to his feet.

"Look I hear you brothers talking but what if you marry the wrong woman?"

Kobe takes a hard look at Jalen and speaks in a mad tone.

"Man what in the hell are you talking about you and Reagan been together for years and I'm sure you two will be together for years to come." They give each other pounds.

"Sho nuff we been together forever but I'm not sure what to think or say to Reagan about marriage hell I see what it is you go through Kobe, and I don't want the same thing you know it seem as if we get along better living together okay!"

"Man you're dreaming if you think that Reagan is going to let you continue to live with her. She don't need you playa she has education and a career she has a lot to offer not to mention she's fine as hell nigga you better get on your job, and that meal she whipped up for that dinner party man you better make her your wife ninja."

Kobe smiles as he think about how he use to talk with Jewel and how smart and creative she is he enjoyed being around her because she was the most loving and kind hearted woman he ever met. She also was supportive and didn't give him attitude unlike Keisha.

"Man I have to bounce I have to go and pick up Shayla from my mom's house I will meet you guys later at the club alright." They all give each other a man hug as they see Kobe off, Byron smiles to himself as he shakes his head then Cory look at Byron and says.

"Man what's wrong with you?"

"Nothing man I feel for a brotha he has something else going on with his ass trust me."

I decided to walk off because Kobe wasn't the only one with something going on with him I had some issues as well. I love Reagan but wasn't ready for the black tie affair.

I want it to be right and I was just plain scared to be honest. I wondered if Reagan would stop doing the things she do after we get married because I remembered when Kobe and Keisha got married they were so in love with one another they had been together since high school Keisha got pregnant and Kobe wanted to do the right thing by getting married and the right thing cost him not only his freedom but his happiness and I just wasn't ready to deal like that. Byron on the other hand he claims he love his wife but he look at other women as if he is not a married man hell sometimes he meets women and don't even tell them he's married. He has a beautiful queen for a wife and personally the women he looks at don't have a thing on his wife so what's wrong with that picture?

Reagan doesn't ask for anything she's independent and that's what I love about her she loves me I know and I love her as well I just have a damn mental block about making her my wife.

"Look man what are you over here thinking about?" Byron walks over towards me as he grabs his backpack that was full of towels and water bottles

"Nothing I have so much work to do that's all you know Sundays are really busy for me I need to get things ready for tonight I have a new bartender to train for 8:00."

"Oh really what's his name."

"Actually he is a she. She just moved here from the West Coast and needed a job so I hired her because she use to work in a club in Los Angeles one of Vicky's friends."

"Well that's good man I hope things work out for you."

"Thanks, me too man."

Meanwhile Reagan is working out at the gym with three of her hottest star players Kristy Black, Rosland Williams, and Zola Cooper they always like to hang out with Reagan so they could get in some extra workout time that's what made them super ball players.

"Hey ladies that will be all for today. I'm tired and I will see you on Monday."

Zola fixes her braids up in a ponytail she then takes off running to end her training for the day she always ran five laps around the gym then walks two to cool off Rosland would work on her jump shot and wouldn't quit until she made ten shots in a row Kristy would work on her lay-ups at the end of practice. While Zola, Kristy and Rosland do their thing Reagan begin to pick up the loose balls and stack them onto the basketball rack as she pick up the last ball Zola walk over to her and ask.

"Coach, will you walk the last two laps with me because I need to talk to you."

"Sure Zola what's up?"

Zola had a worried look on her face she always was the coolest of the three star players and she never worried about anything, she was a beautiful soft brown A student with a plan. She pulls her braids up in a ponytail and says,

"Well coach I don't know what to do about my boyfriend Kelvin he quit school a year ago and he's doing nothing with his life and I'm quite concern about that."

"Well Zola what concerns you?"

"Well he quite college like I said a year ago and went to work off shore for about six months with his brother who owns a rig out in the gulf. I don't know what happen out there but he came home. He's been living with his sister for about a month. Kelvin is doing nothing not to mention the heavy drinking. I'm concern because it's messing up our relationship and I don't need this sort of thing right now I need him to be supportive and loving to me and he has done some file stuff to me lately."

"Like what?"

"Well, coach I know I can trust you and I need you right now to just listen and please do not judge me alright."

"First of all Zola you can feel free to talk to me about anything and don't hesitate to come to me whenever you need to talk that's what I'm here for okay and who am I to judge." As Zola eyes start to fill with tears they decide to walk out to the track so that the other girls wouldn't see her cry as they finish up their training.

"Well coach here is the scoop I been with Kelvin for three years and I put up with a lot of his mess and he put up with mine but now it seem as if he is so damn different it's like he's a new person. I felt that quitting school was a mistake we both came to college together on a full scholarship his grades were excellent so I didn't know what he was thinking about when he decided to work off shore. I know the money was good because he worked there during the summer when we were out of school but never in a million years had I thought he would quit and that's when our problems began. Now that he is not working it's been really hard and his sista is about to kick his ass out on the streets because all he want to do now is party hang out late bring his thug friends to the house and check this out smoke weed. Kelvin never smoked weed before and now this is something new for him and I don't like it and I have told him this but he seem to do what he want to do I don't have a problem with that but when he come to see me now he acts as if he's angry about something and he always picks with me. It's getting on my damn nerves."

Reagan smiles as she sits down on the grass and cross her legs and motion for Zola to do the same.

"Look let's take up some sun while I school you for a minute do you love Kelvin?"

"Yes, I love him so much."

"How much do you love him sis?"

"What do you mean?"

"What do I mean is how much do you love him?"

"I love him with all my heart."

"No, do you love him more than life itself kind of love or do you love him as in you're my friend kind of love?"

"Well now that you put it that way I love him more than life because he is my boyfriend and I don't want anything bad to happen to him nor us."

"Oh, I see what you mean and I know how you feel about

that. A friend of mine once told me that I have to first love myself enough to let go of all the bad seeds in my life and live life the way God planned for me to live and that's to be happy and joyful. Sometimes the things we want don't always be what God want us to have and accepting that Zola is so damn hard because we struggle with this every day."

"Coach you don't seem to struggle with anything I see that you have it made in the shade and you seem so well put together how do you do that?"

"Girl its hard work and I do struggle, but I have to manage to work things out and do what is best for me and I'm doing some things right now that makes me happy and some decisions I'm making about my life are not easy ones, but later I will be blessed to have made those right decisions about my life and you will too."

"Do you think I will, I really love Kelvin and I don't want to let go, but I feel it's time to do so what do you think?"

"To be honest with you Zola it's up to you, you have to live with the decisions you make about your life. I'm not saying to drop Kelvin, but maybe you need time apart to think on something's and do some soul searching and see what it is you want out of this relationship or if this relationship is right for you."

"Coach you make a lot of sense and I'm glad we had this talk. I think I will do just that because you know life is too short to let something so small grow into a bigger problem later. I have to go and do some soul searching and I'm going to talk to Kelvin and let him know what I'm doing and all that good stuff thanks."

She gives Reagan a hug and they both get up and walk towards the gym as Zola walks into the gym Reagan takes a break and sits on the steps. She begin to think about her set of problems at home that she had to fix she thought about her friend Braxtine and some of the things she had told her. Knowing she had her own decisions to make because it's been seven years and it was time to lay down the law, fear had settled in her stomach and pain has balled a fist in her throat as the tears rolled down her dark cheeks.

Chapter 20 - - Kelly

"*I can't believe its six* o'clock already."

So much work had to be done; the furniture was going to be changed around curtains needed to be washed and febrezed. It was clean up time but before that happens I had a date with Billy Blake Tybo workout plan to set the pace. I roll out of bed, head for the bathroom, wash my face and brush my teeth. I ramble in the closet, pull out a pair of sweat pants and sports bra. I really needed to get to the gym today but that wasn't happening so Billy and I needed to kick box our calories off.

After an hour of jumping around kicking, huffing and puffing I begin to lose my breath. I then decided to go down the hallway to get a cold washcloth to wipe my face. Suddenly I hear a knock at the door I really wasn't feeling this but I couldn't pretend I wasn't there so with much attitude I ask,

"Who is it?"

The voice on the other end of the door spoke loudly,

"Open the door and you will find out who it is!"

I really wasn't for all this today but to be on the safe side I slid my chain on the door and opened it slowly thinking it might be Ethan and I certainly didn't want any drama not today. I opened the door and there stood Cory with his black baseball cap turned backwards and a cup in his hand.

"Girl, open the door and stop playing."

I couldn't help but grin like a chess cat.

"Oh hell no Cory, go home!"

I slammed the door in his face as I laugh out of control. Cory stood there looking dumb founded.

"This girl is crazy."

After playing for a minute I open the door laughing.

"I had to do that I'm only joking come in."

He takes a sip out of his cup.

"Girl you throwed for real you know this right?"

He walks in and has a seat on my Ashley sectional.

"Well, how are you?"

"I'm fine thank you for asking."

"I had to come and check on you because I notice you been gone for about a week."

"It's been a good week I went to New York the first night and flew to Atlanta Georgia from there I went to Oakland California and came home."

"Your job sounds like fun."

"I love my career, I meet a lot of interesting people some are nice some are not so nice. We have good days as well as bad, I really don't like working first class so every chance I get I work with the people that are flying coach because they keep it real you know what I mean? Those first class people bug the hell out of me just because they paid more money. I like to treat everyone the same hell, were all on the same plane if that bird goes down guess what first class will be the first to go." We both burst into laughter.

"I hear you but when I travel on one of your flights you better treat me like a king." We laugh again. "I'm only joking." He then looks down at his coffee cup and says.

"Let's be real for a minute." I wipe beads of sweat off my forehead. "OK what's up?" He then breathes heavy and says, "Are you really okay?"

"Why you ask?"

"I just wanted to know because I like you and I'm just concern that's all."

"It's good to know that your concern but I'm doing just fine now that I'm getting my house in order you know?"

"I know what you mean I need to get my house in order as you say."

"It's always good to love others and do for other people, but when you give and give and don't find yourself getting from the person you give to and that person treats you like crap, you chalk it up as an experience and move on and that's what I find hard to do."

"I know what you mean when you say that because I find myself thinking about my past and it hurts so much between you and I men cry too."

My eyes got wide and my eyebrows went into that McDonalds arch look.

"Oh really I didn't think you did."

"You didn't think we cry, oh yes but only in the dark."

"I can understand that but Cory, may I get in your business for a minute while I fix breakfast?

"Sure ask away and what are you going to fix me for breakfast? You know I won't turn down food especially if it's free!" We both laugh as we walk in the kitchen Cory sits down at the bar and pick up my copy of Essence magazine. I look in the cabinet and pull out a box of pancake mix then start to work on my meal taking some strawberries out of the fridge so I can hook it up.

"Cory I need to know why you haven't settled down." Cory scratches his head as he looks me directly in the face and smiles half heartily.

"Well to be honest with you I'm not quite ready to get caught up simply because I'm not ready to get serious with anyone my plans involve me right now I have so much I want to do and so much to do for my mom and my sister."

My pancakes were just about ready to hit the skillet.

"Cory you have so much going for you right now and you're so handsome I can't believe you don't have one good woman you would like to settle down with. Maybe it's because you want to be a playa."

He gives me a sharp look as he stands up to help me with the meal placing the turkey bacon in the skillet.

"It's not because I want to play around I just want to chill that's it I love women but I just don't have time to settle with one."

I shake my head smiling from ear to ear listening to his foolishness.

"Look you're not fooling me I know we only been friends for a short time but there's something else going on with you. You been hurt and you don't want to tie yourself down like that and Cory it's okay to cry."

"Look I told you it's not alright to cry not cool for a man well it's not cool in public, besides I'm all right I don't know what you see but it's all gravy train baby girl, I'm keeping it real with myself so it's all good!" I find myself laughing and smiling giving him a crazy look crossing my eyes as if I'm not buying that bull not today!

"What are you laughing about girl? And you're going to keep doing your eyes like that and one day you're going to look in the mirror and find them stuck like that and no man wants a crossed eyed flight attendant. "

We both find ourselves cracking up from that comment.

"Seriously, Cory I'm laughing at you because you're so damn cool and want to keep it so real until you believe that lie but you believe that man."

He grabs a piece of bacon that he had on his plate and stuck it in his mouth talking with his mouth full.

"Look I just want to live life to the fullest and not get hurt you know what I mean?"

"I know what you mean because I don't think I will ever marry again simply because Ethan James Jackson taught me well about trust. Cory I trusted that man with my life my soul my spirit and he betrayed me in ways you can't even imagine."

Cory slowly sips his orange juice giving his undivided attention to what I was talking about.

"If you don't mind me getting into your business for a minute what exactly did Ethan do besides sleep around?"

I took a deep breath on that question because the pain was still fresh and raw I find it hard to talk about at times without crying.

"Ethan was very kind to me in the beginning there wasn't anything he wouldn't do for me he was God fearing so I thought, we prayed together we went to bible study and church. It all started when he took on this second job at a fast food joint near the military base where we lived. I wasn't too happy with him working a second job simply because he worked really hard doing what he did for Uncle Sam but I didn't say anything I just did what any good wife would have done for her husband and that was support whatever he was trying to do. He was determined to have his own business someday and I stood by his side for whatever it was he wanted to do. I loved this man he was everything to me I couldn't see any wrong in him."

"Kelly you sound like you still love him."

Cory interrupted with intense concern.

"I do and that's what makes this so hard for me because I love him but he loves himself too much to love anyone else, this man knew I would do anything for him and he took advantage of that he started working late and coming home past midnight and the co worker which was a female became really close to him they went to lunch together she would call my house late. One day she called me at home and said that she hopes I didn't mind her being friends with Ethan because they had a lot in common and she really liked him and enjoyed his conversations. Naturally being the Woman that I am I told her that I was secure in my relationship and that I wasn't worried about her or my husband so I found out shortly thereafter I was all-wrong. Once the company had a party and so Ethan was getting dressed up, had his smell good on and I tell you this man was looking good from head to his ugly pale feet" Cory smiles and interrupts.

"What you say he was looking good girl"

"Oh shut up Cory, you're crazy and yes he was looking good this particular night I asked him where he was going? He replied that it was a party that he and his co-workers were going to. I asked him why he didn't tell me about the party so I could go and he said that I wouldn't feel comfortable there I thought that was a little strange so I didn't say anything about it at that moment but I was very hurt."

Cory chews his food slowly as he watched me get emotional and reaches over and grabs my hand. He starts to drift into his zone about his emotional mess with Latisha.

"Look, if this is going to be hard to talk about let's talk about something else alright"

I offer him a pleasant smile while wiping a tear from my eye.

"No, I need to talk about it because that's healing I had all this bottled up inside me I'm glad you care enough to ask."

Cory replies with a gentle tone in his voice "You are so beautiful and with that sweet personality of yours you will find the right man, don't give up I see how these men watch you. I think you all that and a bag of chips and dip myself." I smile knowing he was just being nice.

"Thank you but first I have to love myself. As you know beauty is vain. I loved Ethan more then I loved myself at times. I guess what I was hoping for was him loving me always and forever you know?"

"Are you crazy or just dumb?"

My mouth dropped open.

"What?"

"I said_"

"I know what you said but why you ask that question?"

"I want to know why you feel that sorry no good for nothing Nigga deserved you."

"I don't know my family says the same thing. I guess I have to learn to be happy with myself first."

"What's with you? Don't you know you can get just about any man with your personality alone?"

"Cory, I'm better now I'm learning to love myself and be content in my own skin the most I want out of my life is peace and happiness within me. In time I will heal and make peace with God. Well allow me to finish telling you about that night that broke me in two. Ethan didn't come home until six o'clock the next morning and talk about mad as hell I was just that. I cried from midnight until six that morning when he walked through the door. I asked him where he been but he seem to have had an attitude so I left it alone at the moment, I have to say I was crushed because my husband never seem to have had a problem staying out late, the latest he would be out would be twelve o'clock but he really had some stuff with him at that time. I don't know what he was thinking. He smelled like smoke and he didn't smoke so I know he been around people who was smoking he seem as if he had just a wonderful time. I felt unloved and just plain stupid because he didn't want me to go to the party with him."

"I can't believe he did that to you."

"Neither could I it was so wrong and I never thought in a million years he would try me like that."

"Well to be honest with you men will try you and see how far they could go it's in us I hate to say that but it's true it's in the player handbook."

He smiled trying to be funny but I didn't see anything funny because I was one step from hating all men but I really didn't want to be that way.

"Cory I know this now it never fails but, this is what really hurt me he said that I was tripping and there was nothing to worry about and I was just acting foolish and he told me to go to bed and stop crying it's not that serious. He made me feel as if I was being crazy for feeling the way I did."

"That was stupid on his part and sounds to me that Ethan is really pond scum you know."

" Your right he is worse than Pond scum you know he made me feel like I was going crazy and check this out the next day was even worse he got up put on his clothes and said he was going to a company picnic. I asked him could we talk about last night he said it was nothing to talk about and for me to stop trying to fix something that wasn't broke." Cory then picks up his fork and put a piece of pancake in his mouth and chews slowly as he listens.

"Cory I really don't know what Ethan was thinking but he made me feel very insecure!"

"Well what did he do? And why were you feeling that way?"

"Oh his girlfriend called me and said that Ethan told her that I was jealous of their relationship I said ain't that a_"

Cory frowns and says, "What the hell he did that for and why was he tripping like that and what did you tell her?"

"Well I told her that I was ok with their friendship but I wasn't ok with the fact that he stayed out all night and couldn't let me know where he had been nor what he was doing because that was so unlike him to do what he did. She said that I didn't have anything to worry about and that I had a good husband and she talks to him a lot about our marriage I then asked her has she ever been married."

With suspense in his eyes Cory asked, "And what did she say?"

"She said no but she said that she gives him good advice! Cory I blew my damn top at that moment I felt this whore was giving me a lot of bull and I wasn't going to take this crap from neither her nor him so I started looking into that. What I found out was that he had been taking her not only to lunch but, to the movies and has taken her out of town twice. Once she came to my house while I was gone out of town of course he denied that. He had sexual relations with her no doubt, I came home early and she was coming out of my house." Cory interrupts. "What in the hell do you mean she's coming out of your house what is this hookers name?"

"Her name is Lisa Barns and Cory what made things so bad she wasn't even cute this over sized big face, moon head, huff neck, bald head scaly wag, wide nose heffa had some nerve to tell me after I went off on her days later that I should have been taking care of my husband then I wouldn't have to worry about her!" Cory pounds his fist on the table

"Oh hell no and what did Ethan have to say for himself?"

"Oh my dear sweet husband had nothing to say, he was there when she and I got into it. All he said was that I was wrong for doing that and that she was upset with me and I should apologize for acting like that simply because I had no reason to be insecure."

"He didn't go there did he?"

"Yes, Cory he did and I felt like crap. I asked my husband to try and talk about this better yet could he consider taking another part time if he feels the need to work a part time job. He said I need to get pass all that because it makes no sense to him the way I'm acting.

"Kelly you need someone who respect you and that's all to it this boy is not a man he is a true butt and you deserve better and don't you forget it I don't even know playa but he sounds like a punk to me!"

"Well I married the punk and that was the biggest mistake I could have made I tell you. I thought he loved me but I was all-wrong he only loves himself and it took three years to figure that out! He treated me like a second-class citizen I tell you he made me feel like dirt so when we finally split up after all the run ins I had with Lisa and him I gave it up! You're not going to believe what happen next!" Cory then gets up and pulls me by the hand to the living room.

"We need to sit in here on your couch my back is getting stiff in this chair." As we both move to the living room to the sectional I reached over to turn the lamp on.

"Well this was really bad I knew he only thought about himself when he came into our home and said that one of his friends just came to Ft Polk and his family didn't have their furniture just yet and he was going to take our bed that we slept in and let them use it."

"I asked him why our bed and he said it was his bed before we met and he could do what he wanted to do with it he no longer lives there and I will have to leave soon anyway. Cory I was still sleeping in that damn bed as a matter of fact I was in the bed when he came to pick it up."

"Oh hell no I know you didn't let him have the bed did you?"

"Cory I didn't have a choice in the matter I was calm I even gave the man new sheets that we just bought for the bed and I tell you that was the hardest thing I had to do without crying in his presence. After he left I went to my friend Monica and pitched a fit. Cory I was so hurt that he would do something like that he also told his commander that he was going to clear housing and that I was no longer living there so they came and I had no clue what was going on and had to move in thirty days. I asked him what was going on and he treated me raw. Talk about mad that I was I didn't know what I was going to do because at the time I was only working part time for the airlines not making enough money to even live in the projects okay!"

"You are so sweet and I can't imagine anyone treating you like that thanks to God you two didn't have any children together."

"Glory to God but that never happened and besides he had one of his own with his first wife who was just as sweet as she wanted to be to me but she hated him and I always wondered why Jamie acted like that towards him and now I can see why. "Later after Ethan and I split up I called her to see how her son was doing and she said fine and asked me how I was doing and she told me some horrible things about Ethan and why they split up he use to do her the same way. He cheated on her as well, and would make it seem as if it was her fault he cheated! Also I didn't learn until after we split that he slept with her before we got married. She didn't know he was getting married until the week of our wedding that bastard was so dead wrong! He use to talk bad about Jamie, said she didn't take care of his child. He said she didn't want him with me and things like that but it was a different story when we met he also said that she was trying to fool me into thinking she was kind but who was in sheep's clothing was his yellow big belly out of shape ass! My heart has been torn into a million pieces but it's beginning to heal and now I can talk about this and I don't feel too bad."

"Kelly I'm glad you feel better and that you're able to talk to someone about this because you need to get out and live a little because you are a good woman as I can see you work and you're doing damn good for yourself keep your head up." I offer my friend a smile and reach for the remote turning the TV to BET watching the new video by Usher.

"I like this song I didn't know it had video that's cool"

"Girl where you been you need to come go out with me this weekend to my boy's new club called the Black Onyx."

"Yeah I heard about that club my friend Monica was telling me about it maybe we can check it out sometimes."

Chapter 21 - - Jada

Byron sits on the couch drinking a Bud light while watching the Lakers put a beating on Orlando while I feed Jordan in the kitchen. The phone rings, "Byron, honey can you get that? I'm busy right now and you know how she gets when I stop feeding her."

His ass didn't move, this was getting really old the phone continues to ring for the fourth time. Still sitting on the couch not saying a word with his eyes glued to that damn TV I put the spoon down and Jordan starts to cry at the top of her little lungs while I answer the phone.

"Hello"

"Hello, how are you today?"

"Who is this?"

"This is Cole"

I found my heart pumping blood as fast as it could go I didn't understand why this man made me so nervous. Just listening to his voice was a treat it was deep and sexy he spoke clear and slow.

"I would appreciate it if you could please come in I'm drowning in paper work that need to be done by Tuesday."

"Well, Mr. Sinclair I don't know, I have so much to do and I'm spending time with my family right now, as you can hear my daughter screaming in the back ground I _"

"If you can't I understand not only would I pay you overtime I will also pay for travel time, I really need your help, I apologize for calling you in such short notice."

"Well, Mr. Sinclair_"

"Please call me Cole."

"Ok, I have to see what I can do."

"Thank you so much."

"Well, give me two hours I have to finish feeding my baby."

"I appreciate you."

I put the phone back in the cradle giving Byron a hard look.

"Why didn't you answer the phone?"

"Look I'm trying to watch the game I didn't hear you, besides you were in the kitchen closer to the phone anyway!"

"Well, can you watch Jordan? I have to go to work."

"Sure, Jordan and I will be alright you don't have to worry about us you have a good day."

He never took his eyes off the TV screen.

"Well, if you didn't want me to go I will stay home."

"I said I will keep the baby bring her here."

I was disappointed in his behavior so going to work is starting to become the highlight of my life because home life was just a little bit boring. This man wasn't interested in what I had to say or do so what was the damn point of it all!

Meanwhile I decided to dress down for work since the office was closed; I picked out a pair of faded hip hugger jeans and tank top alone with my white K Swiss tennis. I finished dressing, sprayed on my Journey cologne and walk into the bathroom to make sure my hair was okay. I grab my lip liner before putting on my Downtown Brown lipstick, Byron walks in behind me.

"Hey didn't you say you were going to work today?"

Rolling my eyes I say with attitude.

"Yes, I'm going to work."

"Oh you have to fix your face up to go to work?"

Laughing to myself I pick up a comb to pick through the strings that were sticking up in my hair, after doing that I blotted my lips while looking in the mirror.

"Honey, I'm going to work but it's very important how I look."

He raises his eyebrows.

"You don't need all that on your face to look beautiful."

"It's a woman thing I don't expect you to understand."

"I guess, you have a good day!"

"I'll try I wish I could just spend the day with you and Jordan."

I give my husband a hug and kiss.

"I love you."

"Me too, now you have a great day don't worry about Jordan, she and I will be just fine."

I walk to the living room to find my daughter asleep in her swing with her little head hung to the side.

"Would you just look at her she's so precious."

I decided to lay her down on a blanket in the floor; giving her a kiss on the cheek.

"Bye my sweet little angel mommy loves you very much."

I turn to Byron. "I'll see you two later."

He waves as I walk out the door.

Meanwhile at the office Cole sits at his computer going over inventory the phone rings. He pushes the speaker phone button.

"Cole speaking"

"Cole, baby that you?"

He knew who it was the moment she spoke his name. With a smile upon his face he says, "Grandma how you?" He stops typing so he could focus on the call.

"Baby I'm fine, I was just thinking about you, and decided to give you a call because I miss my grandson." Cole's grandma lived in a small town outside of Atlanta Georgia.

"I miss you too grandma, I will be there soon to see you, give me a couple of weeks, how pop doing?"

"That old fart is doing just fine with his mean self, he's gone fishing with your daddy and some of his fishing buddies were having a fish fry tomorrow, I'm cooking a lemon pie and peach cobbler for desert. I wish you could be here, your cousin Brandy is getting married to Todd Chambers finally. I am so happy for them because they had been living together for two years. I had a talk with Brandy and told her that if he gets the milk for free there's no need to buy the damn cow. I love my family and I want to see them in the kingdom you know. I married that old fart of mine and I wouldn't trade his no teeth having behind for no amount of money well__ I have to think about that again for the right price they can have his gummy bear ass." They both laugh.

"Grandma you a mess so tell me when is the wedding?"

"Baby their getting married April 3 and I can't wait, another one of my grand children getting married. Speaking of which when are you getting married son? You're in your thirties and you should turn in that playas card it's time."

He laughs because his grandma was so hip.

"Well grandma when I find the right woman."

"I have someone I would like for you to meet when you come home to visit and she is a cutie baby!"

"No thanks grandma I will find my own woman."

"Look boy! I want some great grandchildren so you better get to it and find that woman and I mean soon!"

"Grandma I will do that for you I just might bring someone home with me I don't know we will see what turns up alright!"

"Well baby we will see, if not I think you will like this young lady she's not only smart she is very pretty and she's going to school to be a doctor."

"You two will have a lot in common she is knocking on thirty herself she has no kids which is a plus because you don't won't to have no baby mammas drama."

"Grandma you are something else I love you and be sure to tell the family I said hello thanks for calling."

"I love you too son and call more often and stop working so damn hard you heard me!"

"Yes, I hear you bye grandma" "Bye baby." Cole places the phone on the receiver, while laughing to himself and shaking his head. He then hears a knock at the door pushing his chair back from his desk he ask loudly and in a strong voice.

"Who knock?"

"Who are you expecting Mr. Sinclair?" Cole clears his throat.

"Come on in its open."I was standing there with my Coach on my shoulder and hands on my hips.

"I would like to say thank you for coming at such a short notice, you are indeed a team player and I really appreciate you I will give you a bonus I promise."

"Really I didn't mind coming in simply because I didn't have any plans."

"Regardless it was your day off again thanks!" I place my bag on the table and pick up some papers off the desk. "Are these the papers you need me to go over and file?"

"Well, yes I was trying to do most of them so you wouldn't have much to do when you come in."

"As you know Mr. Sinclair_"

"Wait let's get something straight I told you to call me Cole, cut the Mr. Sinclair act okay, everyone else calls me Cole and so should you!"

"OK Cole, what I was trying to say was that it's my job to do this and if you don't mind let me do my job because when you go over stuff you don't type nor file things the way they should be filed and that messes me up I never told you that, but it do, and I hate to work behind you."

"Well excuse me Miss Thang I will let you do your job, I apologize for getting in the way."

"I like it when you help, I just don't like to have to look for my work after you have tried to do my job for me."

"I'm sorry my bad."

"Please don't get me wrong ok."

"I don't, I like your work and I like you as a person."

"Well, the feeling is mutual." Smiling from ear to ear Cole walks over to the coffee pot to make fresh coffee, so they could get started.

"Say before we get started would you like to go to the donut shop to get something to eat?" Looking over the work that needed to be done I politely smile and says,

"Would you just pick me up something because I would like to get started so I can get finish?"

"Ok what would you like from the shop?"

"I have a taste for a grill cheese sandwich also bring a dozen of donuts with you so I can snack on them throughout the day if you don't mind."

"You know I don't mind doing that for you! I will be right back, if you need anything just call my cell."

"Sure will do, now let me get started!" Cole walks out of the office I have a seat in front of my computer wondering where to start. It wasn't much work; maybe I could get finished before 5:00.

While typing I hear my cell phone ringing in my bag. I reach down into it grabbing my singing phone with Beyonce calling

When the Honeymoon Is Over

all the single ladies looking at my caller ID it read: Madison Courtney

"Hello Madison what's up?"

"Hey girl I have some good news!" I continue to type, while I listen.

"We'll tell me what's up? You got yourself a man or what?"

"You will never believe what happen to me!" I stop typing and prop my arms on the desk.

"OK Madison what happen? What did you do or what happen to you? Tell me now because I can't wait to hear, what's new?"

"I won a cruise!" I scream, "What! A cruise how and when do we leave?"

"I won the Tom Joiner fantastic Voyage cruise it's going to be off the hook!"

"I am so excited for you who are you taking?"

"To be honest with you Jada I really don't know, I'm thinking about Cory because we've been dating for a while. I really like him, but were not that serious with one another, and when I think of a cruise I think couple. I haven't made a decision about that just yet."

"Look at you girl you sound so happy. You and Cory might be a couple by then you never knows, are you seeing someone else besides him?"

"Jada this is Madison you talking to."

"So, you can see other people you single. You just have to get out there, date and be merry you don't have to sleep with those ninjas get a free meal and a movie from time to time."

"I hear you loud and clear I like Cory, we spend time with one another, but he gets no pie at this moment because we said were not ready for anything serious."

"You go girl I'm so happy for you."

"Well it's all good Jada I just want to finish school and be able to take good care of Collin although Collin Sr. is active in his life you know."

"Sure I know what you mean and things will be just fine with you and Collin and I'm sure that Cory will also be there for you he seems like a keeper."

"Yeah your right, Hey where are you? Because I called your house first and your husband told me to call you on your cell."

"I'm at work."

"Work, I thought you were off on the weekends."

"I am but, Cole asked me to come in and so here I am."

"Oh I see its Cole now what are you two up to?"

"Nothing I'm making money that's all."

"I bet I told you this man have a space in his heart for you, keep on."

"Well if he does he hasn't told me and I have a loving husband at home that doesn't pay any attention to me but he is still my husband alright!"

"I hear you just be careful girl"

"I will and I will call you soon take care smooches."

"Smooches right back at ya" I cut my phone off and place it in my bag as I continue to work. The phone rings again this time it was the company phone.

"Jada speaking"

"Hey Jada this Cole I'm at the donut shop, I was wondering if there was anything else you would like to have?"

"No just the grill cheese and the donuts I asked for is plenty thanks."

"You're welcome I will be back in a few minutes."

"Take your time I'm fine"

"I know your fine."

"What did you say?"

"Oh nothing I was just looking at this woman that walked in the shop let me go I will be back soon bye"

"Bye Cole."

For one moment I wished I was single so I could ride Cole like a roller coaster that man was just too damn fine. I want to just lay one hard core kiss on this brotha's lips. What the hell, Byron and I had been through too much together and why was I thinking about Cole like this, the devil is a lie. I have a good husband not to mention he is a good father, he just needed to take care of his business in the bedroom, which he wasn't doing, and I was quite tired of it.

Every night going to bed wondering if he was in the mood or if I touched him he was too tired, that was getting old and it was making our relationship weak. This bedroom business was my only complaint of Byron I never knew of him cheating and he never gave me any reason to think he would be cheating until now, because of the burning volcano between my thighs frustration became my best friend. A knock at the door interrupted my devilish thoughts.

"Come in."

There stood a well dressed young man with an envelope in his hand, alone with some beautiful pink and white long stem roses dressed with baby's breath, in a clear glass vase with a beautiful pink bow wrapped around it.

"Oh those flowers are beautiful" I said with a wide grin on my face in hopes they were for me. Then the man asks, "Do you know where I can find a Mrs. Jada Knight?" My smile broadens with great surprise as it lit up the room I then stand up pulling my shirt down around my waist so I can collect my beautiful flowers.

"Thank you, that husband of mine takes my breath away." I reach to grab my coach bag as the young man raises his eyebrows and shakes his head I pull out a ten and hands it to him.

"Thanks again you have a good day!"

"You enjoy your day, as well as the beautiful flowers; your husband is one lucky man if you don't mind me saying so."

"Well thank you so kindly you have a blessed day sweetie." The young man walked out as I smiled at his comment making my day all worthwhile.

The flowers smelled so good and looked just lovely sitting on the table next to my cherry wood desk. I begin to cry, because guilt started to show his ugly face, how I dare think about another man, when my husband thought enough of me to send me two-dozen roses. I was excited to have such beauty grace the room. I decided to open the note: *You are such a special woman; words simply couldn't express how special you truly are, thanks for everything you do.*

I knew my husband had at least one romantic bone left in his body. It's been over a year since he last sent flowers and this was the best yet! I pick up the phone to call home only to get the answering service. "You have reached Byron and Jada Knight were not home at the moment but if you will please leave a brief message and one of us will gladly return your call; however we apologize for the inconvenience so after the tone please leave message beep-"

"Honey when you get a chance please call me at work."

I begin to think about the fire below and I'm going to make sure Byron put it out tonight. I pick out one of the white roses, and place it up to my nose, I walk over to the window that overlooks the city and see all the people walking and enjoying their day. I suddenly hear the door open; I slowly turn around with a wide chess cat grin on my face holding the rose close to my nose.

"Cole I was just looking____"

"Save it I see you like the flowers I sent you."

"You sent me these flowers?"

"Yes, to just say thank you and___" my heart stood still as my emotions took over my eyes fill with water as I place the flower back with the group.

Cole walks over, wipes my face with a tissue he pulled out of the box on my desk.

"I didn't mean to upset you I apologize for_"

"It's not you Cole I just thought my husband was thinking about me. I wish he would have been the one to have sent the flowers that's all."

"I don't like to see you cry do you want the rest of the day off so

When the Honeymoon Is Over

you can go home I just wanted to send you something nice because you always have my back here and I ___"

"Look you don't have to explain I love the flowers really I do and they are beautiful, and the card was just lovely."

Cole sits down in a chair by the window as he listens.

"I just wish my husband do something like this again because he use to be romantic, but now all he ever does is watch games, play with Jordan, and sometimes hang with his damn boys." Cole stands up beside me and places his arm around me as I burst into tears.

"I am so sorry that this upsets you and just maybe you need to talk with Byron about this, have you ever told him how you feel?"

"Not really I just pretend that everything is ok and hope things get better."

"Sometimes we take things for granted and I'm sure your husband doesn't mean any harm I'm sure he loves you very much if he don't I think he's a fool."

"Well I just want things to be like they use to be that's all." Cole places his arms around me and kisses me on the forehead. I embrace him with a tight hug it's been awhile since I've been held like this, it felt good to be lost in someone's arms, and I slowly sucked in some air and exhaled.

Chapter 22 - - Madison

I hear music playing in the living room, I decide to get up and see what was going on. To my surprise I see my son and Cory dancing to the sounds of Charlie Boy I look fly they were popping their collars and jerking their bodies as if they had some type of seizers going on. I stood there with my arms folded smiling and laughing a silent laugh as I lean against the wall until they spotted me I then ask,

"What yawl doing?"

Cory looks and grins. "Well I'm teaching little man how to dance." Both Cory and Collin laugh as they reach for me pulling me in the middle of the living room floor. "Momma, please show me how to dance." Cory walks over to the stereo and turns up the music. "Your momma can't dance Collin she only thinks she can." I give Cory a sharp look and smile as I lift my hands up and say,

"Step back let me show you brothas something."

I start popping my fingers and shaking what my daddy gave me not missing a beat.

"Momma, is that what you're going to do when you step on that ship?"

"Yeah, baby momma is going to show them what I'm working with." Cory gives me this look of confusion.

"Are you going somewhere and didn't tell me?" I walk towards the stereo and turn the music down. Collin walks down the hall to his room and close the door.

"Yes, I'm going on a cruise"

"So you're going on a cruise." Cory shakes his head as he tightens his lips.

"Yes I won a trip."

"No kidding you won it how?"

I turn and walk into the kitchen to start breakfast I open the icebox to look and see what was in there; I pull out eggs and bacon and walked over to the pantry for a box of grits.

"I registered, and they drew my name. They announced it over the radio."

"That's good, I hope you have fun." I could see that Cory had a disappointed look in his eyes.

"I really hope to have fun I always wanted to go on a cruise and now here's my chance to shine I have to lose a couple of pounds so I can look good in my two piece." Cory looked at me with those bedroom eyes scanning my body up and down.

"What weight? You're thick and curvy and I like that on a black woman and your feisty as hell and I have to say I'm loving it so that's all that matter."

I couldn't help but blush while I pull a sauce pan from under the cabinet and place it on the stovetop.

"Well, thank you, you're not bad yourself. I been checking you out lately and your six pack is tight and I would like you to be my guest on the cruise since your fine, I can't take anyone with me unless he is fine."

"Really, you would like for me to go with you?" I crossed my eyes being silly.

"No I don't want you to go jackass."

"Look stop playing girl I need a vacation because I'm due one. I have to look over my schedule to see if I can have that time off so get back with me on that."

"No you get back with me."

I place some bread in the toaster. The phone rings Cory picks up and hands it over to me,

"Hello"

"Hello may I speak to Collin please"

"May I ask whose calling?"

"This is Deshay Hall Collin's date for the dance tonight."

"Oh hi honey, sure you may speak to him, but first I would like to speak to your mom if she's there."

"Yes she's in I'll get her hold on." I whisper and points to the phone.

"This is my baby's date tonight." Cory sits down, pick up the Essence magazine on the table and folds his leg across the other.

"Girl, you need to get over that he is not your baby anymore he is almost grown." I give Cory a hard look and point my finger at him and say.

"He's still my baby no matter what."

"Hello, Jill speaking."

"Hello Jill, this is Madison Courtney, Collin's mom."

"Hi Madison it's nice to meet you finally, my daughter talks about your son all the time."

"Oh really Collin speaks a lot about Deshay as well, and I look forward to meeting your daughter because she has that boys nose wide open." We both chuckle,

"The reason I wanted to talk with you Jill is because I wanted to know what time shall we pick Deshay up for the dance? Also I wanted to take pictures; you know how it is with the first dance and all."

"Girl, I know I think I'm more excited then she is about this dance. You can come to my house around 7:30 because the dance start at 8:30 and ends at 12:00 that will give us plenty of time to take pictures."

"That's okay with me I have to get ready to take this boy to the mall and pick up his tux."

"I understand I have to get Deshay to her hair appointment, so she can do something to this wig of hers. Her hair is so long and thick I can't seem to do anything with it right now so were going to see what Patty can do to it."

"Oh you take her to Patty over at the Beauty Hut?"

"Yes, you know Patty?"

"She hooks me up every week I wouldn't know what to do without that girl." We laugh, "Well Madison I better let you go so you can do your thing and we can do ours. I look forward to meeting you and I will see you at 7:30. "

"Likewise, I will call you around six to get directions to your house."

"Oh before you hang up Deshay is having a fit to get on the phone, is your son around so she can say hi and bye."

"Let me go get him." I walk to the end of the hallway and yell.

"Collin baby pick up the phone!"

"Alright ma I got it you can hang up." I walk over to Cory and give him a kiss on the cheek.

"What's that for?"

"I want to thank you for spending time with Collin that means a lot to me."

"You don't have to thank me for that I like the kid he have some mad skills on the court did you know that?"

"Oh yeah I know he and I play every now and then. My baby will play in the NBA one day he's going to be like that cutie pie Kobe Bryant."

"I wish Collin much success in that area I'm just going to teach him that we have strong black women out there that will have his back when he reaches to that point in his life."

"I hear what you're saying."

I reached for the toast and turn over the meant sizzling in the skillet and places two more slices of toast in the toaster oven.

Cory developed a glaze look in his eye.

When the Honeymoon Is Over

"What's on your mind?"

"Oh nothing really"

"Wait baby I know you, you have something on your mind you can talk to me this is Madison remember."

Cory scratches his chest and look at me while I turn the meat over in the skillet. I couldn't imagine what he was thinking, I knew he had something on his mind, but I just couldn't figure it all out just yet. I know it couldn't be me because I'm not stressing him about a relationship, I don't ask him about other women, and it's almost too good to be true, to have such a woman in his life I know that sounds a little cocky but true. It's the same for me because he hasn't even touched me sexually yet. I say yet because I want this man he's attractive, intelligent, and a gentleman and most importantly, he gets along with my son that's a must. We haven't even shared a real kiss I often wonder what his kiss taste like I look forward to that day because it's going to happen and when it do well it's going to be worth the wait.

"Madison I don't have anything on my mind I'm cool."

"Alright if that's what you say Cory Wash I believe you."

"Ok trust me." Collin comes into the kitchen.

"Momma, when are we going to the mall?"

"As soon as you put on clothes we can head out."

"Can Cory go with us?"

"Yes if he wants to, Cory?"

My son and I both give him looks of hope and compassion.

"Yeah, yeah I will go."

I grab Cory around his neck and give him a big huge bear hug. "Thank you so much maybe you can help us out today!" Cory wonders what he has gotten himself into he hates going to the mall especially on a Saturday.

I put on my black True Religion Jeans and tank top, my hair

was pulled up in a ponytail, and I didn't like to wear too much makeup so I went natural with a little powder and a smoky color lip gloss. Collin was dressed to impress with his platinum jeans and tee shirt by FUBU. His hair was twisted, which he just got done yesterday for the dance. Cory on the other hand wanted to keep it very simple with his blue and white Nike tee shirt and wind pants and tennis to match with his matching fitted baseball cap.

"Girl, you look like a teenager, I might get in trouble."

"Boy please I will never see my teens again."

"No, I'm serious if I didn't know any better I would think you're a teen at least a senior in high school."

"Momma, Cory is right some of my friends tell me at school that they think your fine." Cory and Collin both laugh Madison stop walking while smiling.

"You two need to stop."

"Momma I'm serious Michael Wilson told me that and I told him he better stop looking at you like that because that's my mom and you ain't going to disrespect her like that."

"What you say Collin your momma have it going on like that?"

"Yeah, mom has it going on at times."

"What you mean at times I have it going on son."

"You got that right."

Two women with hair piled up on their head a mile high walks by and eye ball Cory down.

"I see you have two ladies watching you are you going to say hi." Cory winks his eye at me and smiles.

"Girl, that's him and he looks damn good in person." The girl with the blue hair says.

"Sho do and honey did you see the arms on the man I can really do some things with him baby." The other girl with the fire red hair said.

Cory offers a smile and walks by and grabs my hand. The girl with the blue hair yells out, "You go girl we ain't mad at you toil."

I shake my head and laugh to myself as we walk pass the girls as they watch and whisper.

"How do you put up with that all the time?" He rubs his chin.

"I've gotten use to it, it's not bad, sometimes I like the attention but other times I just want a woman to know the real me you know?"

"I guess you have a point." A little girl with gray eyes, dull brown skin with a white cap on steps up to Cory, " Hello Mr. Washington" She was really cute but looked very sick she weighed about 60 pounds and about thirteen years old." Cory smiles as he stoops down to greet this little angel he grabs her hand.

"Hello beautiful, how are you today?" She smiles as she look him in the eyes.

"Fine thank you, I don't know if you remember me but about a year ago you came to St. Jude hospital in Tennessee and visit the cancer patients, well I was one of those patients." Cory eyes widen with compassion.

"Really what's your name?"

"Solea Hampton." A woman calls her name "Solea, leave that man alone." Cory smiles and greets the pretty woman that speaks her name.

"Its okay I met your daughter before."

"Hey wait a minute your Cory Washington the super model, actor guy."

"Yes I am and you?"

"I'm Solea's mom Sharon." Shaking her hand "It's really nice to meet you; you have such a beautiful daughter."

"Well thank you so much."

"Oh this is my friend Madison and her son Collin."

"It's nice to meet you both. I have to apologize for Solea bothering you." The woman just smiles as she places her purse over her shoulder.

"It's really no problem." Solea smiles

"Mr. Washington I would like to take a picture with you if you don't mind. My friends won't believe who I saw in the mall." Cory smiles and says. "Sure do you have a camera on you?"

"No, I don't have a camera but there's a booth over there."

"Hey, Solea do you own a camera?"

"No sir I don't own one" Cory look at Madison and Collin then across to Solea's mom.

"Well, let's go into circuit city and see about getting you one of those fancy cameras so we can take lots of pictures so you can make a scrap book to show your friends alright."

"Oh Mr. Washington you don't have to_"

"I want to do this for your little girl it's the least I can do for her besides, she have to go and show her friends some real pictures, I will not take no for an answer got it!" Shaking her head and smiling at her daughter.

"Well, let's go get a camera then." As they walk into circuit city a young blond woman with ocean blue eyes greet them at the door.

"Hello, how may I help you today?" Cory greets her with a huge smile. "Yes, can you help us find a video camera small enough for a little girl to use?" "Sure here is our video selection this camera takes digital pictures as well it's easy to use and you get an extra battery pack as well."

"Solea would you like to hold this camera in your hand to see if you like the feel of this high tech machine." Solea smiled as she looked with those big gray eyes of hers.

"I love this camera it's great but I thought you were going to get a regular camera Mr. Washington."

"Look I will get you what you want today now if you want something else just say so little cutie I don't do this often.

"No sir this is fine."

"Mom, do you have anything you need going once going twice?"

"No, Cory you have done enough and thank you." Sharon eyes

When the Honeymoon Is Over

fill with tears. Cory consoles her by putting his arms around her. My eyes fill with tears as I reach in my purse for a tissue and hands it to Sharon. " Thank you, your such nice people and you made my daughter really happy today she has had a hard time and I can't thank you two enough, Madison your really blessed to have such a giving and wonderful man in your life."

"Thank you, you have a blessing as well your daughter is really sweet and polite."

"That she is I can say she has always been my backbone when I was supposed to be hers." I looked over at Collin and thought how blessed I really was to have a healthy son and how grown up he has become in such a short period of time. "Excuse me I was wondering if you like the camera?" The sales woman asked.

"Sure we will take it can we take pictures with it now or do we have to charge it up for a couple of hours?"

"No, you can use it now if you like sir would that be cash or credit?"

"I will pay cash you ladies can step outside until we finish up our business in here." Solea, Madison and Sharon step to the door.

"Collin, come on,"

"Let Collin stay with me we will be out in just a minute alright. We walk outside the store; Solea sits down on the bench outside looking drained. I walk over to sit next to her. "Your mom tells me that you're a brave little girl."

"My mom is the one who is brave Miss Madison she has to deal with me leaving here someday. I ask God to take care of her when I'm gone, because I'm all she has my dad died two years ago with the same thing and now it's just us. I'm going to a better place and God promised me that he will take care of her so I can go in peace." My heart melt at this child's courage her eyes fill with tears as she places her hand over her mouth and wipe the tears from her eyes as she look up at her mom looking at a dress in the window of JC Penny's.

"You have a heart of gold Solea and I can't express that enough."

She smiles and watch Collin and Cory walk out the store with the camera in Collin's hand taping them as they watch. Solea yells at her mom.

"Look mom I'm on TV this is such a cool camera thanks a million Mr. Cory it's so cool now mom will have something to remember me by I love you for this." She grabs him and gives him a huge hug around his neck.

"Well let's take some pictures. Oh Solea before I forget I engraved something special at the bottom of the camera" It read: *To a brave little angel God bless you Love, Cory.*

"Thank you Mr. Washington this is a dream come true."

"You're so welcome I want you to send me some pictures here's my address." He hands his card over to Sharon and she sticks it in her purse. Also Solea when you need to talk call me my cell number is on there as well all right.

"Thank you again." The day was a definite unexpected miracle and all I could think about was how I would lose my natural mind if something would happen to my son.

"Cory, that was really a nice thing you did for that little girl she was really cute too."

"I count my blessings son and that little girl is fighting a deadly epidemic called cancer not knowing if she will see tomorrow and that's the least I could do for that child." "Oh I see, that's so sad and I feel guilty because I make so many plans for the future and she don't know if she has a future." I was simply at a loss for words but had to say something because life is truly too short to sweat the small stuff.

"Honey count each day as a blessing from God because really we don't know if today is our last day or not Solea is such an angel and God has blessed her with great courage she worries about her mom instead of herself and that to me is wisdom knowledge and understanding that she may not be here and that she want her mom to be of great courage." Cory smiles as he stops at a red light on the corner.

"Look that little girl will be just fine I know it and I look forward to getting pictures from her and her mom. I also look forward to taking pictures of you Collin going on your first date tonight look in that bag on the floor in the back seat and hand it to me." Collin reaches down to get the bag and hands it to Cory. Cory passes the bag to me.

"Reach in there and get that camera out" I look at Cory and then look into the bag and pull out a digital camera.

"Cory you shouldn't have."

"I notice you had a throw away camera and I saw the way you were checking out those cameras in that store so I wanted to do something nice for you as well."

"Well thank you Cory you're so sweet." I move closer to Cory and reach over to give him a kiss on the cheek." Collin laughs to himself and watches as they pass over the bridge.

"Ok let's take a picture of you." Collin had on a black tux and a white tie and vest he had on his mom 2ct diamond ear rings in both ears just bling, blinging looking sharp as a tack. With a smile big as China he poses for his first picture with two of his fingers up in a peace sign.

"I'm cool as ice don't you think?" I snap the picture.

"You're my baby and you look so cute." I snap another picture in front of the fireplace in the living room.

"He's handsome not cute girl."

"Ok my baby is handsome your happy now."

"Mom I will be happy when we go and pick up Deshay she is waiting for us." The phone rings Collin runs and looks at the caller ID box first.

"Mom its daddy,"

"We'll pick up the phone.

"Hey, daddy"

"Hello son how are you?"

"Fine,"

"Well, you sound like your excited are you dressed in that tux you told me about."

"I have to say I look fly nobody can't touch my swag."

Collin laughs at his son wishing he could be there with him but he couldn't get away.

"I want you to have fun tonight and you remember to be a gentleman you understand me?"

"Yes sir."

"Where is your mom?"

"She and Cory are in the living room waiting on me?"

"Oh really who is Cory?"

"Mom's friend who comes to see us every now and then he is so cool daddy you ought to meet him he's a super model."

"Oh that's really nice Collin let me take a moment to speak with your mom for a minute alright."

"Ok dad I love you thanks for calling."

"I love you too son call me tomorrow and tell me how things went, wish I could have been there to see you off send me some pictures okay."

"Cool I will do that. Mom telephone dad wants to holla at you."

"Ok Collin I got the phone you can hang up now. Hello"

"Hello right back at ya say what's with you and this Cory dude my son talking about?"

"Well, I don't think that's none of your business." I smile and hold the phone away from my ear shaking my head.

"Well, I got that loud and clear you're a little spunky thing huh?"

"Well, you know me I don't take any crap off anyone."

"Baby I know that better than anyone." I look at Cory and blow him a kiss as I hold the phone up and point to it and shake my head from side to side. Cory smiles and waves his hand giving me the signal to go ahead and talk as he flips through the channels with the remote.

"Well you're doing okay Collin?"

"Yes, and I see your doing alright your damn self with this super model dude you go girl I ain't mad at ya."

"Well, thank you for not being mad at me I feel blessed."

"Oh now you're being funny I'm glad you have someone and Collin seems to like this Cory guy and its all gravy with me if he likes him."

"I know, we must talk some other time Collin is having a fit we need to get going thank you for calling and I will have him call you tomorrow to tell you all about it."

"You do that and tell him to take plenty of pictures."

"Will do, goodbye now."

"Good bye Madison you take care and talk to you soon."

"Look people are you ready to go so we can get the ball rolling." Collin looks in the mirror and fixes his tie he then turns to look at me standing there smiling. He walks over and gives me a hug and says, "Mom I love you." Cory looks at his watch grabs me by the hand and says.

"Girl I hate to see Collin graduate from high school because you're going to be just tore up when he leaves for college." We burst into laughter but I knew there was some truth to his words because I wanted to just cry and this was only his first dance.

"Come on let's go meet little miss thing."

Chapter 23 - - Kobe

Going home was almost like a chore, not only I was at war with a woman I once loved, but I find myself stressed all the time just thinking about this situation. Keisha was now my enemy and I needed a break from this nagging woman I called my wife, it was 2:00 a.m. and here I sit in the parking lot where I live, hanging out with the guys at the club was cool but reality steps in. Wishing like hell I had somewhere else to go, I know my daughter's asleep; Keisha might be up waiting to fuss about something. I look at my cell and thought about calling Jewel, just to say hello and to let her know that I will be opening my shop in one week, I also wanted to thank her for being so supportive unlike my wife, Jewel was more of a wife then Keisha will ever be I know that's hard to say but it's the truth and I wish I could change this whole situation because it simply gives me a headache thinking about it.

I didn't know how to say how sorry I was for hurting Jewel the way I did. I often wondered if she had someone else, and if so could we at least be friends, because I needed her in my life. Jewel was my support; she always had something positive to say. I never met such a woman who had goals and a sense of direction, that's what made me love her so much there was something about her I couldn't explain.

Keisha however, is still my wife and I may be a fool for living like this but she is the mother of my child. She has one goal in mind, which is to make my life a living hell. She places these lame threats of divorce in my face and I'm just sick and tired of it. Deep down I wish Keisha would once pack her stuff and just leave and never return then I wouldn't have anything to feel guilty about.

I pick up the phone and start dialing Jewel's number I let it ring once and hang up. It's been a while and I'm feeling a little nervous about this, hell, it's almost 2:30 in the morning. I fold the phone up and rub my chin. I find myself opening the phone again and dial the number as I clear my throat. The phone rings three times, someone picks up, I heard the sound of clutter in the background. I could hear my heart pounding, I felt as if it was going to beat right out of my chest. I started to hang up but soon remember she has caller ID so there was no need to panic. A soft voice answer in a whisper,

"Hello"

"May I speak to Jewel" looking at the clock as she wipes her eyes.

"Who is this?"

"I apologize for waking you up but I couldn't sleep and I haven't talked to you in months, I wanted to know if you were alright."

"Kobe?" Jewel sits up in her bed as she wakes up.

"How are you?"

"I'm good; it's good to hear your voice."

"Likewise, I'm just surprised, so what's new?"

"Everything is still the same, but one thing."

"And what may that be?"

"I will be opening my shop in one week, I wanted to call and tell you myself."

"Kobe that's great! I'm excited for you and I knew you could do it."

"You have no idea do you?"

"No, tell me I'm lost."

"I will tell you this you're the only person that believes in me."

"I always told you that you can do whatever you put your mind to and you did just that, I'm proud of you and know that your business will do well just keep thinking positive."

"Thank you you're really a Jewel I miss you so much."

"I miss you as well."

"Really,"

"Yes, I miss you, we had a thing going on and you don't think I miss that?"

"Well_"

"Well, nothing it's all good I know what you had to do and I can't say that I understand all of it but I know why you did it. I couldn't stand in the way, besides you have a wife and child to think about I still love you because that part of me will never change, you needed to see if this thing will work out."

"I'm just there and I miss being with you and I wish I would have met you perhaps, another place another time."

"Honey, you didn't and this is now and if we don't stop talking about this I'm going to break down and cry because you're the best thing that has happened to me in a long time."

"Can we be friends, may I call you sometimes?"

"Do you think that's wise?"

"I don't know I just miss talking to you."

"Yes, and if you need a friend you can call me but I need and want to get on with my life because you know I will not be the mistress I'm too smart for that."

"I know and I'm not asking you to do that not unless you want to be my woman on the side."

"What did you say?"

"I'm only kidding with you don't come out of your thongs." Jewel laughs, "I won't come out of my thongs trust me."

"I know woman, it's a quarter to three I have to go I will call you later and tell you more about my shop alright."

"Yes, do that I have to be at the hospital at 5:30 in the morning we have a woman coming in for a gallbladder operation for six."

"So you finally got into the operating room?"

"Yes and I love it, being a scrub tech is something I love doing but I finally passed the test to get into nursing school, I look forward to that and you never know where I might end up, girlfriend is living large and in charge."

"You go girl I ain't mad at ya."

"Well let me get at least another hour of sleep and call me later, here is my cell number hit me up you have a pen?" Looking in my glove department rambling for a piece of paper I find a black ink pen as well.

"Yeah what's your number?"

"Ok its 201- 6847 got it?"

"Yeah I got it I will call you later alright."

"Okay Kobe you take it easy baby bye." I listen as she hangs up the phone I look at her cell number and places it in my phone memory data so I would have it at all times I didn't want Keisha to find the number and trip so I tear the paper up because she knows nothing about my cell phone or should say know how to unlock my codes. I closed my phone and place it in my glove department. Still feeling the buzz from drinking all night with Jalen and Byron I get out of my car and hit the alarm. I walk slowly up the stairs to my apartment I see a young couple kissing in the hallway as I pass by. I put my key in the door and turn the knob; damn all the lights were off except my bedroom light. I walk in; Keisha lays across the bed reading a book she never looks up at me.

"Hello" I say with a low tone not knowing what to expect as I pull off my shirt. Keisha looks at me out the corner of her eyes.

"Good morning to you."

I look and sit on the side of the bed next to her and bend over to kiss her on the cheek Keisha pulls back and sit up on the side next to me as I pull off my tennis.

"Look Kobe we need to talk about your late hours your keeping here."

When the Honeymoon Is Over

"What do you mean late hours I keep? Hell I don't go anywhere and all I do is work and maybe once in a blue moon I may go out and drink a couple of beers with the brothas what are you talking about?"

"I want to move to Dallas I think we would do better there."

"What about my shop that's going to open in a week?"

"What about it? It's not open yet." I stop messing with my shoes and look up at her with a frown.

"Tell me something what are your plans? You have a full time job there?"

"No but I'm going in a couple of days and look for a job my sister said we could live with her for about a month until we get on our feet I think that would be nice." My buzz exit and the aggravation start to set in at this point.

"I'm not moving! I have too much invested here already, it's a week before I open and you think I can just pop up and move, that's crazy girl I can't do that."

"Kobe, I love you and I want us to start our life over."

"You love me?" I start an evil laugh of pure frustration as I strip down to my blue silk boxers, and grab a towel out of the closet to take a shower.

"You make me sick! You're selfish all you talk about is this business that's going nowhere I'm to the damn point I can't stand your ass." Keisha gets up and walks into the living room with me in tow; I throw the towel on the bed.

"Look I don't want to fight with you tonight but, what the hell do you mean selfish? I give you what you need, and half of what you want, you work part time, you don't spend your money, I work overtime to have things in this house and you call me selfish hell I think it's the other way around. Girl you're driving me up the damn wall, do you know that?" Keisha turns around and places her finger in my face in which she's about to lose because I feel the blood pressure slowly rising,

"You make me so damn sick you no good punk!"

"Look girl it's best you get your damn hands out of my face before__"

"Before what nigga you're going to hit me!"

"Hell no, I'm not trying to go to jail just get your hand out of my face damn!"

"Daddy!" A small voice is heard and standing in the hall with tears in her eyes Shayla stands there.

"Girl, go take your ass to bed!" Keisha yells out of control.

"You lost your damn mind? She's hurting and you treat her like this? I will not have it Keisha; you need to calm down for real."

"Daddy I will go back to bed if you and mommy stop fighting please stop." I was furious this woman has lost her natural mind. I bend down to give my daughter a hug taking her to her room I was ready to hit the damn roof at this point but needed to keep my cool.

"Look baby, daddy is so sorry mommy and daddy are not fighting were having a really loud discussion we didn't mean to wake you up, it will be alright go to sleep." "Daddy why mommy had her hand in your face what's wrong?"

"Hey, don't you worry about that it's going to be alright I love you more than life itself baby girl you have no idea how much goodnight."

"Night daddy I love you too." I turn on her night lamp and close the door. I walk back in my bed room looking at Keisha sitting on the bed shedding her fake ass tears I say nothing; I begin to put my socks back on alone with my pants.

"Where are you going?"

"I have to jet because if I stay here tonight it's going to get downright ugly and to see my daughter upset hell no I need to think."

"Please stay Kobe I'm sorry for how I acted"

"Sorry Keisha you yelled at our child because your pissed with me not to mentioned cursed her , hell that little girl didn't do a damn thing to you and this is how you treat her because your mad with me this is not the first time you did something like this. Why are you acting like this please tell me?"

"Look I said I was sorry and I love you."

"I don't really want to hear that word love come out of your mouth because I think you misuse that word quite often I'm waiting on love because I'm certainly not getting it from you."

"Well whatever you think." I lace my shoes up and head towards the door as Keisha walks behind me in tears.

"Please don't leave."

"Hush you're going to get my baby up again."

"We'll stay because she's going to get up when she hears the door open so please stay."

If looks could kill this bitch would be dead I roll my eyes and close the door and walk over to the hall closet to get a blanket out to spread over the couch again.

"I will stay because I don't want her to ask where I am I'm tired and I'm going to sleep you go in your room."

Chapter 24 - - Jalen

"Good morning Baby." *Reagan* says in a soft raspy tone as we wake up slowly and make our way to the sit on the side of the bed.

"Good morning love do you want to go to the gym with me this morning?"

"No, I have some things to do today and I don't want to waste any time you go ahead alright."

"Are you coming to the club later?"

"I might, you need me there tonight?"

"What you mean by that statement?"

"I'm saying if you need me there to help out I will be there if not I might just stay home and read a book."

"No, I don't think I need you there I would like for you to be there if that's alright with you."

"Well don't look for me."

"Ok Reagan what's wrong with you today? You've been acting crazy lately."

"I'm going to pretend you didn't say that, because for one I'm not crazy." Reagan gets up and walks into our closet to look for something to put on. I walk into the closet behind her and grab her from behind and pull her close to me as I feel my nature rise against her backside. I slowly kiss her neck and place my hand across her breast. She turns around and kiss me back holding me tightly as she moves her hands slowly down to my private area where I was standing tall and strong!

"Jalen may I ask you a question without you getting mad, because we both been tense lately and I'm quite tired of it." I stand there all hard and sexually frustrated but was ready to listen to her concerns; I take her by the hand and sit on the bed as I position her on my lap.

"What's wrong baby?"

"I would like to know where I stand and if this relationship is going anywhere?"

"What do you mean? We have this house, were both successful, and doing what we wanted to do what more can we do girl I love you?" Reagan looks back at me with piercing eyes in which I never seen her do before.

"You really think that too and that's scary."

"What are you saying?"

"Jalen you say you love me but you haven't mentioned marriage what else is there?"

"Look we will someday get married but not now baby we have_"

"We have what, what do we have to do? We been living together since we graduated college, we came here and bought a great house what else do we have to do can you tell me that?" Reagan then stands up and places her hands on her hips as she wipes the tear that was forming in the corner of her eye.

"Look Reagan you know I love you and I have been good to you and you to me. Hell what's with this marriage thing all of a sudden? You never really said anything about it before. I'm not going anywhere I wouldn't have bought a house with you if I didn't love you can't you see that?"

"Don't you get it? It's not about all that it's about making a commitment to me, and God."

"Look Reagan don't throw this in my damn face I love you and

I told you I'm not going anywhere and I'm committed to you what the hell do you want? It's like were married already."

"You really think I'm concern about you leaving me? You think I'm a weak sista? Brotha you got me twisted."

"Honey I didn't say that_"

"Hell, you didn't have to your damn actions speaks loud enough!"

"Look, why are you tripping?"

"Baby I'm not tripping not at all you just told me where I stand in your life and I think maybe I have placed too much faith in this relationship and not enough in myself and God." I shifted on the bed and placed my hand on my chin and look Reagan in her eyes only to see that my words really did hurt her. But she wasn't going to make me do something I simply was not ready for.

"Look baby I'm sorry that I'm not ready to walk down that road yet, can you forgive me?" Reagan offers me a half hearted smile and walks off into the damn closet and come back with a Ed Hardy T shirt and jeans and throws it on the chaise. I watch her walk over to the dresser and gather her makeup. I'm sitting there looking dumbfounded because this woman is simply ignoring me.

"Reagan you hear me?" She turns slowly and looks me square in the eyes not blinking not showing any kind of emotion and places a kiss on my unwashed lips morning breath and all and said in a stern tone with light attitude.

"You don't have anything to worry about I won't mention this again. We have a trip to plan to Jamaica remember Braxtine is having her wedding there and the trip is paid for your still going right?"

"Oh I see where this is going."

"This doesn't have a damn thing to do with her wedding it's about you and I and I don't care to talk about this anymore, subject closed." Just like that Reagan shut it down went into the bathroom to finish her morning thing and left me sitting on the bed looking puzzled. I decide to clean things up in hopes I wasn't in the dog house so I yell in ear shot.

"Well yeah, to answer your question I will be going to the wedding with you besides it's a trip we both need maybe we can go a couple of days earlier than planned." I walk into the bathroom as she pulls her hair up in a ponytail to get into the shower. I lean against the door to watch her and fold my arms.

"Maybe, Braxtine will be here tomorrow and I really would like to get some things done around this house were going to pick out the dress I will be wearing in the wedding and things like that so were going to be busy."

"That's cool" I walk to the sink and grab my tooth brush and start to clean my funky mouth I already had on my basketball shorts and T shirt for my workout in which I need more so then ever. "Well I have to go to the gym I will be home around six don't worry about cooking I'm going to grab something while I'm out."

Looking as if she didn't give a damn about what was being said Reagan say's,

"Alright have a good day."

"Reagan I love you more then you know."

"Bye Jalen have a nice time at the gym."

"I can't believe that man!"

⁓

Sitting in the lobby of the airport waiting for her best friend to arrive Reagan had on her blue D& G tank and black shorts and black sandal hills showing her well-painted toes. With her hair pulled up in a French roll and bangs hanging down on one side of her face she had her makeup done lightly and looking as natural as she could be. Reagan was excited because she hasn't seen her friend since she moved and had to play catch up and get things together for the wedding. Although she was feeling sad and very pissed about her own situation she made a promise that she would be happy for Braxtine and not let what she's going through mess up Braxtine's visit. Reagan listens to the woman over the loud speaker.

"Flight 123 will be arriving at gate 7B in 10 minutes. Reagan runs to the bathroom to potty and make sure she look okay because deep down she was hurting but didn't want Braxtine to know how she really felt. She somehow always had a way of knowing what was going on with her besides, they only been friends since forever. As she goes to gate she notice a small crowd, she moves closer to see what was going on she couldn't believe her eyes he looked so much better in person, the ladies were just having a fit she stood there and watch then moved back to see if she could spot Braxtine, because she certainly was a fan but not a groupie. She saw Braxtine walk up the aisle in a snakeskin pants suit that was slamming alone with the purse to match. Her hair was cut in a cute short crop style with small curly waves she had at least 1ct diamonds in her ears she carried with her this bad suit case that matched her out fit the girl was together as always, she noticed Reagan standing there with all thirty two teeth showing they both scream like little girls.

"Damn, girl you look good."

"Reagan your butt look good as well what have you been doing with yourself you lost heck of weight since I saw you last but it looks good on a sista." They both hug and scream again.

"Hell the way I saw you walking up that runway I thought I was looking at Halle Berry girl you really look good your butt been pushing the steel yourself."

"Hey, I want you to meet a friend of mine."

"What?" Reagan looked puzzled as Braxtine pushes her way back through the crowd she hoped no one else came with her because she really wanted to play catch up but if this friend is going to help out and she's fun they all can hang. Reagan eyes bucked as she stood there watching Braxtine work her way back towards her with this fine man on her arm.

"Reagan this is Ginuwine, Ginuwine this is Reagan my best friend my maid of honor I was telling you about on the plane."

"Hello Reagan." He extends his hand out and kisses her hand."

"Well hello it's nice to meet you." Reagan looks at Braxtine with this look of disbelief.

"So this is where you live Alexandria Louisiana?" He was looking good, hair lade and shiny, goatee looking sharp as a tack he had rocks in his ears that was bling, bling for sure, Reagan was thinking that this man will make you cheat on yourself.

"Reagan do you remember I told you over the phone that I had a surprise for you at my wedding well he is it he will be in Jamaica the same weekend and so he will be singing in my wedding isn't that great?" Reagan looks again at him and smile.

"Girl, that's wassup how did you two meet?"

"I have to tell you all that later I'm ready to jet out of here G I hope you have a safe fight to New York I will call you later alright." He smiles as he looks Reagan up and down and kisses her on the cheek.

"It was really nice meeting such a beautiful lady when we meet in the island we have to spend more time together I apologize for leaving in such a short notice but I have to catch another plane. Bye Reagan, see you back in Atlanta Braxtine you ladies take care." He then grabs Braxtine's hand and kiss it and walks off. Reagan screams as they walk to the car.

"Girl you're going to have G singing in your wedding? You have to tell me all about this stuff, that man look good you two sat together on the plane?"

"Yes, he is really a nice young man that brotha is down to earth and that's why I like him so much. I also talked with him about doing a show at the Black Onyx I talked with Jalen about this, I told him that I knew G and he said he was trying to get a couple of groups down to perform live to make his club stand out more he's trying to do things for Alexandria."

"Really and why didn't you tell me about this you holding back on me girl!"

"No, I wanted you to meet him I know you like G and I wanted my maid of honor to know what was going on. No one else has a clue and they won't know until the night before the wedding so we won't have a crowd of people we don't want there. He agreed to do this for us and I agreed to not spread the word, I will have video to show friends and family that are unable to attend our wedding. I am so excited and I'm really excited about spending five wonderful days with my best friend in the whole entire world."

Reagan and Braxtine both smile as she turns into the driveway of her house. Braxtine look around the neighborhood and was impressed it wasn't ATL but she approved pulling her shades down to her nose as they get out of the BMW.

"Reagan, this is not bad at all girlfriend, I love this house. This gray stucco is slamming and you didn't tell me it was two stories." Reagan smiles as she pops the trunk to get the bags out.

"I'm planning to landscape this place and plant a nice rock garden in the middle of the yard and set a Bird bath in it I think that will look cute what you think?" "Now that will be nice you have plans for your living quarters huh?" Reagan squint her eyes to keep from thinking about her conversation with Jalen on yesterday she promised herself not to worry about that while Braxtine was here.

"Say let's go on in so I can show you the rest of the house." Braxtine grabs her bag and walks behind Reagan, she looks girlfriend up and down and knows something is wrong but decided to keep quiet for now.

This room was simply amazing red paint covered the walls in the living room the furniture was white the blinds were cherry wood the energy was inviting, warm and vibrant. There was a shelf with a collection of black art in a corner. A tree sits behind the contemporary love seat on the other side. The walls were full of pictures of red and white roses; Braxtine takes in the smell of a light scent of febreze oils.

"Girl, tell me how do you keep this room up? I couldn't have white furniture in my house, I would be afraid of it getting dirty and it smell so clean and fresh."

"We really don't be in this room much if you notice we don't have a TV in here, when we have company we sit in here. Let me show you where we spend most of our time." They went down the hall into another huge room. This room was black and gold there was a huge painting of a black panther in a gold frame. She also had a picture of a tiger in a black frame on the other wall. The room was full of trees, plants set up like a jungle. Braxtine places her hands on her hips shaking her head up and down.

"I have to give it to you and Jalen you have a beautiful set up here I love that flat screen, I take it this is where you two spend most of your time huh?"

"Yes, I have to say that we do I love this room the best because we come together here to watch DVD listen to music and enjoy our set up as you would say."

"That's really nice I know from your apartment back in Atlanta I knew your house would be on point."

"Now can you show me where I will be sleeping so I can put these bags up?"

"We have a guest room down here unless you wanted to go upstairs and sleep?"

"No, down here is fine where is it?" They walk down the hall and turned to the left and there was this cute room with its private bathroom the colors were pink and green. The bed was a queen size iron canopy with a pink and white lace fabric around the beautifully crafted iron post. Braxtine walked into the bathroom that flowed with the bedroom it too was pink and green she looked at the tub.

"Girl, this is too cute and I love this tub you know I like the jets a girl can get lost in here. I know you and Jalen have a huge gig up upstairs because the guest room here is really a suite." Reagan smiles,

"Sure we have a nice suite we have a Jacuzzi tub we both can fit in, when we do girl it's on like popping corn." They both laugh and joke for hours just enjoying one another's company.

"Braxtine I am so glad you're here I miss you so much because true friends you can't find often and when you do you take care of one another."

"I'm glad I could come I miss you, and Tipsy miss you also." They chuckle,

"Hell no that dog act as if she didn't like me."

"Yes, she did you just acted as if you were scared of her and she got off on that you know. Hey are we going to the club tonight or what? I know it's going to be jumping and I want to see the business man in action, speaking of Jalen is he still coming to the wedding?"

"I talked to him about it yesterday and he said he would like to get there early so we can make this trip like a vacation for us if that would be alright with you."

"Yeah, I have you two covered don't worry about a thing just have spending money!" Reagan rubs her head "Sure"

"Reagan what's up girl things hasn't gotten better with you and Jalen? Talk to me." Reagan pushes her hair back out of her face as she look at Braxtine.

"You seem as if you got your stuff together and my stuff is falling apart."

"What you mean?"

"Don't get me wrong I'm happy for you and being jealous is not me we been knowing each other forever so don't think I'm trying to rain on your thing here."

"Wait first of all don't you ever think if you have a problem my head is so far in the clouds that I can't hear you screaming for help you're my sister my friend we been through too much stuff together not to notice when one another is hurting so tell me what's up and if I can help girl I will, advice is my middle name." Reagan turns her lips up into a smile.

"It's good to know this because I didn't want to feel as if I was burdening you with my problems at a time like this."

"Girl if you don't stop I'm going to slap you right here right now."

"Well, I mentioned marriage to Jalen and he says some crap like he's not going to leave me like I'm some weak ho or something." Braxtine eyes buck,

"What?"

"Yeah, he thought I was concern about him leaving me if anything he should be concern about me leaving him right here right now because I'm really tired."

"No girl"

"Yes girl this is so and I really don't know what the hell is going on and I'm about two minutes from a jet flight right up out of this camp."

"Well let's not get emotional just yet Reagan let's get to the bottom of this before you fly off the handle alright."

"I hear you Braxtine but it's about to get real ugly around here because I don't know if I'm going to spend another month here with his attitude because he seem as if he is happy or should I say comfortable just us living here."

"I know what you're feeling and I can't say not to feel that way maybe you need to leave and show him what being alone is about, now I know this is easier said than done my sista because you invested a lot into this relationship and to just walk away from it is simply a test. My saying to you is why buy the cow when the milk is free."

"Your right about that because this brotha really thinks I'm not going anywhere and he don't have a clue what I'm feeling."

"Just play it cool while I'm here because the worst thing you can do is act a fool with a black man when you have company."

"Oh I'm too damn classy for that." They both chuckle and give one another high fives.

Chapter 25 - - Cory

The phone rings I wake up and look at the clock to see what time it is.

"Its 2:30 in the morning who in the hell is this." I clear my throat

"Hello"

"Cory is this you?"

"Yes, and who is this?"

"Tisha, I apologize for calling you this time of morning, but I have to talk to you its important."

"It must be important for you to call me at this hour what's wrong?"

"Cory I need to see you face to face because there's something I should have told you a long time ago."

"You can't tell me this over the phone Tisha it's not like you live next door."

"Hell I know that better than anyone Cory I need to see you and I need to see you soon this is important!"

"Alright you want to plan this weekend."

"Sure, I will purchase my ticket today all I needed to know if you would see me." "No problem, I have to arrange a place for you to stay."

"I thought."

"Please don't think; I will call the Hilton hotel down the street I will pay for the room you just plan to spend your nights there alright."

"Ok I can't disagree with you right now because I need to go I will see you this weekend alright."

"Yeah, bye"

I hang the phone up and I start to think about Tisha my heart starts to pound loudly at the thought of how this woman and I use to make love laugh have fun and all that other stuff lovers do and I'm not feeling this meeting.

I told her not to call me anymore and now I'm going to see her this weekend. Damn, I just thought about the plans I made with Madison because Collin leaves for New Orleans on Thursday and Madison wanted to do something special with me. I rub my head and sit up on the side of the bed Tisha have me all twisted she side swiped me this round I'm not ready for this meeting for real. Now I have to think about what I will tell Madison about this weekend.

I seriously don't think Madison will understand this, what black woman would. Women just don't understand stuff like that especially if they don't have any ties. What was I thinking telling her she could come? I need to talk to someone about this situation and my sister will have to do; besides I need a woman's intake on this scenario. I pick up my phone and start dialing. Her phone rings about two times someone picks up the phone she sounded wide-awake.

"Talk to me daddy" I narrow my eyes and look at the phone totally caught off guard.

"What?"

"Look boy don't play with me you said you were going to call me when you thought I would make it in and you're just in time I made it back to the dorm safely."

"Excuse me this is Cory, Nina this you?"

"No, Oh I'm so sorry I thought you were my boyfriend Jackson he was going to call me to see if I made it back"

"You don't have to explain, I apologize for calling so late but I need to speak to my sister if she's there."

"Sure she's right here laughing her head off at me." Nina comes to the phone chuckling.

"Hello"

"Nina baby sis what's up?" Nina stops laughing and starts to panic.

"Cory what's wrong? Is it mama? What's wrong?"

"Hey girl calm down I know it's late and there's something wrong but it's not mama I need to talk to you and no it's not an emergency, alright, well to me it is but not to anyone else." Nina calms down and catches her breath the phone beeps.

"Hey Cory can you hold just a second I think this is Jackson for real." She clicks over to the other line.

"Hello"

"Hey Nina what's up pretty girl can you talk?"

"Julius I can't chat right now I have my brotha on the other line I will call you back smooches."

"Alright you do that I will be here by the phone waiting to hear your sexy voice."

"Good Bye Julius" She clicks back over.

"I'm back"

"So your roommate talked to her sugar daddy?" We both laugh.

"No that was Julius"

"Julius? I thought you two broke up after graduation so that you could be free while you were in college."

"Well we tried and with him here it's hard I love that boy."

"I know, you two only been together forever."

"Yeah I know I can't believe he followed us here but he said he was going to school in the south this wasn't planned, but we're not talking about me and Julius what's up with my big brotha?"

"Well I have a problem."

"And, what's new?"

"Be quiet Nina and listen."

"Okay I was just making a funny I'm here for you big brotha."

"Okay I talked with Latisha she called me this morning and told me she wanted to come down and talk to me about something important and needed to see me face to face and I told her yeah."

"Say I know you told me to be quiet but Cory didn't this hooker, break your heart?"

"Yeah but she sounded worried and I'm really concern,"

"Well if you called me to tell me you two are getting back together I really don't want to hear it but if she makes you happy__"

"See there you go I didn't say a damn thing about getting back with this chick as a matter of fact I told her I will get with her this weekend but I will pay for the room she has to stay in because she can't stay with me."

"To be honest with you I wouldn't pay anything for that B_"

"Nina, I know how you feel about Latisha."

"I couldn't stand that long nose, cat face, Jezebel, especially when she lied and told you she was single and wasn't."

"Well"

"Well nothing I didn't trust the whore since that day she was caught up in that bull, mama didn't either she thought you could do better but that's what you wanted and so on and on."

"Nina, hold on girl let me talk you're so damn dramatic."

"No I just don't want you to get caught up in that hooker's web again. She's a black widow and you're the next damn victim. I love you Cory."

"Nina I love you too and that's why I called because I needed to talk because I'm going through some stuff right now."

"You don't have to go through if you just let go. When she get here Cory just tell her it's over and to leave you alone, hell she chose to go back to her husband and his crazy ass took her back let him deal with her alright."

"I'm not going back to Tisha because she's not the one for me."

"Say let me ask you something what's going on with Olivia?"

"What you mean?"

"Well you know I was home last week and saw her and she looked mad as hell. I asked her about you and she just looked at me all crazy and said, as if your little ass didn't know"

"I rolled my eyes and said excuse me for asking and no I don't know and walked off."

"Well Olivia has issues and I care not to get into that right now because that's another long story."

"Oh I see playa"

"Nina I'm not a playa and don't want the title. I'm too old to be a playa I have turned in my playa's card a while ago." Nina holds the phone up looks and point to it smiling at her roommate.

"Oh really that's nice I heard you were playing daddy to Madison's child."

"Who told you that?"

"Mama told me, she always liked Madison I can't believe you two hooked up again hell this is a small world because she went into the air force right?"

"Yeah Madison is really beautiful sweet smart and not to mention fine as hell and check this out Nina her long silky hair is real."We both burst out into laughter.

"I always liked her and I think she's cool just be careful because she has a baby's daddy."

"Thanks for looking out for me, but this situation here, is so cool and I really like her but were only friends but I want more."

"Yeah, but be cool and see what happens."

"Well, Madison and I had plans this weekend that I have to break because Tisha will be here."

"See what I mean about that damn girl! She is going to catch you in her web, now Madison has to suffer for that hoe."

"I don't know what to tell Madison that's the real problem."

"What you mean you tell her the truth and hope she understand you know mama always told us to be honest with people even if it hurts because they will respect you for being honest."

"I'm going to call her today and let her know what's going on."

"You do that hell this phone is beeping I know its Jackson you call me later okay love you."

"I love you too thanks."

I get up and go to the bathroom by this time it's 3:40 am I know not to call Madison at this hour but now I can't sleep because I'm worried about how she's going to take this news. Hell she's intelligent and seem to be understanding but really, what woman in her right mind will understand that her man or future man is going to spend a whole weekend with his ex girlfriend. In a way I'm excited about seeing Tisha but at the same time guilty as hell because this is starting something that I worked hard to get over. I wash my face in cold water as I look into the mirror I see myself for the first time in a long time. I break down as I think about the pain this woman caused me. I treated her well and I sure as hell loved this woman and now she want or need to talk. What did she want to talk about what's left of this damn relationship she's looking to destroy. Now that I said yes to this weekend I guess I have to wait and see what happens. The phone rings again I look towards the phone as if I was afraid to answer it.

"Damn who could this be?"

"Hello"

"Cory you sleep?"

"No I haven't been to sleep all night, who is this?"

"Olivia"

"Hello Olivia"

"Damn you don't have to sound so excited, I was thinking

about you and I was up doing paper work and packing for my leadership meeting that starts this weekend."

"Oh really"

"Damn Cory, don't sound so ecstatic."

"I apologize for being this way I have some things on my mind that's all."

"Why don't that surprise me you always have something on your mind."

"Olivia please don't start alright I'm not in the mood not at this hour."

"I won't start with you I wanted to apologize for getting all emotional the last time we talked. You're a good person and I took what happened between us to heart. You said we could only be friends and I rather, be your friend then not have you in my life at all you feel what I'm saying?"

"Sure Olivia I feel ya and I would like to apologize for going that far with you your worth more than that you were right when you said that you're a good woman. Your beautiful, you're smart, and you have your own business and I admire you for that you go girl."

"Cory what we did, we did it because that's what we wanted to do and I have no regrets okay so don't feel bad if it happens again."

"Well Olivia, I need to be honest with you, my sister said something to me this morning that made a lot of sense sometimes being honest may hurt a person but as long as you are honest with them they will respect you later for your honesty."

"Cory what are you trying to say to me."

"What I'm saying to you Olivia, is that we can't sleep together anymore simply because it's not right nor is it fair to you. You deserve a man in your life that's going to love you and treat you well and I know you will find that."

"Cory but I want to connect with you who says we won't be together in the future and baby I have needs."

"Sure you have needs so do I and I'm a man with big plans,

but I can't make a promise that I'm going to make that move with you." Olivia's voice drops to a small tone as her throat feels a knot forming.

"Cory if you feel that way, I have to respect that because this is what you want. Tell me something and be honest since your being honest today."

I shake my head from side to side as I hold the phone down then put it back to my ear again.

"What Olivia?"

"Are you gay?" I start to laugh.

"What in the hell is so funny about that question are you gay or what?"

"No I'm not gay far from it I'm all man but if you would like to know why I'm not seeking you as my woman it has nothing to do with you trust me."

"Tell me then what's this all about?"

"I'm interested in someone else." Suddenly silence fill the air and I felt bad because I knew this woman had a Jones for me and I just couldn't return the feelings.

"Okay, glad to know you're not gay you must really like this lady huh?"

"Yes, I do."

"Well I wish you all the best really I do because you're a good man and I have to give that to you."

"Olivia I really would like to be friends."

"Sure thing buddy but I have to go right now and finish packing my cloths and finish up this paper work I will talk to you when I come back."

"Alright you do that."

I thought that went rather smoothly now will the conversation with Madison go like this only time will tell.

It's been a long stressful day and all I want to do is relax and go to bed. I walk in the bedroom to find my answering machine blinking, the counter said I had five messages the first message was from my sister.

"Hey big brotha I was hoping I would catch you home but you're not there so I just wanted to see if you talked with Madison yet give me a call later I'm out going to a party tonight love you." The second message was from his mom,

"Hey son I wanted to just speak to you before I go to bed but I see your not in I will call you tomorrow love you." I check the time my mom called. The third message was from Jalen he sound troubled.

"Man I don't like talking into these damn machines but when you get in call alright." I listen to the next message from Tisha.

"Hello Cory, I hope everything is set for this Friday because I will be there at 6:00pm I will be flying American Airlines I look forward to seeing you. Again thank you for saying you will see me this weekend I still love you."

Those words hit me like a ton of bricks because she don't know the real meaning of the word love it was just something to say. It didn't stop my chest from hurting from the pound of my heart beating so damn fast! I haven't seen her in over eight months. Surely I couldn't be falling into her web again like Nina said. Well I pushed the button to listen to my last message, it was Madison.

"Cory honey I have to apologize for telling you this on your machine but baby I have to cancel our plans for this weekend because I have to fly to California to see my baby brotha he's home and I'm leaving out tonight I hope you understand I looked forward to spending time with you but I haven't seen my brotha in over two years he's in the Marines and we don't spend much time together again I apologize about this weekend I will call you when I get to Oakland alright Smooches." I scream,

"Damn, damn, damn I don't have to tell Madison anything but hell I have to spend this time with Tisha and I don't know if I can handle all this right now." I pick up the phone to dial Jalen back to see what was going on with him. The phone rings twice Reagan answers.

"Hello"

"Hi Reagan, um how you doing?"

"I'm fine how you Cory?"

"I'm okay is Jalen there I apologize for calling at this hour but I need to speak to him for a minute."

"It's cool Cory."

"Alright"

"Please hold for a minute while I go get him he's upstairs."

While I wait for Jalen to get to the phone I think about this meeting with Tisha wondering what it is she has to say and will it make any difference in my life trying to get over someone is hard when you love them .

"Hello"

"Jalen man what's up I got your message you sound really concerned about something what's up?"

"Look man I can't get into it right now but I need to talk with you about something what are you doing tomorrow around noon?"

"I have a commercial to shoot and after that I'm good."

"Man hit me on my cell if you get a chance, maybe we can hook up alright."

"Will do son you take it easy and again tell Reagan I really didn't mean to disturb you two alright."

"Man no problem you didn't disturb anything trust that, don't forget to hit me up on my cell."

"Man I got you."

I take a look at my Rolex to see what time it is, I had to be at the airport at least by 5:30 so I wouldn't be late, it was already 2:00 I had time to go home shave and shower. I jump into my car, my cell phone rings it was Madison I push a button to place it on speakerphone.

"Hello"

"Hi Cory what's up?"

"Hey baby how was your flight?"

"It was good my brother and I are spending time together, he will be here for a month in a half he will be leaving for Japan after his vacation so I will make a few more trips out here before he has to leave I'm going to miss him because we're really close thank God I work for an airlines so I can at least fly for free you know?"

"I hear you."

"So what are you doing this weekend?"

"Well not much I have something to share with you when you get back okay."

"Sure but is everything alright? You sound as if you're worried about something."

"Baby I'm alright; you have fun with your brother okay."

"Well you have a nice weekend I miss you."

"I miss you too."

"I will call you on Sunday."

"You do that."

I press the end button to hang up the phone as I make my way into my apartment complex and back my car up next to my Range Rover. As soon as I step out of my Impala I hear a voice calling me.

"Cory"

I look up and see Kelly standing on her balcony.

"Hey girl what's up you been gone a week where have you been?"

"Come see me for a minute."

I wave at Kelly to let her know to meet me down stairs. I walk

Holly M. Jewell

to my apartment she walks out in her blue shorts and white tee shirt.

"Damn girl you're looking good what's up with you?"

"I'm doing okay and you look nice where you going?"

"I'm taking care of some old business this weekend."

Kelly hit's me in my arm softly and says, "don't let me stand in your way I wanted to holla at you since I been out of town all this week, you know how it is when you have to work over."

"Oh do I know, well I don't mean to be rude but I have somewhere to be at 5:30 and I'm running I will catch up with you later ok."

"Sure you take care I will talk to you later."

◦~◦

I decided to put on a pair of Sean John shorts and tee with my matching fitted ball cap and Jordan Tennis I threw on some Polo Sport Cologne and my new 2 ct platinum diamond earrings. I'm so nervous and I have no idea why or what to expect the plane just landed.

Looking cool was natural but feeling anxious was not I had to hide my nervousness behind my Kenneth Cole shades and stance; I did a breath check so I wouldn't smell wrong in the mouth. I then walk to gate five so that I would be there when she stepped off the plane. My heart is doing a dance of some sort in my chest this is not cool at all. The young woman standing beside me gives me a sly look and I shot her a smile back. My hands start to fill with sweat my stomach turns with excitement. The passengers start to exit the air craft.

I first spot a lady with her baby coming off the plane. I also noticed this black man with a brief case, he looks as if he was a lawyer or something. I spotted a middle age lady with salt and pepper hair, she was walking and talking to Latisha, but she didn't spot me just yet, my eyes grow wide and I try to smile I was afraid to move, afraid to speak, I didn't know if what I was looking at was real or fake my eyes were playing tricks on me. This fat round belly woman greets me.

"Hi it's been a long time I really miss you."

My words were paralyzed I couldn't do anything but look at her round belly that stood in between us.

"Earth to Cory can I get a hug."

My eyes blink furiously at her stomach.

"I'm sorry"

Latisha grabs me and starts to hug me and a tear reaches the corner of her eye as she notice I wasn't hugging back.

"Latisha did you have a safe trip?"

"Yes, I did we had a thunder storm to start off with but things got better as we went above the storm that was a little shaky for me and little lady here."

"Well let's go and get your bags so we can get out of here."

I ignored her little comment about that belly of hers I was feeling anxious and beginning to feel the heat rise throughout my body.

Chapter 26 - - Cory

I crudely watch Latisha unpack her clothes; I couldn't take my eyes off her round figure, I watched her walk around the room as if nothing was wrong. I didn't have a clue as to what was really going on; suddenly anger hit the shore. "Tisha sit down!" She walks towards me and sit on the bed licking her lips, wondering what I was planning to say next with pleading eyes.

"Cory, before you say anything_"

"No wait! You've been pregnant for some time now; you mean to tell me you haven't thought enough of me, to let me know you were packing a load?"

Tisha gives me a sharp look while she bites down hard on her bottom lip while twisting in her hair; she nervously speaks in low tone.

"Baby, look I wanted to tell you that I was pregnant but didn't know how, and I thought if I told you over the phone you wouldn't see me and_"

"And. my ass, don't give me that bull, Tisha, you've been playing games with me for a long time girl and this is simply not the time!"

"You think this is easy for me, hell no! It's hard because my husband thinks that this is his baby!" My eyes drew tight as I watch her rub her stomach.

"What did you say?"

"I said_"

"Dammit! I heard you, are you crazy or what?"

"Look Cory I couldn't tell my husband that this was some other mans baby because were_"

"I don't want to hear another word, you really have out done yourself and what do you plan to do when you have this child? What do you want me to do, shut my mouth and say nothing?"

"No Cory, I felt it wasn't right not to tell you but I figured that you wouldn't want anything to do with us."

I instantly find my stress level pop up as I walk over to the blinds and peep out at the crowd of people below to clear my mind. Things seem a little out of control at the moment.

"Tisha, you got me twisted girl, I simply think this is a test of my faith seriously."

"Cory, I love you."

"Don't say that word love, you don't love me, you don't love your husband, and it seems as if you don't love your damn self you know nothing about love! Your full of crap and I should have dropped your ass the moment I found out you were married but hell no you said this and you said that and now it has come down to this! " Tisha starts to cry.

"Cory I'm sorry."

"Sorry is all I ever seem to hear from you, you're nothing but a damn liar, and cheater and I wish to God I never even met you!"

I slide down in the corner of the room and place my head in the palms of my hands. Tisha walks over to me and try to hug me. I never looked up I begin to speak with vicious force.

"Get your damn hands off of me I don't want you touching me!"

Tisha backs up and sits on the bed as she watches me break down and cry she has never experience my anger.

"I know you said you didn't want to hear me say that I'm sorry but I am. I never meant to hurt you baby I really care for you a lot could you just listen to me?"

When the Honeymoon Is Over

I stand up slowly and walk over to the little table in the corner and sit down with tears in my eyes as I look out the window.

"I don't know if I want to listen to anything you have to say."

"I can understand that but it's time I tell you the truth because you deserve to know."

"You've been telling me the truth for a long time now and I can't determine truth from fiction with your scheming ass."

"Cory I understand what it is your going through because I been there."

"Girl I don't understand you, and hell no you don't understand a damn thing I'm going through, you can just get off that little trip your on!"

Tisha walks over to me and stands in front of me forcing her belly in my damn face.

"Look I know you're mad and I wish you wasn't so angry."

"Angry! Hell angry ain't the word I'm pissed because I wouldn't listen to my family nor friends when it came down to you and now that I'm getting my life in order here you come with this story about this baby and your husband! What's with that Tisha can you tell me?"

Tisha walks over to the sink, turns it on as she throws water over her face she then turns back and looks at me as I stand up watching her with one hand under my chin and the other holding my elbow.

"Look Cory I didn't come here to make your life difficult! All I wanted to do was let you know what was going on with me, that's it baby."

"Oh really now,"

"Yes, I know I should have told you a long time ago but I'm telling you now I'm not asking you for anything other than your support."

"Support, what do you mean?"

"What I mean is that I told you that this baby is yours but I don't want you to say anything because it's going to be taken care of."

My face drew tight in a frown.

"What are you really saying Latisha please tell me."

"I will send you pictures and let you know what's going on with our daughter but you can't_"

"Wait a damn minute! You don't expect me to have anything to do with my baby? You lost your damn mind? I have nothing to discuss with you as a matter of fact I will see about getting test done and I will make damn sure that my child is a part of my life you hear what I'm saying? Latisha now this has nothing to do with you because I have danced by your music long enough and I have to draw the line right here right now!"

"Wait! My husband knows nothing about this he don't have a clue I'm here with you this weekend he thinks I'm at a wedding which is tomorrow but___"

"See you lie too damn much! I think its best you prepare your husband for this baby, because I can't see myself going through this so get yourself together and fast. You have a whole weekend to think about what you plan to say to your man your husband your whatever I'm out of here I will have my lawyer contact yours so get one."

I walk towards the door as Tisha starts to lose control she rushes up to me and stands in front of the door to block me in.

"Look girl you need to get out of my way!"

"Hell no you can't do this to me I didn't have to tell you but I did you want me to lose what I have huh?"

"This has nothing to do with you but have everything to do with what's going on inside of you right now!"

"Cory."

"Move out of my way girl!"

Tisha starts to cry out loud and scream in my face.

"I hate you for what it is your doing to me right now, you will never see this child, damn you!" I grabbed Tisha before I realized it to move her out of my way when suddenly this shortie slaps me in the face and scratches me on the neck with her cat claws I push her onto the bed not hitting her a lick trying to keep my damn cool which was not in my favor at the moment.

"You need to stop this your stressing the baby, me and yourself with all this childish shit your doing and I refuse to hit you now stop it! I will be back tomorrow to check you out of this hotel and pay for your plane ticket home, simply because we have nothing else to discuss now leave me the hell alone!" Her eyes fill with water she could cry a river right now and I could care less at this point. I jump up and walk towards the door I look back at her as she coughs and catches her breath.

"I'm sorry it has to be this way and most of all I feel sorry for you."

I walk out never looking back.

Chapter 27 - - Kelly

I stepped out the beauty shop rocking my fresh new light bronzy brown hair color that I had cut into a stylish Mohawk over lapping my face. I'm feeling this look because it's very becoming of me, if I have to say so myself. I couldn't stop looking in the mirror admiring my new look that enhance my swagger. I throw on my Prada shades and grab my seatbelt and snap myself in. I reach in my bag for my lipstick. Suddenly, I spot in my rear view mirror my soon to be ex husband pulling up behind me I try to pull off but he pulls his black jeep in behind my BMW. He jumps out, runs to my window tapping on the glass I hold up my cell phone as I look at him and say,

"Look I will call the police so leave me alone and get out of my way Ethan."

"Look Kelly I don't want any trouble, all I want to do is talk to you, I don't want to go to jail, I don't want any trouble alright I promise I won't cause any let's talk."

I decided to crack my window because he looked harmless but I simply didn't trust him.

"Look what do you want? I don't really have time for this today we really don't have anything to talk about now do we?"

"You're still my wife and I want to talk to you if you don't mind. I can't stay parked like this can we go to Buffalo Wild Wings across the street please?" I nod my head as I look at my watch.

"I guess so I will follow you over there." He then jumps back into his vehicle pulls off and pulls into the parking lot as I follow behind him pulling my car next to his. I get out of the car, grab my cell phone and Prada bag, I lean against my car waiting on him to make his way out of his. He steps out with a dozen of roses and hands it to me. Not impressed but I smell the flowers as I look at him through my dark shades and didn't bother to crack a smile I open the door of my car and place them in my front seat and slam the door. I push my alarm button walk in front of him as if we were not together towards the sports bar with him in tow.

A young lady dressed in all black with a long silky pony tail on her nappy head and lashes that look like she belonged in a circus greeted us at the door. Her teeth were dressed in platinum; instead of a tooth brush she needed some jury cleaner.

"Hello welcome to BWW Sports Bar and grill."

I stood there looking in this ghetto queen's mouth trying not to laugh I thought she looked ridiculous.

"I would like a spot at the bar if there's room."

The young lady looked around to see if she could spot room at the bar it was happy hour and this place was packed with people the Lakers were playing and people were yelling and the place was just loud and the atmosphere was happy and fun.

"Well I don't see any room at the bar but there's a small table with bar stools in that corner next to the window I think you may like."

I look over towards the table while smiling at the young lady as I spot her nametag.

"Veda thank you you're so kind."

I reached in my bag and pull out a five to give to the young lady then we walk over to the table to be seated. Ethan follows me like a puppy as he tries to be a gentleman, he pulls the stool out I stop him by saying,

"I got this."

Ethan grabs his stool and sits down. A young waitress greets us at the table.

"Hello my name is Shawn I will be your waitress this afternoon what can I get you two lovely people to drink?" As she passes us our menus I offer her a smile

"Yes, Shawn I would like to have a Bahama Mamma please."

She smiles and look to Ethan and ask.

"And what would you like to drink?"

"I would like a coke and a smile thank you."

"Sure I will be right back with your drinks."

The waitress bounces off across the room. Ethan looks at me grabbing a straw that was placed on the table, opens it and places it in the corner of his mouth.

"Tell me something?" Kelly snaps back.

"What!"

"When did you start drinking?"

"I drink every now and then is there a problem with that?" Ethan raises his eyebrows.

"Excuse me Miss Thang I just asked a question I didn't want to get you wired that's not why I'm here."

"First of all I'm grown and drinking relaxes me from time to time to answer your damn question and second why we are here?"

"Look lets order our food and then we can talk about why I'm here okay, is that alright with you lady?"

I looked around the room to see if I knew anyone and to see if anyone was listening to our conversation.

"I guess your right we should eat besides I'm hungry I been busy all day doing this and that."

"What have you been doing all day?"

"It's a woman thing you wouldn't understand plus I needed time for myself."

"Oh really I see."

"Next week I will be flying to Jamaica alone with some girlfriends of mine we had this trip planned for about six weeks now and I need that time off just to relax in the sun and have some fun."

"You go girl I see your looking well."

"Here is your coke and smile and here is your Bahama Mama I hope you enjoy."

"Are you ready to order?"

I look at the waitress and say.

"Yes, I would like to have the spicy hot wings and chili fries with creamy ranch dipping sauce please."

"That sounds good and sir what would you like to order today?"

"I would like to have the same thank you."

"Okay that will be right out if you need anything else please let me know."

The waitress goes to the back I pick up my bag.

"I will be right back I'm going to the ladies room."

"I will be here."

"I'm sure you will."

I walk to the back of the room the men that sat at the bar watched me work my way through the crowd. I walked in the ladies room, checked the mirror to make sure my hair was in place and to check my nose to see if it was clean. I open my bag pulled my phone out I had one missed call and message from Cory.

"Hello Kelly, I hate I got your voice mail, call me when you can I'm at home but if you get this message and I'm not in give me a call on my cell."

I start dialing the number and catch his answering machine so I hang up to see if I could catch Cory on his cell, I get his voice mail and leave a message.

"Hi Cory honey this is Kelly I'm returning your call I'm out right now but I will be home in about two hours if you need to chat I will talk to you later smooches."

I hang up the phone. I take one last look in the mirror before

When the Honeymoon Is Over

returning to our table. I begin to walk out with my head up; I shoot a smile and wink at the gentlemen sitting at the bar.

"Hello" They smile among each other as they speak back.

"Hello" They watch me as I return to the table they speak among themselves as I smile to myself thinking " *I Know I still have it going on this Negro at the table knows it too and it's too damn bad he lost this bag of chips and dip".*

I start to laugh out loud Ethan smiles as he watches the men watching me Ethan asks,

"What are you smiling about?"

"Oh nothing I was just thinking about something someone once told me that's all."

"Do you care to share?"

"No it has nothing to do with you at all."

"Oh I see."

The waitress returns with our food placing it down she turns and smile.

"Is there anything else I can get you?" Ethan says.

"No thank you."

"Alright then you two enjoy your meal." Ethan fixes his plate up with hot sauce and adds salt to his food and starts to talk while chewing.

"Kelly I'm happy to be sitting here with you eating lunch it's been awhile." I poked my lips out and rolled my eyes slightly, because I didn't believe a damn thing that came out of his mouth.

"Look let's cut through all the bull Ethan because I really don't have time for the drama nor the lies." Ethan stopped chewing and picked up his glass and slowly drinks. "Look Kelly it's been very hard dealing with this and__" I interrupted by slamming my fork on the plate trying to not make a scene. I spoke in a soft but hard manor.

"Look you; I don't want to hear anymore of your lies because you made it your business to hurt me. I loved you more than life itself and did you give me the love in return? Hell no you did everything in your power to hurt me treat me like I wasn't human now you sit there on your round out of shape ass looking like your pregnant with two baby elephants and tell me it's been hard for you, Nig please"

Ethan clears his throat to speak as he look around to make sure no one was listening to their conversation.

"Kelly I'm asking you to please give me a break I made a mistake and I want to make things right again."

"What do you mean make things right again are you crazy you will never make things right ever it's too late for that you made your choice now you have to live with the decisions you made trust me it's over. I'm just happy I didn't have any kids with your sorry ass so I don't have to deal with you after the divorce."

"Don't do this to us Kelly please."

"Ethan where were you when I begged you to stop cheating, stop treating me like an outsider you can go straight to hell as far as I'm concern and take your little girlfriend with you because it's over."

"So you're saying it's over that's it?"

I pick up my chicken and dipped it in my ranch ignoring his sorry excuses.

"Are you listening to me girl?"

"You better eat your food because I really don't have too much more to say to you Ethan James."

Ethan rubs his hands together as he watches me eat. He knew he messed up and there wasn't anything he could do to fix this situation this marriage was over and it was time to accept the fact that he was in a no win situation.

"Kelly I really know now that I hurt you and I never meant to do this to you if given another chance to redeem myself I will do better by treating you with love and respect. I was wrong I admit, but you have to understand that I'm only a man and I make mistakes please don't do this, just think about what we had together and what we can have together."

I wipe my mouth with my napkin and clear my throat and start to slowly sip on my drink as I watch the man I once had respect for beg for my forgiveness.

"Look the food was great I see you haven't finished yours."

"Do you hear me talking to you?"

"Yes I hear you talking to me and what you say right now isn't important not to me."

I look at my watch and calls for the waitress.

"Shawn could you step here for a second please,"

"Sure would you like another drink?"

"No I would like the check please."

"No problem I will be right back."

"What's wrong with you?"

"There's nothing wrong with me I have to go simply because I have important things to do I told you we have nothing to discuss I have to say that this has been real and I certainly enjoyed my meal." The waitress return,

"Here is your check."

I reach in my purse and pull out a fifty-dollar bill and pass it to the waitress.

"Say you keep the change.

"Thank you"

Ethan had a surprise look upon his face.

"I was getting this thank you very much."

I stand up and place my purse on my shoulder.

"I don't need you to get anything for me you just take care of yourself I will have my lawyer contact yours, you have a great day!"

I walk off as Ethan watch me walk right out of his life if he didn't know it was over he knows now.

Chapter 28 - - Jada

I walk into the house only to find my husband and daughter playing on the floor. The music was loud the house was a mess. I walk over to my baby and pick her up Jordan starts smiling and giggling, oh how I love to hear her laugh she cracks me up. Byron stretches out on the floor throwing his hands behind his head looking like the sexy daddy that he is.

"We need to talk; mama is coming over to get Jordan so we can have some time alone."

"Well is this going to take all night I'm going out to the club for a couple of hours if you don't mind."

"Byron did you hear me my mother is coming to get Jordan we can do something together for a change."

"Baby, all that is fine but I told Kobe and Jalen I will meet them out tonight can we do this some other time."

Byron gets up and places his arms around me and kisses me on the lips softly.

"Look whatever, do what you like I'm going to step out with Madison I will drive up there to see her since I don't have Jordan tonight, and I may spend the night."

"Well that's cool we will do something tomorrow me and you I will call my mother and see if she want to keep Jordan if your mom has something else to do I promise."

"Yeah sure,"

I didn't believe a damn thing Byron was stressing, I was too tired to stress about it I pick up the phone to call my best friend.

"Hello"

"Hey girl what's up?"

"Hey sis Cory and I are about to go to a party my boss is giving at her house. I have to go and finish getting ready."

"Ok you two have fun."

"We will, I will call you tomorrow give Jordan a kiss for me sweetie."

"Will do, tell Cory I said hello don't have too much fun ok."

"I promise I will give you a call tomorrow smooches."

"Hey, Madison I need to get away for a while, will you do me a favor I will call you tomorrow don't call me I just remember that I won't be here and I will contact you when I get back."

"Are you sure?"

"Most defiantly, I will contact you."

"Ok bye now."

"Good bye sweetie."

I have to get away I wish Madison was available but it's cool, I just need to get my head together so I packed clothes anyway. Byron steps into the room.

"Honey what time you coming back tomorrow?"

Raising my eyebrow up a notch, "I don't know Madison and I might do some shopping why?"

"I was just asking no particular reason I was just wondering that's all."

"Yeah right,"

Byron walks up on me getting in my space; I'm at least 5 inches shorter than he is.

"What the hell you mean by that comment?"

"Nothing not a thing, now move out of my way so I can finish packing my clothes."

"I thought that's what you meant."

He begins to pick me up, throw me onto the bed and start tickling and kissing me gently on the neck. I start to kiss him back on the neck as my nipples harden and my womanhood starts to get moist.

"Let's get you dressed and packed."

"Byron, I want to make love to you before we go."

"Baby I have to get dressed we can take a shower together."

"Damn a shower I want to make love to my husband."

I start to kiss him around his neck then down his chest area and begin to unzip his pants.

"Baby stop I have to meet the fellas in one hour and you have to get on the road."

"Look Byron I'm trying to be patient with you, dammit never mind."

"Baby we will do something tomorrow I promise."

"Tomorrow just forget it!"

Byron walks into the bathroom and turns on the shower.

"Come in here and take a shower with me."

"Never mind I have to get my things so I can go you go ahead there's the doorbell I think that's mom."

"You don't want me to wait on you baby."

"No you go ahead."

I walk down the hallway mumbling out loud.

"That man is going to make me get stupid on his ass if he keep holding out on me for real."

I open the door trying hard to show that everything was ok in my household. There stood a woman that look young enough to be my sister instead of my mother. Her hair was black long and silky her skin color was sugar brown she had a small mole in the corner above her thick lips.

"Hi baby, where my granddaughter?" I kiss my mother on the cheek and give her a hug.

"Jordan should be in here somewhere I just walked in here."

"What you mean, how can you lose a baby?"

Jordan crawls into the living room as she sees her grandmother's face she reaches up.

"There's my baby come to granny."

"You have little momma spoiled when she comes home after you keep her on weekends Byron and I can't do a thing with her little butt."

"Girl this is my first grandchild and I can spoil her if I wish."

"Your daddy and I are taking her with us tomorrow were going to south Louisiana and won't be back until Monday will that be alright with you two?"

"Sure."

"So you and Byron can have the whole weekend to do what you like."

"Are you going to see Aunt Reyna this weekend?"

"Yes, we told her that we will be there tomorrow so were going to have a blast and you don't have to worry about Jordan she will be just fine don't worry about a thing okay."

"I'm sure you guys will be just fine I need a break and thank you momma for everything."

"Jada honey you know it's no problem, hey where is my son in law?"

"His butt is in the shower."

"Let me take Jordan in there so she can tell her daddy bye you know she loves her daddy."

"Ok I will put her things in the car."

"Ok." I grab Jordan and take her to see him when we stepped

into the room he was wrapped in nothing but a towel I smile at my sexy hubby trying to get pass my anger and disappointment.

"Momma is here so Jordan will be with my parents for the rest of the weekend she will bring her back on Monday I'm sure after I get off work."

"Ok I won't have to call my mother then." Byron gives her a kiss on the cheek. Jordan lets out a huge smile as she pulls his ear to her mouth.

"You be good little lady." She laughs as if she knows exactly what he was saying then she reaches for me standing there.

"Well let me get her to mom."

I walk back into the living area where my mom was waiting.

"So lady bug are you ready for some fun?" Jordan reaches for her grandmother and looks back at me. I offer her a huge smile as I watch my daughter play with my mother's hair; she then reaches over to give me a kiss on the cheek.

"Bye baby girl."

"Well were off you and Byron have a good weekend and please don't make another grandbaby right now although it would be nice but wait until this one gets to be of age like five at least she will be in school."

I rustle up a fake laugh because if only she knew you have to have sex to get a baby and Byron isn't giving up the manhood to me lately and I'm sick of this. My mother winks her eye while she holds my child as they walk off the porch.

"You just don't spoil that little girl too much. Bye Jordan mommy loves you." I wave as they get in the car and drives off.

Meanwhile in the house Byron stands there in the mirror fixing his earrings and smelling good and looking sharp as a tack. With his black slacks and white polo sweater vest and black Polo boots. He was indeed a man on a mission tonight.

"Are you sure you're going to the club with those brothers or are you going to meet some hooker off the streets?"

"Girl stop playing you go and get dress and do your thing it's the weekend and we should be having fun hell."

"I know we should be having fun."

"Look Baby I will make this up to you tomorrow I promise."

"Yeah have fun."

Byron kisses me on the cheek. "Be careful call me when you get to Madison's okay to let me know you made it alright."

"I will be just fine you have fun."

"I love you Jada Knight."

"Hell I love you too."

I walk my husband to the door to see him off. While standing in the glass door I wave as Byron gets into his truck the phone rings.

"I wonder who this could be."

I look at the caller ID to see who was calling before I pick up the phone. It read: Cole Sinclair 352- 6898 I smile like a chess cat I couldn't help but wonder why he was calling. I let the phone ring for the fourth time I clear my throat as I decide to pick up.

"Hello"

"Hello Jada"

"Who's this?" Pretending I didn't know who it was.

"This Cole I don't mean to bother you at home but you left your purse here in the office do you need me to bring it to you?"

Breathing heavy and trying to clear my voice so I could speak clearly while my heart beats a hundred miles to the minute.

"Look I'm about to leave could you just wait for me because I really need my purse and I was just about to walk out the door so if you give me about 30 minutes I will be there if that's alright with you."

"Sure I will wait for you, just be careful and there's no need to be in a huge hurry because I'm doing some things on the computer you know me its work seven days 24 hours so take your time."

I was glad he said that wondering what I was going to throw on so I could look like I was going somewhere.

"I will see you then."

When the Honeymoon Is Over

I jumped in the shower and started to sing I wash my hot body down in the steamy water while the soap runs down my smooth silk skin I begin to think about Cole as the water wash across soapy body.

⁓

Meanwhile Cole sits in front of his computer waiting for Jada to walk through the door at any time. He thinks to himself how upset she was when she found out it was him who bought the flowers instead of her husband. He thinks that her husband is really lucky. Only if he could find a woman as real and pleasant as Jada, he would never in a million years take her for granted. He wondered how it would be to just kiss her and make love to such a beautiful woman like Jada Knight; her husband must be out of his damn mind to not want to tap that nightly. The phone rings he snaps out of his day dream.

"Hello"

"Cole this is Jada I'm outside could you please open the door I forgot my key."

"Sure no problem," He reaches in his desk grabs his Joop cologne so he would smell fresh, rush to the bathroom to make sure he was looking ok, then opens the door.

"I can't believe you forgot your keys. I thought you sleep with those keys girl."

We both share a nervous laugh and turn away feeling funny about the moment.

"So you say I left my purse?"

"Yeah it's there on the table."

"I see it."

I grab my purse and look at the flowers picking one out of the bunch to smell. Cole smile and says,

"I have to apologize for making you sad by sending you those flowers."

"Look Cole you're a great friend as well as my boss and I'm glad someone thinks about me every once in a while my husband don't these days."

We both sit down on the small love seat that sits in the corner of his office.

"Jada look I really don't like to see you cry and if you don't mind I would like to see you smile because you have such a beautiful smile." Blushing from ear to ear I turn and say,

"Thank you so much I really do like the flowers."

Looking at his watch wondering if she really had somewhere to go he says politely.

"You're going somewhere special tonight?"

"I really don't have anywhere to go at this moment I would like to go somewhere because my baby is out of town with my parents, my husband rather be with his friends tonight and I have nothing else to do." Cole looks at his watch again.

"I want to get out of here and do something now if you like we can go to my place. I have to change clothes and then we can go grab a bite to eat how about that?"

"Yes"

Smiling from ear to ear Cole picks his keys up off the desk alone with a flower and passes it to me. I put the flower up to my nose he reaches over and greets my cheek with a small kiss.

"Will you be my date tonight?"

"I haven't been on a date in a while." He grabs my hand and we walk out the door.

The house was very neat and clean it smelled fresh like pine. His living room was filled with Ashley show room furniture his sectional couch was white. His Plasma TV hung on the wall with his surround sound in every corner. The walls were decorated with fine art pieces He had huge large plants in the corner the ambience was breath taking.

"Would you like for me to put on some music? Or would you like to watch TV. He hands me this huge universal remote and points to the button.

"This baby controls everything from stereo to lights."

"Lights stereo sound system for real?"

"Yes, baby everything, I got it like that. One of my frat brothers had a set up like that and I had to have it, it cost a grip but it was worth it trust me!"

"I can just point and this control will do what I want it to do."

"There's a button for everything and if you read it, you can see that it's not hard to control."

I point the control to his surround sound stereo system; you could feel the music in your chest even when it was on low. I look into his CD case that looked like a curio cabinet to see what kind of music he was into. I open the door as I listen to the radio shaking my head from side to side listening to the sounds of Aaliah, (your love is a one in a million.) I notice that he had every CD in order of artist and style of music, he had Blues, gospel, pop, rap you name it he had it in this pretty cherry wood cabinet. I pulled out this CD by Musiq Soul Child and started reading the cover. Cole walked up behind me.

"You like Musiq?" I slowly turn around and look Cole in his dreamy bedroom eyes.

"I like his music it has real flavor, there's something about it that gets me in a mellow mood."

"You too, I also like Jill Scott, Maxwell and a few others, keep it real artist I call them."

We both smile as Cole rubs the back of his hand against my cheek.

"I like to see you smile. I want to see you smile the rest of the evening if that's not too hard for you to do alright."

"I will do just that."

"Well I want you to make yourself at home here I want you to also be comfortable I'm going to get into the shower and put on some clothes so we can get out and have some real fun." I look at Cole and ask, "If you don't mind can we order a pizza to be delivered maybe we can sit and listen to some of your music and talk I really don't feel like going out?"

"You sure about this I don't mind taking you out."

"I'm sure I feel like talking and relaxing right here in your spot this pad is so laid out I could set up shop right here."

"Well let me order Pizza let me go check out my wine selection and see what I have to go with Pizza is that alright with you or do you drink wine?"

"Yes, I drink wine but you don't have to pull out your best for me."

"Look girl you deserve the best and I don't mind doing something nice for a friend and I do consider you a friend of mine."

Two hours and two bottles of wine later we both sit in the living room laughing, talking about things we both did when we were children.

"Cole, I can't tell you how much fun I had tonight, I also can tell you I'm tipsy as hell."

"Baby you're just feeling good that's all."

"I wouldn't mind feeling like this every weekend with a man that cares how I feel."

"Were not going there, I tell you what you're too tipsy to drive home I want you to get real comfortable and I'm going to draw you some warm bath water and find you something to slip in okay."

"I can do that." Meanwhile I look around his house. He had candles everywhere so I found a lighter and start lighting up the room and dim the lights. I pop in a CD by Luther Vandross. Turning up the volume I start to sing, "(Can I take you out tonight)" I shake what my momma gave me to the rhythm of the music and pop my fingers as I begin to close my eyes. Cole steps into the room and begin to dance with me he grabs my hand also moving to the beat of the music singing alone getting this party on as the mood set in. As the CD changes to another song Cole stops me and points me to his room where he had my bath water ready he says,

"You better go and take your bath lady we can finish talking when you get out and if you need anything please don't hesitate to let a brotha know what it is you need, I have you set up really nice, enjoy your bath."

My eyes were half shut as I stare into Cole's eyes and intake his sexy smile. Cole takes me by the hand and leads the way as I walk down the hall to his room. I notice the black art on his wall in the hall way I noticed one picture of a woman breast feeding her child. This was such a beautiful picture. The woman was sitting in a rocking chair with a soft pink blanket wrapped around her child as she look down at her new born with a smile painted across her face. This made me think about Jordan, a smile came across my face. The next painting was quite interesting as well this picture was of a man and a woman. The man had long braids chocolate skin tone, he was on one knee with a huge diamond ring in his hand looking up to this beautiful golden skin tone woman with soft brown wavy hair who had a tear rolling down the side of her rosy cheek with a smile looking down at her lover.

"So you like my paintings?"

"Yes, this art tells a story and says something about you."

"You wouldn't believe me if I told you?" Jada turns around.

"Yes, I would I believe just about anything you say because you're an honest man and that's why I like you." Cole laughs as he points at the painting with the man and woman and says,

"This one is by this teenager name Jarkin McCain I spend lots of time with him. I pay for him to go to art school, he has real talent he's my little brother in this group called the big brother little brother program at my church."

"Oh, I heard of programs like that?"

" Well I have to keep busy when I'm not working because

staying around here will do nothing but take control of my mind you know what I mean?"

"Well, tell me what made you pick this picture of a mother breast-feeding this child this is rather odd for a single man to have such a painting in his home."

Cole had a glassy look in his eye as he looked at the painting.

"Your right and I didn't pick this painting my girlfriend did." Jada looked as her eyes widen.

"I thought you didn't have a girlfriend?"

"I don't anymore."

"Oh you two split up?"

"No, she died"

"I am so sorry." I put my arms around him. He strokes my hair ever so gently and says to me.

"It's okay I have to talk about it, not too many people know only my family, that's why I moved here from Georgia to get away from the area where we lived. We planned to get married; the day she bought that painting she had hung it on the wall in our living room. She had candles lit everywhere I will never forget that day the house was clean smelled pine sol fresh. I can still smell the scent of the apartment we lived in. She had on a pink gown her hair was pulled up in a bun. She asked me to sit down she had something to share with me. As she massaged my neck she told me she was pregnant. I was so happy because I loved Jena with all my heart and soul we had been together since the beginning of college. She meant the world to me."

"So what happen to her?"

"She was having problems throughout the pregnancy that she didn't want to share with me, but she told her mother, she set up a life insurance policy that only her mother knew about for me. She found out that if she had this baby it could kill her, the doctors wanted to terminate the pregnancy."

"Cole, I'm so sorry this happened to you."

"No I'm sorry this happened to Jena, when she went into labor she was in great pain. I was there for her, right there holding her hand and telling her to breath. We were there for twenty-four hours I never left her side. The last hour approached. She looked up at me and told me.

"If something happens to me baby go to my mother and talk with her."

"Me thinking she was just talking because she was in a lot of pain I didn't think much about it. I watched her give birth to a seven pound 6 ounce beautiful baby girl with a head full of curly black hair looking just like her mother. Jena looked at her and gave our daughter a kiss on the forehead before they cleaned her up and she kissed me and said. "I love you two so much. She had tears in her eyes and smiled and looked at me with glassy eyes. I knew she looked funny but I didn't know she was leaving me at that moment. She closed her eyes and that was it. Two hours later my daughter had a heart attack and died as well. We buried them both in the same casket they looked so peaceful."

"Cole, you never know what people are going through until they sit and tell you what's going on."

"I don't talk about it much because it's been two years sometimes it feels as if it happened just yesterday. I love my daughter and Jena so much." Cole glanced at the painting with a distance look upon his face.

"What did you name her?"

"January"

"That's a pretty name"

"Yes, Jena and I decided to name her January before all this happened but we really didn't know what we were going to have we wanted it to be a surprise but I found out later that Jena knew because she didn't know if she would live to know what she had so her mother told me everything after this happened.

"I can only imagine what it was you were feeling."

"Well at first I was angry at Jena for not telling me but at the same time I understood why she decided not to."

"It seems as if you two were really close."

"Yes, we were she was my everything the only thing I regret is that we didn't get married because she wanted to marry me and I asked her to wait until the baby was born so we could do some things together all three of us but__"

"Hey don't beat yourself up over this you meant well and you can't do that to yourself."

"I know my grandmother tells me the same thing she is so wise she wants to see me happy, besides it's been two years."

"Yeah, I agree with you on that we both have some issues to workout we will pull through this thing together."

"Thank you Jada for listening to me because I haven't told anyone about this situation of mine I rather leave it in the ground where my girlfriend and daughter is it's too painful to keep bringing up."

"Sure thing, hey show me where my warm bath water is so I can jump in." Cole leads me into his bedroom where his Jacuzzi tub sits in the middle of the room. His bedroom was like being outside on a private island. He had big beautiful rubber trees that sit in the corner candles around the tub not to mention the huge king size rice bed with a lion comforter that really set it off.

"I am really impressed with this house of yours to say you're a single man you have taste."

"Well thank you some of the things I had in our apt. I brought to this house but most of the stuff I set up and a friend of mine from Georgia came down when I bought this house and she helped me out."

"Oh really!"

"What's up with her are you two__"

"No Mona is just a friend of the family she and Jena were best friends and she promised to make sure I would be alright. Mona knew about Jena's situation and so she felt bad for not telling me but she kept her promise so when I moved she came with me and helped me get settled and then she moved to the east coast to start a new job with a literary agency. Her new husband is from New York so she was blessed with that job. We still keep in touch and every now and then I fly to New York to see them."

When the Honeymoon Is Over

"Oh I see."

"Well you better get settled and take your bath and when you finish we can watch a movie or something."

"Okay."

"Hey if you need anything just holla at me alright all the towels are out and the soap is on the side of the tub and don't hesitate to make yourself at home, you can have my room and I will sleep in the guest room."

"Oh okay" I smile as I walk him to the door I look over only to see another stereo system in his room so I walks over to it and get 102.4 and hear the sound of Janet Jackson I look into the huge tub of water and then I turn and look over at the bed and see a pair of black silk boxers and big white tee shirt. I smiled and said to myself. "He pulled out his best but I forgot I have clothes packed in my car but, I can wear his stuff and feel his silk boxers next to my skin and his tee rub against my chest." I slip out of my clothes and into this tub filled with bubbles and hot water waiting to soothe my very soul.

Meanwhile Cole listens to the music in the living room trying to think good thoughts but he was still a man, his manhood was getting hard as he thought about the beautiful woman that's necked in his room in his tub. It's been too damn long since he had a beautiful woman this close to him. Since Jena he hasn't felt this way about anyone. Why Jada, she's married she's off limits she has a husband and right now she's half drunk and in the tub and he's horny and half drunk himself and things can happen but he can't let it happen like that because it's wrong but the more he tries to think spiritual thoughts the more his flesh want to just inject his manhood into her ocean abyss. This was about to go down and he didn't want to come off as a punk if things start to happen. With a whisper Cole slaps his forehead and whispers to himself. "Wait one minute Cole Sinclair you have to keep a cool head this is a woman who works for you and she respects you."

Cole looks down at his little man and points to it as if it has a mind of its own standing there looking him dead in the face.

"You better calm the hell down you can't do this I have control over you and I said no! I have to take care of you later not now so calm the hell down and go soft I said!" While standing there Cole can't believe he is having this conversation with his hardness but he was so serious. Jada slowly walks into the room and finds Cole looking at his manhood and she said.

"Who are you talking too?" Laughing, as she already knew because she heard every word he said she thought that was so funny.

"Oh I was thinking out loud that's all." Embarrassed as hell Cole was standing tall and his manhood couldn't help but salute the woman before him. Jada blushed as she walked up to him and stood there in front of Cole and looked at him as he stood there blushing and feeling guilty for what has happened. She then started to feel his hardness and said,

"It's okay I feel what you're feeling and it's alright, Cole looked at Jada as his heart starts to beat at a fast pace he bends down to kiss her on the lips. Jada closes her eyes and begin to embrace Cole as her nipples harden to his touch and they both breathe deeply as the heat turns up. Cole whispers to her.

"You are so soft." As he rubs his hands across her left breast Jada moans softly she then starts to kiss him down the neck as he picks her up and carries her to the couch. All of a sudden a big clap of thunder sounded outside and the rain starts to pour heavy as they kiss deeply moaning with passion and excitement of two bodies that's about to become as one. Cole looked at Jada as the lightning flashed across the room and into their face the weather was indeed getting the mood set. Cole was hard as a brick and Jada was soft and wet from all the heat that covered her body. Cole smiles as he stops for a moment to look at Jada and ask.

"Are you sure you're ready for me."

"Yes baby I'm ready" Cole begins to kiss Jada's breast as she arched her back to his touch and moans. He gently slides down her perfectly shaped body and kiss her belly button where she wore her belly ring and plays with it with his tongue as he glides down and begin to kiss the unknown. Jada screams with passion as he gives her pleasure he watches her body move up and down as he feel beads of sweat roll off her soft gentle skin. All of a sudden Cole jumps up and pulls Jada up from her position.

"Jada looks at Cole and says,

"What's wrong?" Cole looks at her and kisses her on the forehead.

"You are indeed a beautiful woman and I want to make love to you_"

"Well what's the problem Cole I want to make love to you also so why don't we go in your room and just do it?"

"Jada it's not that simple."

"What do you mean I'm feeling this and you're feeling this as well?"

"Baby, you're married."

"Yes, and_"

"I can't do this I really like you and this is just wrong."

"Wrong?"

"Yes, wrong you work for me and if we do this now it will change things." Jada slides up and fixes her clothes, pulls the boxers she had on back up.

"So you're telling me that you place your lips in my privates and kiss me and make me feel your touch and that if we stop now things will be the same is that what you're telling me Cole?"

"Baby I'm sorry I can't do this you have to understand?"

"Understand my ass; to hell with all that I want you, you want me what's to understand? I don't get it Mr. Sinclair."

"Jada don't do this okay you had quite a bit to drink and so did I and I don't want it to seem as if I was___"

"Don't say it I know what the hell I'm doing I took a long hot bath in your tub and I'm fine I know what I'm doing and so do you so don't try to brush me off okay it's been so damn long since I felt like this and I like you too and things can be the same between us maybe better."

"Tell me how can it be better? You are married and it was wrong of me to come onto you like this I apologize let's just cool off a bit alright." I didn't understand what went wrong I was feeling good and all of a sudden this fine brotha wants to stop what's really the deal.

"Cole what's with you?"

"Look it's nothing I got out of hand and it's wrong, see I'm not the average brotha that just see a woman as a sexual tool I really think about what's ahead so please don't take this the wrong way and don't allow it to come between us."

"Take this the wrong way! Please I don't want to hear this crap all right. I hear the same thing from my husband and he acts as if he doesn't want to touch me anymore and now you, to hell with all you men!" Cole stands up and reaches for her and she steps back.

"Look don't touch me I have to go!"

"I really would like for you to stay it's storming outside and you been drinking please don't leave!"

"Hell no I have to go!"

Running in his room she scoops up her clothes puts on her tennis and storms out the door. Cole rushes behind her but seem to be too late she's already in the car the wind was blowing the lightning was flashing and the thunder was rolling it was indeed a very bad storm that was moving across the area and no one should have been in this kind of weather. Cole watched Jada as her tires slid across the wet streets. He grabbed his coat and his keys and headed out the door to make sure she didn't hurt herself. While driving in this weather Cole couldn't keep up with Jada she was racing down the street like a mad woman she ran two stop signs on her way out of the suburbs she then lost control of her car as it slid into a ditch and flipped over the car was smoking. But the engine was still humming. Cole dialed 911 on his cell phone he then jumped out of his car screaming.

"Jada baby I'm sorry can you hear me?" Cole was standing there with tears running down his face helpless and feeling scared as the rain dumped buckets of water on him not able to hear a peep out of Jada as she lay there turned upside down with blood everywhere. He tried to get inside the car to get her out but was unable to move anything. Cole just sat there waiting for help to get to the scene.

Chapter 29 - - Madison

I had to have me some me time so I lay in the hot tub filled with bubbles eyes closed relaxed and thinking about some place tropical suddenly the doorbell rings, I open my eyes half way wondering who could it be. I yell for Collin.

"Son get the door don't forget to ask who it is before opening it."

"Okay momma you got that." Collin runs to the door and asks.

"Who is it?" A deep voice from the other side answers,

"Little man it's me Cory." Happy to hear his voice he swings open the door.

"What's up man?" They both give each other dap as they greet.

"Where's your mother?"

"She's in the bathroom taking a bath let me go get her for you."

"No, allow me to surprise her alright."

"Ok cool I'm going back into my room and finish up the conversation I was having with Shay."

"Oh you two still got it going on strong huh?"

"Yeah, that's my boo"

"Man go do what you got to do."

"Will do holla," They shook hands and departed. Cory starts lighting all the candles in the bedroom by the bed and turns on the radio to see if he could find the quiet storm. Madison yells.

"Collin, who was it at the door?" No one answered but Cory decided to knock at the bathroom door.

"Who is it?"

"Who do you want it to be?"

"Cory is that you?"

"Yes it's me may I come in?"

"Sure you can come in, you know what? You're going to live a long time, I was just thinking about you because it's been a while since I seen you."

"I know, I have a couple of days off and I want to spend it with you and Collin if that's ok.

"That will be nice have a seat let that toilet seat cover down and have at it." Cory smiles as he looks around the bathroom and sees nothing but the light from the candles he lit, he was feeling relaxed.

It's been awhile, since the visit from Latisha, he's been stressed and so he decided to throw himself in his work and take on project after project. He started missing Madison, trying to figure out how he was going to tell her the news. He wanted her to stick by his side because she was just so down to earth and the best woman he dated in a long time no drama no fuss and he wanted very much so to keep it that way.

"Hey what's on your mind tonight?"

"What you mean?"

"You seem as if you have something on your mind."

"You think you know me huh?"

"Yes"

"Well since you ask can I wash your back?" Madison looked surprised because Cory always respected her not that he was disrespecting her now but he has been a perfect gentleman and she wanted this to happen.

When the Honeymoon Is Over

"Sure you can wash my back."

He smiles as he bend down on both knees and kisses me on the forehead then on the nose and lightly on the lips. I close my eyes as I feel the water from the towel that he squeezes triple down my back. Cory takes the bar of Ivory soap and lathers the towel down and begins to wash slowly up and down my back. His eyes take in the beauty of my flesh. His heart starts to beat out of rhythm as he washes up and down and circles the lower part of my back. I close my eyes as I enjoy the moment of this man who is not only fine as wine but knows how to treat a woman. It's been so long since I had a man's attention like this; I almost forgot what it felt like.

Cory thinks about how sweet Madison is, and what it would be like if they would spend the rest of their lives like this together. It's been a long time since he felt like this towards a woman. Sure he had friends and so on but he hasn't allowed himself to get too close since Latisha, speaking of which Cory needed to think about how he was going to tell Madison about his visit from Tisha three weeks ago. He was feeling uneasy about the situation because he had no idea what she was going to say or do and he didn't want to lose Madison. She seems to be enjoying the moment.

"Cory I been thinking about you."

"I been thinking about you also, and I have something I need to talk to you about."

My heart fell to the bottom of my stomach because I certainly didn't want to hear any bad news I breathed deeply and spoke softly.

"Look let me get out of the tub and we can go into the living room and talk if you don't mind." Cory stood up and smiled nervously and winked his eye.

"Yeah okay I will be in the living room."

"Sure" As soon as Cory stepped out of the bathroom I jumped out of the tub and dried myself off. I begin to look at myself in the mirror and start to think about the time I spent with Cory and how much I like him to be honest I'm falling in love with him, and I didn't want to rush things, nor feel as if I was putting pressure on him and most of all I wanted to know what this little chat was going to be about.

I heard music coming from the living room I put on my silk Pink pajamas and robe. I had my hair swooped up in a wet ponytail. Candles were lit from my room to the living room where it smelled so sweet and fresh. When I made it to the living room there were a big bouquet of yellow and white long stem rose buds. Holding a Yellow Rose in his hand Cory stood there in the middle of the room with a smile upon his face as he looked at how my eyes widen with surprise. Having Eric Benet playing in the back ground my eyes filled with water as I walked slowly towards him and took the rose out of his hand and placed it near my nose as I closed my eyes and pressed my face against his chest saying softly,

"Thank you"

"You're welcome,"

We both sat down on the couch as we hug and kiss alone the way. Cory stopped kissing me for a second.

"Madison, you know I really care about you a lot?"

"Yes, I know this and I feel the same about you."

"Well, I have something to share with you and I don't want you to be mad at me, and I certainly don't want you to let this come between us."

My heart starts to pound super fast thinking here we go I offer him a blank look to get ready for the big bang!

"What you mean?"

"Well I have to say that a couple of weeks ago Latisha came down to see me."

"Tisha the woman you were serious about several months back."

"Yes her."

"Well what did she want?"

I felt that pain lump enter my throat but tried to remain cool but wanted to explode. I didn't know what to expect. I certainly didn't want to hear that he was planning to go back to this woman I knew nothing about, I just knew he was heartbroken by her and that this woman was married and went back to her husband but Cory never talked about her much.

"Well Madison, Latisha wanted to see me and talk to me about something and I have to say that it was to my surprise that she's pregnant and she says that it's my baby."

I felt like screaming and just doing the fool but I made a conscience decision to keep my cool.

"So you're telling me that she may be having your baby, how do you feel about that?"

"Mad, hurt, confuse baby I have mix emotions about this situation and I don't know what to feel."I crossed my arms and legs as I sat beside Cory.

"How do you feel about her?"

"I hate what she is doing to me and this baby?"

"What you mean?"

"Well she says that her husband doesn't know that this baby isn't his and she doesn't want to tell him and she just wanted me to know that I have a girl on the way."

"What! Cory, I'm mad as hell, one because girlfriend had no right or business to walk into your life like that and expect you to be okay with all this." Cory places his hands on the temple of his head.

"I know baby but, she's not going to get away with this bull she's putting down I can promise you that." Madison stands up and places her hands upon her hips.

"Tell me what you are going to do about this situation tell me!" Cory stands up and places his hands around her shapely hips and pulls her close to him.

"Baby I told you this because I trust you and most of all I wanted you to know what was going on with me." Cory kisses me on the forehead and says.

"I don't know if you realize this or not but I'm crazy about you because you treat me so good and I want this to bring us closer together no matter what the outcome, but I need your support will you be there for me?" I couldn't help but look in those puppy dog eyes of his filled with water due from stress, and place my arms around his neck and say.

"I'll be here, you can count on me."

Chapter 30 - - Kobe

"Thanks for calling The Chrome Zone Kobe speaking how may I help you?"

"Man, look at ya; don't know how to act a black man with a business what's up?"

"Jalen man what's up?"

"Nothing I see you doing things that's great. I had to call you and see what's poppin."

"This place has me pretty busy."

"I feel you; the club keeps me going as well."

"I have to save little momma some cash for college."

"Yeah, I feel you."

"Well, what's up?"

"We got to get with B man, Jada been in an accident and it's been hard on a brotha."

"Jada, accident! When?"

"It's been about two weeks now and I'm sorry you didn't know sooner I know you been busy and all that but Jada is in a serious fix she's been in a coma for about a week now and B blames himself, it happened on the night we all got together at the club."

"Aw man I'm so sorry give me about an hour and I will close shop and head in your direction alright."

"That's cool maybe we can talk to him and see what's going on, I'm about to go and pick Cory up meet us over at the club."

"I will check you later."

"Alright peace,"

I hang up the phone and pull out a cigarette thinking about how short life is and why people choose to do what they do. Byron has a beautiful wife and a lovely daughter but he chose to do other things besides spend time with her and she always seem to be okay with that but at the same time no woman is just pleased with that not even Keisha. Speaking of which I had to call her to tell her that I would be late coming home and don't know when I will be there. I pick up the phone and dial the number the phone rings twice she answer.

"Hello"

"Hey Keisha where is Shayla?"

"She's in the living room watching the DVD you brought her yesterday for the ten thousandth time."

"Oh really"

"Yeah, now when are you coming home?"

"That's why I'm calling."

"No Nigga I don't want to hear that."

"Look girl my boy called."

"I don't want to hear about your damn boy."

"Keisha will you please listen to me, Jalen called me and said Jada has been in an accident and that Byron needed us he was really down."

"Why you have to go?"

"I told you B is my friend and his wife is in great danger."

"And what are you suppose to do about that?"

"You mean to tell me that if you had a friend_"

"What I am saying Kobe is why do you feel the need to go and be with them you have a family right here."

"Girl, is you stuck on stupid or what? I feel like when I call you and tell you something you have to give me the third degree about simple stuff."

"Well I don't trust your sorry a_."

"I'm bout tired of you calling me outside my name and you need some understanding for real and besides if you don't trust my sorry ass why haven't you left for Dallas I won't stop you!"

"Damn you Kobe." Keisha slams down the phone.

"That girl is stupid for real."I dial up Jewel.

"Hello"

"Are you busy?"

"Kobe is this you?"

"Who do you think this is?"

"Boy, don't play with me."

"I'm cool"

"What's up with you?"

"I was just thinking about you and decided to call."

"Really"

"Yes really,"

"Well I'm doing alright how's your business coming?"

"It's great I like being on my own being my own boss is the life you know?"

"No I don't know I punch a time clock every day."

"You wouldn't, would you?" We both chuckle,

"Well, I can say that my boss is always complaining about something. She always has something negative to say nothing the surgical team does is right. She don't realize that she has a good team and we work well together but when she comes out she makes everyone life a living hell. Were all tired of the bull and I dislike the heffa. If things are not done the way she would do it of course it's not right. And talk about controlling she's all that and then some."

"Baby, I see you needed to chat, you needed to get things off your chest."

"I apologize for taking you through this."

"Baby it's alright that's what I'm here for."

"Thanks, you're really a good friend."

I smiled at the comment it was nice to know that she still thought of me as a friend, which meant a lot. But, deep down I wanted this woman to be my wife because she always had that noble character of a wife. She understood me I could go home to her every day with a smile. Most important Jewel knows me better then I knew myself, of course I wouldn't admit that to her.

"Well, I have to go I just called to say hello."

"Kobe, you okay?"

"Yeah I'm cool" Jewel had a way of feeling me out but I didn't want to bother her with my drama fest from that wicked witch of the west I was married to besides I made the decision to marry her ass.

"Okay if you say so."

"All right woman I have to go I'll talk to you soon bye"

"Good bye Kobe"

I hang the phone up and begin to shut down my computer, the phone rings. I reach for the cordless across the desk.

"Chrome Zone,"

"Hey big brother what's up?"

"Hey Brenda"

"Nothing, I haven't talked with you for a minute what's with you?"

"Just chillen, you?"

"I'm chillen, you don't sound too right talk to me."

"I told you it's all good."

"Sure it's all good what you doing?"

When the Honeymoon Is Over

"About to close shop and meet Cory and Jalen at the club and go to the hospital to see Byron and his wife."

"What's up whose sick?"

"His wife was in a bad accident and she's not doing too well so I decided to go and see what's up with Byron because he blames himself."

"Why, was he was driving?"

"No he feels guilty I guess"

"Guilty for what?"

"Brenda, I really don't know can't get into all that right now because I don't know the entire story okay."

"I feel you go see your friend."

"Well, what's with you?"

"Nothing, I just wanted to check on you. I saw your ugly wife today." Don't call her ugly alright she is still the mother of my child."

"I can't stand that hooker."

"Why you say things like that about her?"

"Kobe if I were to tell you something you won't do a damn thing about it so what's the point just forget it."

"What do you mean and what are you talking about?"

"I'm going to say this I love you, you're my brother and I don't want to see you unhappy and that's real talk."

"Brenda you speaking in riddles now."

"No I'm telling you to get yourself together and stop being so naïve."

"Girl, don't play with me."

"I'm not playing with your crazy butt."

"I have to go I will call you later better yet I will stop by to see you later."

"I will cook you up something good and we will sit and have a shot of Patron or something I miss you."

"I miss you too lata."

"Peace." We hang up the phone and right as I hang the phone up it rings again. Now I'm frustrated.

"Hello!"

"Well I thought this was the Chrome whatever."

"Keisha, please don't play with me alright I'm really not in the mood okay."

"I wanted to know when you coming home?"

"I don't know!"

"I need you to come and get Shayla I have somewhere to go."

"I called and told you that I wasn't coming straight home so why are you trying to be so damn difficult?"

"Baby I'm not being difficult I just need you to come home that's all."

"Well I'm coming to get Shayla and drop her off at Brenda's house and I will pick her up later."

"Oh hell no, I don't want Shayla over there!"

"Keisha, please that's my sister."

"I don't give a good hot damn if she was your mammy I don't want my child over there!"

"You acting so crazy what's up with you lately?"

"Nothing, never mind I will take her to my mom's house you go and hang out with your nasty ass friends don't be surprised if all your damn clothes are out on the lawn boo."

"Keisha, I swear if you put my clothes out there you will forever be sorry you met me I'm about tired of this bull you putting down its crazy and you know what? Hell, never mind, forget it do what you have to do as a matter of fact I will be at my sister's place if Shayla needs me!"

I was running out of patients with this trick I call my wife the only reason I try to get alone with her is because of Shayla, but this record is played out its old and Keisha is about to be just a memory for real. The phone rings again but I continue to pull the money out of my register and place it in the green money bag as I head towards the door then I stop to look back for a minute as the phone rings for the tenth time I pick up.

"Hello!"

"Kobe, look you can come over and pick your things up and live with your sister for as long as you wish I won't stop you!"

"Keisha, it seems like every time I tell you I have something to do that don't involve you it's like you go crazy, I don't stay out all night, I don't hang with the boys all the time and I certainly don't have time to cheat on you so what's the deal?"

"What's the deal you say? I want more time and I think you're cheating on me." I slam the moneybag on the counter.

"What do you want me to do Keisha what?"

"I want you to come home that's all."

"I told you that I will be home as soon as I leave the hospital damn!"

"Well like I said before you can pick up your clothes."

"Keisha, alright I will be there to pick my clothes just don't trash my things I'm tired let's put an end to all the madness."

"Fine, you rather leave then work things out." I can't believe this bull; my head starts to hurt instantly.

"What are you saying? You want to put me out! Not once I said I was leaving you, you want to put a brotha out and so I'm not going to fight this time girl do what you have to do alright!" I slam the phone down, Picks up my keys, moneybag and heads towards the door.

༺❦༻

My head felt as if it was about to burst thanks to my she devil wife I swear this woman was about to drive me into the Central State Hospital for the mental. The sad thing is that I want to work this out with this crazy woman, because of my daughter. I just didn't want to be another black man who abandons his family, leaving my daughter in search for a father. Well now I have to put that to the side right now because my boy Byron needed me. I stepped out of my car to greet Cory and Jalen coming out the door. Cory smiled as he shook my hand I throw my third cigarette down to the ground and put it out with my shoe.

"Man what took you so long we started to leave."

"Man it's a long story I can't really get into it right now let's go to the hospital and check on Byron." We all agreed and jumped in Jalen's SUV to the hospital.

Meanwhile Byron sits beside his wife's bed as he looks at all the tubes and wires that hangs from her body. He cries as he caress her face that didn't have a scratch on it, she looked rested and at peace.

"Baby, I'm so sorry for all the mess I put you through lately." He grabs her hand and gently squeezes it and places her hand towards his face.

"I know I have put you on ignore and I was wrong for that but if you come back to me and Jordan I promise you that I will make it right." Byron starts to cry harder as he prays for God to restore his family and not take his wife.

"God, please if you take anyone take me and not the mother of my only child. But if you choose to bring my wife back I promise that I will treat her better then what I have been. I was wrong and I admit that, I want you to know that I'm sorry for all my wrong doings and I promise that I will serve you from this day forward if you bring my wife back."

Byron then opens his eyes to see Jada's mother standing there in the doorway with tears in her eyes holding Jordan in her arms. Children were not allowed but Jada's mom asked the doctor to allow her granddaughter to see her mother. Jordan saw her daddy and reached for him. Byron grab his daughter who he haven't seen in about a week because he been at the hospital day and night, he held Jordan tight as he kissed her on the cheek. Jada's mother hugged both him and her granddaughter tightly. She said,

"Byron I'm so proud of you"

"For what Mah?"

"I heard every word you said to God and I believe that God knows your heart and whatever he has planned it's going to turn out okay." Byron shook his head and said,

"I meant every word and I have only God to trust now."

"I know son it's going to be alright and what problems you and my daughter had will be alright. I prayed for you two all the time and maybe this is only a test of our faith son we just have to believe in what he says is true." Byron looked at Jada's body lying there and Jordan said for the first time momma and started to point. Byron looked at his daughter and smiled yes, baby that's mommy he then embrace his daughter and begin to walk towards the door as he walk someone knocks, he opens the door. It was Kobe, Cory, and Jalen; Byron smiled as he saw his homeboys with flowers and cards.

"Cory walks up to Byron first and kisses his daughter and shook his hand and embraced his friend with a hug. Jada's mom grabs the baby and says,

"Well I'm going to take my grandchild back home and Byron I will be back later to spend the night so you can go home."

"Ma you don't_"

"Byron, I want to spend time with my daughter your daughter needs you so when you leave here you just come to the house and pick her up and I will come back and spend the night I will not take no for an answer."

"Ok ma thanks." Jada's mother grabs the baby and smiles at Byron and his friends and winks her eye at them and walks out. Kobe look across the room at Jada lying there he says,

"Man I have to get out of here I don't want to see Jada like that."

"Man its okay we can go and sit in the lobby down the hall it's nice in there I understand." Cory shook his head and says,

"Man life is too short and when you find someone you love it's time to make a move there's nothing to think about, let's go to the lobby."

Jalen finds himself thinking about Reagan, All she wants to do is get married they been together for seven years. Why is he so scared of committing himself to her? He asks himself that question over and over in his head as he look towards the bed and sees his friend's wife lying there fighting for her life. Kobe taps Jalen on the shoulder.

"Man, what are you thinking about right now?" Jalen turns around and smiles at his friend and says,

"Reagan, I love that woman and to be honest with you she completes me. I know I haven't been doing what I should and when I get home tonight I'm going to tell her this because man life is too short and I want to spend the rest of my life loving this woman." I look off and scratch my head as I think about what was just said. I know that I'm no angel but only if I could work things out with Keisha and stop all the madness but that's not about to happen so it's time I have peace in my life what's left of it anyway.

Chapter 31 - - Jalen

I put my key in the door thinking about my woman and how short life really is, my heartfelt Byron's pain, and I certainly pray his wife get's better and recover from this situation. As I walk through the door I place my keys on the table and find Reagan sitting in the media room curled up on the couch reading a book.

"Hello beautiful."

"Hello" I pull my shirt off and sit next to Reagan kissing her on the cheek softly.

"May I talk with you for a minute?" She never made eye contact with me.

"What you want to talk about?" I reach over and gently pull the book out her hand knowing she's been upset with me and I really want to make things right.

"Jalen, what's wrong?"

"Baby, I have so much to tell you and I don't know where to begin." Reagan heart starts to pound; a lump develops in her throat so she stands up and says,

"Hold that thought I have to go to the bathroom I will be right back." I offer her a sincere smile in hopes she will just hear what I have to say.

"Well hurry because we need to talk."

After Jalen made that statement I couldn't help but wonder

Holly M. Jewell

what it is he has to say I make my way upstairs to the bathroom. I know things haven't been right between us and I was ready for whatever, I know he been upset about Jada's accident but we needed to fix this situation that was going on with us.

"*Reagan girl get yourself together.*" I had to motivate my spirit to go downstairs and face my fears because this man need to put a ring on this or I'm out no matter how much I love him. I feel a lump in my throat and the tears find their way to my eyes at the thought of not having Jalen in my life. I grab a piece of toilet paper and blow my nose I didn't want him to know I was crying. I hear him yell from down stairs.

"Reagan what's up girl?" I wipe my eye with the back of my hand and yell back.

"Okay I'm coming give me a minute."

I look at myself closely in the mirror to make sure everything looked all right. I couldn't punk out now because I had to be stronger than that. I pull myself together and run down stairs to sit and listen to what was on his mind.

I didn't expect that all the lights would be turned off and the candles would be filling the air with a fresh floral scent. The last time this man did the candle thing he asked me to move in with him in Georgia I remember as if it was yesterday, this man still has his way of moving me.

"What's going on Jalen?"

"Baby, just have a seat," She hesitated but decided to take my advice I begin to speak as I held her hand.

"I know I haven't been easy to deal with for the past couple of months and you certainly been good to me, and Reagan I don't want to lose you for whatever reason. I'm surprise you still have anything to do with me. All the pain I caused you baby I want to apologize for that. I know that you complete me and this is why I want to ask you, will you do me the honor of being my wife for the rest of my life?"

I had to do it right and bend down on one knee and pull out a platinum 3ct B class diamond ring and place it upon her left finger. Reagan was speechless all she could do was look at the rock that dressed her hand as she begin to cry.

"Yes, I will marry you, I love you."

"I have one thing I need to tell you." Reagan looked puzzled.

"What is it?"

"I have to be honest with you because I want you to be my wife and I need to make a new start with you Reagan because I need things to be right."

Reagan said, "Whatever it is you just made it right."

I looked at Reagan and at that moment I knew I wanted to spend the rest of my life with her. My heart was full and I don't get emotional but Reagan made me this way I start kissing her softly all over her face.

"May I tell you something?"

"What is it babe?"

"When we go to the islands for Braxtine's wedding I would like for us to get married the following day just us and Braxtine and her new husband can be our witnesses." Reagan laughed and said,

"You're kidding."

"No I'm not kidding baby I'm serious I want you to be my wife and I want to make my life complete and right before God because I want to be right for you and I want us to make this thing we have holy."

I was overwhelmed by what was said I never heard Jalen talk like that before.

"I want things to be right too baby I love you so much."

The phone rings and Reagan picks up.

"Hello"

"Hey girl what's up you excited?"

"Braxtine, I was just about to call you it's only a week away. I can't believe were going to get married around the same time.

"Neither can I I'm so glad things worked out with you and Jalen this is a dream come true, two best friends going to the islands to get married, were going to have a blast!"

"I know girl I'm having a time trying to get packed I have to go and pick up my dress later. In such a short notice I found the perfect gown it's so pretty."

"Reagan, I want to tell you that I love you and I can't wait to see you."

"Neither can I, Jalen said he don't want to sleep with me until were married he's serious about this."

"Well, marriage is serious and you must not take it lightly it's a lifetime commitment"

"I know and now I'm getting scared and nervous when I think about it all."

"It's going to be all right I promise."

"I wish you were here so we could help each other, this is going to be a wonderful weekend; Best friends weddings of a lifetime!"

"I can write a book about it someday better yet make a movie of all the drama it took to get here!"

"I know, I thought I would never marry this man and just think I was going to pack my stuff this coming week and leave him."

"No"

Yes, girl I was listening to you, I didn't want to settle for less then what I deserve. You know I love this man more then slice bread but, I was ready to give up this house and move into this cute little town house I looked at on the east side of Alexandria. It had two bed rooms in a nice clean neighborhood."

"I can't believe what I'm hearing. You been looking for a pad and you didn't call me."

"I was going to tell you after the wedding I didn't want you worried about me. Now I don't have to worry about all that now because I'm getting married. I wasn't expecting to do so this soon but that's what he wanted to do and believe me I wasn't going to say no."

❦

I was sitting at the bar with my buddies drinking and listening to some music. The club was closed and my boys wanted to celebrate with me before the big day, I didn't want to have a bachelor party, so we decided to just have a couple of drinks together before I fly off into the sun set with my soon to be wife God blessed me with. Kobe sits there with both hands around his glass looking at me shaking his head up and down.

"Man, I can't believe you're about to do this, when you come back you're going to be a married man."

"Man I can't believe how blind I been for the past seven years, I'm lucky Reagan wants to marry my black ass she means everything to me." Byron looked at me with great sadness in his eyes trying to fight back tears.

"Man, it took my wife almost losing her life for me to realize how much she means to me." Kobe asks Byron.

"How's Jada doing?"

"She's doing better she comes home tomorrow and I can't wait she says that she has so much to tell me when she get home. I told her that whatever it is I can deal with it because I want us to start fresh and do some soul searching and start loving one another again." I look over at Kobe because he's been quiet for the past few weeks and he haven't been to any Sunday basketball games in a while.

"How is your wife?"

"Well as of yesterday she says she would like for us to be friends because of Shayla and try to work things out. I'm tired of trying to work things out with her it's not working out we been working things out for 10 years now." Byron asks,

"What about your daughter isn't she worth you trying to work it_"

"Man I been there and done that. It's nice that you got your wife back and all that, but that's not going to happen with Keisha and me. We are on two different pages and I'm tired. I'm going Monday and file for my freedom papers for real. Jalen man marriage is a good thing when you're with whom you suppose to be with so please do not let my problems question what you're doing."

"I know and I hope things work out for you and most of all I want to see you happy but think about what you're doing that's all." Kobe takes a sip out of his drink.

"I know what I'm doing _____"

"Well I have to ask what's going on with Jewel you're going to get with her that woman is so fine and not to mention beautiful." Byron said.

"Dude, I told Jewel that I was going to file and she told me to try and work it out with my wife. I thought maybe we could get together and start over, but she says that I need time for self before that happen because she has to look out for herself she didn't want to be caught in the middle again and that was the end of that." I look over at Kobe.

"Man, it's going to be all right_"

" I know it's going to be all good, well look it's not about me today Jalen it's about you and I don't want to discuss what's going on with me let's chill on me right now and talk about you for a minute you're ready to hang yourself?"

"Yes I'm ready besides; Reagan would kill me if I come home and say I've changed my mind."

We sit and laugh for hours at a time, drinking and listening to music. Cory finally walks into the club.

"Sorry I'm late"

"What you want to drink playa?" I ask while standing behind the bar washing glasses.

"Give me a Bud." I reached into the cooler behind me and passed Cory his drink. "Man what's up you had to work today?"

"No, out shopping"

"Shopping it's not Christmas." Kobe laughs alone with Byron and me.

"I went to Patton's" I clear my throat because Patton's was a jewelry store.

"Patton's for what playa?"

"To buy this," Cory pulls out this beautiful 5-1/2ct-diamond ring. He passes it to Kobe first, Kobe passes it to me and Byron looked at it last.

"Don't tell me you're going to tie the knot too what's up with that?" Byron asks.

"You're wife experience made me realize that life is too short and when you love someone you need to show it because you can love someone today and they can be gone tomorrow."

"Well what about old girl that's having your baby that she wants to pass off as her husband's?" I asked as I dipped my glass in the hot Clorox dish water full of bubbles.

"Madison and I are going to deal with that when we get back from our cruise."

Kobe asks with raised eyebrows. "Does she know she's getting this ring?"

"I haven't asked her yet so she has no clue." Kobe yells as he slaps his hand across the bar.

"Man if she say's no what are you going to do with the ring." Cory seems a little aggravated with Kobe at this point

"If she says no she can have the ring besides you need not to be so negative because I bought it for her."

"I don't mean to be negative good luck. So when are you going to ask her the question?"

"When we go on our cruise," Kobe shakes his head and says,

"Man you better be good to my cousin." Cory sips on his drink

"I love her and I will be the best thing that happened to her I hope anyway." Kobe says.

"You hope now look who's talking all that negative stuff now man to be honest she's the best thing that happened to you."

"I don't mean to sound negative I just want it to be right because I don't plan to do this twice and she is the best thing that has happened to me." Kobe shakes his head in agreement.

"I feel what you say really."

"Fellas your company is good and I enjoyed you but I have to go and get my stuff together for this trip. We plan to have a reception when we return." Kobe stood up first and gave his friend a man hug.

"I wish you the best and hopefully you can bring me one of those island women back." We laugh; Cory gave me a pound and a man hug and said.

"I wish you all the best."

"Good luck with your situation as well."

"Thanks." Byron stood up tilts his beer and says,

"You are indeed the man of the hour and I will be sure to tell my lovely wife that she messed all your lives up."

We all laughed as we walked to the door. I was happy and pleased that my closest friends could join me before I hang myself knowing this was something I should have done a long time ago.

Chapter 32 - - Cory

*T*he phone rings.

"Hello"

"Hey baby you ready?" I walk back and forth with the cordless phone to my ear.

"Yes, I'm ready, I'm about to put my bags in the car now."

"I can't wait to see you I'm so happy you were able to get the time off to go with me."

"You think I was going to let you go off without me you must be out of your mind."

"I wouldn't have gone if you couldn't go with me shug." I roll my eyes.

"Yeah right,"

"You know it."

"Where is Collin?"

"He's in his room finishing his packing his daddy is here to pick him up."

"We'll tell him to have fun and I will have to talk with him when we get back."

"Would you like to talk with him now?"

"No, I will talk with him when we get back just tell him what I said alright."

"Will do I guess I will see you in about an hour right?"

"Yeah"

"Tell Collin hello for me too and have a safe trip back to the Big Easy."

"Ok baby I will see you soon bye."

"Bye sweetheart." I hung up and looked around the room to see if I forgot anything. I take one last look at the beautiful black velvet box on my dresser and smile to myself.

"I really hope she likes this piece of ICE." The phone rings again.

"Hello"

"Hello big brother, hi son"

"Hi mom hi Nina," Nina spoke.

"We decided to call you on the conference line to wish you the best time on your trip."

"Well thank you I was going to call you guys once I got to Madison's house but I'm glad you called."

"Son, I just wanted to tell you that you have a wonderful wife to be and I love Madison."

"Well momma I haven't_"

"Honey, I know you haven't asked her yet but I know she will say yes and as soon as you two return home Momma is going to cook you two a nice meal at my house alright."

"Momma you don't have to do that."

"Look Cory I know I don't have to do that but I want to do that for you and my new daughter in law."

"Yeah big head, Momma wants to do that. I like Madison she's really sweet when we went shopping the other day she couldn't stop talking about you that girl loves you Cory, I know for a fact she will say yes." My eyes widen I started to shake my head up and down biting my bottom lip.

"Really what she say?"

When the Honeymoon Is Over

"Well we just talked about love and marriage and I asked her would she marry you."

"Well what did she say Nina?"

"Well she said that she would marry you but she didn't want to push the issue."

"Are you telling me the truth girl?"

"Yes, I'm telling you the truth."

"Look your sister and I just wanted to call and tell you that we love you and we know that everything will turn out just fine."

"Thanks ma I appreciate that."

"I know one thing big head you better bring me back something nice." We all laugh.

"I will."

"Most important you have a good time and be safe."

"I will well I have to get out of here so you guys take it easy and hold it down while I'm away I will bring Madison up to visit when we get back."

"Alright you two have fun." We all hung up. I picked up the black box throwing it up in the air and catching it while thinking about what Nina said.

Madison's hair was in micro braids pulled back in a ponytail. She dressed comfortably in her Gucci blue jean sundress and slip in sandals. She wore her Gucci sunglasses and her silver ankle bracelet. Her nails and toes were painted red. She stood at the door waiting for me to arrive. Looking at her watch, as I make my way in the driveway with my music blasting to the sounds of Tray Songzs I pop my trunk. I later step out of the car looking cool as ice with my stone wash Burberry blue jean shorts and tank with my tennis to match. My hair was freshly cut and goatee was in order. The diamonds that dressed my ears were so bright a blind man could see the bling.

"Hey baby you look nice." Madison smiled from ear to ear.

"So do you I don't know if I planned to let you out my sight on that ship because you look so fine." I winked my eye at my beautiful angel that appeared to be standing before me.

"Well, I can say that you look like a diamond yourself, and what is that smell? It smells so nice."

"That's something new my Mary Kay consultant brought me last night she helped me pick out some new fragrances and try some new colors for fun in the sun and believe me I'm ready!"

"I can see that." I said looking her up and down. Madison looks at me and begins to laugh to herself as she grabs her bag.

"Honey, is that all you have?"

"Yes, that's it everything I have is in this bag except my evening gown for the Captain's ball and dinner it's in my room on the bed can you go get it for me."

"Yeah I'll go get it."

"Thank you."

"The phone rings Madison run to pick it up setting her suit case down.

"Hello."

"Hey, girl you ready?"

"Jada honey how are you today? I been so busy I forgot to call you back." Jada voice was light and a little weak from the tubes that lived in her throat for over a month.

"I'm feeling alright I'm still having problems with my back."

"I hear you girl when I come back we have to get together and talk how's Byron?"

"Honey, he is so good to me Madison since I got out the hospital he has been wonderful I see a great change in him. I'm feeling really guilty about_"

"Hold up what did I tell you about that it's in the past so you leave it there alright."

"I know but sometimes I feel really bad about all that because

I was ready to give up on my marriage and I almost died because of it!" Madison takes a seat on the stool in the kitchen as I pick up her bag to put in the car.

"Honey, you didn't die and you must go on and live your life, enjoy the treatment your husband is giving you. It's been three months since you been out the hospital, continue to be happy with your husband and child isn't that what you wanted?"

"Yes, it is but sometimes I still think about Cole and how foolish I_"

"Girl, forget about all that foolishness it's over and he understands because he's a real man and real men are very hard to find these days it's all good sweetie believe me."

I slip behind Madison pulls her braids up and kiss her behind the neck while she finishes her conversation with her friend.

"Well Jada honey I have to jet we have a plane to catch."

"I know but may I speak to Cory for a second I want to thank him for talking to Byron for me."

"Sure and I will be sure to bring you something back from the islands okay."

"You do that smooches."

"Smooches back at ya." She passes the phone to me and run to the back of the house to make sure everything was cut off and that she didn't leave anything behind.

"Hello Jada."

"Well hello Cory, my hubby told me that you were going to ask my friend to marry you on this trip I want to tell you that you don't have anything to worry about she's good people and she loves you very much!"

"Thanks how are you?"

"I'm doing better my legs and back give me problems from time to time but its all gravy."

"Well I hope the pain subside really soon so you can get back to your regular routine."

"Thanks well you two have a bless trip talk to you guys when you get back maybe I can cook you two up something really nice just have lots of fun and think about us not, we will be here when you get back bye."

"Bye Jada and tell Byron I said he better be ready for our game when I get back." Laughing out loud Jada says, "That's if I let him out the house he's been so good to me lately I don't think I want to share him with anyone bye."

"Goodbye."

Madison looks at the ship it was unlike anything she has ever seen. It was huge she pulls out her camera to take a picture. She then saw Tom Joiner getting out of this Black van alone with a couple of people including his wife and another woman and man. She taps me on the shoulder as she points and wave at Tom.

"Cory there he is Mr. Fly jock himself. He's waving at me."

"Honey, you're going to see a lot of celebrities on this cruise so don't get your thong in a knot."

Madison punches me in the shoulder as we walk towards the loading dock. She still couldn't believe how huge the boat was. She knew this trip was going to be a blast! Excitement filled the air as friends join one another and groups of people who haven't seen each other since the last trip.

Madison heard two women behind her talk about me. One woman says,

"I know that's not that super model standing there." The other one said laughing. "Girlfriend that is him he is so fine and he looks better in person."

"That man looks good I tell you I just know he's going to be at the party tonight and I'm going to ask him to dance with a sista."

"You wrong for that because he might be here with someone."

"I don't see him with anyone I been seeing him talk to that

When the Honeymoon Is Over

other brotha that's standing in front of him." Madison smiles to herself as she listens to them talk and lust over me. Finally we reached our goal getting on board the ship.

"You alright miss?"

"Yes, I'm all right how about you?"

"I will be better when we get to our room."

"Me too you know I won a room with a private balcony so I know we're going to enjoy that!"

"I didn't know that"

"I wanted it to be a surprise."

"I like surprises I have to come up with a surprise for you since you surprised me."

I winked my eye at her as we make our way through the crowd. Madison looked around only to see that it was a big hotel on water. The lobby was filled with beautiful paintings and a huge area where people would be able to sit and relax. She saw that the ship had everything from a day spa to a hair and makeup shop. Wal-Mart didn't have anything on this place. This was only the lobby and it was beautiful. Madison and I push our way through the crowd to get to the elevator so we could go to our room as we wait; we both looked at one another and just smiled.

"Attention ladies and gentlemen welcome to the fantastic voyage. I am your captain Marcus Pane we plan to have seven days of entrainment, food, and fun. Right now I would like for you all to get to your room as quickly as possible before we get started with food fun and entrainment we must have a drill. When you get to your deck your stateroom attendant will be there to assistant you with everything, thank you and happy sailing!"

There was a welcome aboard party on the 11th deck at the pool site. There was another Ship across from the Voyage and they set sail first waving goodbye as their music played loud enough for the people on the other ships to hear. Then the music started to play on the voyage and people were full of drinks and having a good time dancing by the pool on the deck watching the waves slam against the boat. It was fun in the sun time. Madison had on her beautiful Red and black two-piece and hip wrap on with her towel hanging over her shoulder. Her braids hang down her back and her drink in her hand watching the sea as we begin to move out of the shipyard. I stood behind her in my black swimsuit boxers and slippers with my drink. Three women stood beside me smiling and giggling like school girls.

"Excuse me aren't you Cory Washington the super model?" One lady asked.

"Yes it's me in the flesh." The other lady smiles and says,

"I can see that." Her friend nudged her in the side and whispered to her.

"Can't you see he is with someone?"

"I apologize, I don't mean to disrespect anyone but your man is fine." Madison smiled and said.

"It's okay I trust him." The ladies smiled and laughed among one another.

"It's good to have a man you can trust these days because a good man especially a good looking one is hard to find." One of the girls said as she bob her head up and down to the music that was playing loudly,

"Well I had to leave that nig I had alone, that's why I took this trip so I can get away."

They all laughed as they danced among themselves drinking their drinks and giving one another high fives. Madison hugged me tightly and said to the ladies.

"I can count myself lucky and say I trust him but I have to say to you ladies that you have to learn to love self before you can love someone else and loving self means you wouldn't do anything to hurt yourself." They all shook their head in agreement. One lady said, "She has a point there and may I add that when you love who you are you choose to be with someone who will treat you right and love you for you, which means dealing with your faults as well." We all smiled and laughed with one another as we set sail

When the Honeymoon Is Over

across the sea and listened to the music with great expectations of having fun in the sun.

───※───

It was the third day on the Voyage and everyday there was something new to do. The excursions on shore were really nice. So far the weather was beautiful the water was clear and the parties were uncontrollable. The people that worked on the ship were more than friendly. Madison was having the time of her life and I was enjoying myself by watching my wife to be.

"Honey, you know it's the captain's dinner and ball tonight." I sit there on the bed watching the game on TV. She looks at the daily planner as she sit on the bed to see what time it was. I begin to kiss Madison on the neck.

"Now you better stop." She laughs as she falls back on the bed in my lap looking up towards me.

"The dinner starts at 6:00 and the ball starts at 10:00 until, this is going to be so much fun! I like dressing up it's going to be like prom all over again." I rub her hair gently as she lay across my lap.

"Madison?"

"What?"

"I love you"

"I love you too babe." The phone rings Madison gets up to answer it.

"Hello."

"Hello girl what's up?"

"Jasmine what's up what you about to do?" Jasmine was someone Madison and I met while sitting at dinner the first night on the ship her husband Raymond and I got to know one another and we been doing things together as couples since the voyage begin.

"Well I'm about to go to the spa and I wanted to know if you would like to come alone so we can look good tonight. I'm going to get a massage and body wrap it's going to be fun!"

"Well___"

"Come on girl you deserve to get out besides were divas." Madison looked at me and winked.

"Yeah I'll go meet me in the lobby in about ten minutes alright."

"Okay cool I'll see you there." Madison hung up the phone and looked at me.

"Where are you and Jasmine going?"

"To the spa"

"Well I hope you two have fun."

"I'm sure we will sweetie"

She grabbed her purse as she heads toward the door. She stopped, turns around and blows me a kiss I send one right back at her and wink my eye.

"Have fun."

"I plan on it."

The spa was full but they finished about 5:30 just in time to go back to the room and get ready for the biggest night on the ship. Madison looks in the mirror as she admires her skin it was just lovely it felt so clean and fresh. She rubs the back of her hand across her cheek to feel how smooth it was.

"Girl my skin feels so smooth." Jasmine rubs her face as well.

"I know don't this make you feel good. I go to the spa at home at least once a month. I started doing that for myself when my first husband and I got a divorce." Madison looked at Jasmine with a surprise expression upon her face.

"Really?"

"Girl yes, my ex was something else I don't talk about it much because Raymond is everything he was not. The difference is Raymond's my soul mate and Ethan was not he was something else girl. Now I hear that he is about to get another divorce. He was rude, selfish and most of all a user. If he didn't get what he wanted he would find ways to make you feel guilty." Madison listen to her new found friend as she spoke about her past issues Jasmine continued.

"Girl, this man would even try to use God." Madison frowned and said, "What do you mean?"

"What I mean is he used God as his cover up. Make people think he was a holy and saved man, whom he wasn't because if he was he wouldn't have treated me the way he did."

"Well do you have any children by this man?"

"Yes, I have one, a little boy his name is Patrick he's ten." Jasmine reaches down in her purse to grab a picture of him. He was a charming little guy his hair was long and pretty. He had some pretty green eyes. Madison couldn't get over his hair and how long it was.

"Girl his hair is so long how do you deal with it?"

"People ask me that all the time he won't let me cut it. At first I was going to cut it but I thought about it, it's his hair and if he wants to look like a girl so be it." They both laugh with one another.

"He doesn't look like a little girl he's a handsome young man and I have a son myself who keeps his hair in twist and it's pretty long but not quite as long as your son's hair." Madison pulls out the picture of him and his little girlfriend Deshay at the dance.

"Girl, he is handsome and she's cute as well they make a nice little match." Madison was very proud of her son.

"Thank you I know were both going to have something on our hands." Jasmine agreed.

"Now that's the truth." They both walked to their deck as they continued to talk with one another.

"Well here is my room I guess we will meet you in about an hour?" Madison said.

"Yeah, we can all walk up there together I'm so excited about tonight it's almost like going to the prom."

"I was telling Cory that earlier. Well I'll see you in a little bit call me when you guys are ready"

"Will do bye"

Madison walked in the room to find me lying across the bed asleep. I felt so peaceful I didn't hear her come in she didn't want to wake me, but she knew she had to do so because it was almost time for us to get ready. She knew I had to be tired because it's been non-stop since we board the ship. Madison crawls in bed beside me and rubs her hand across my face and kisses my forehead. That is when I begin to wake up I breathe deeply.

"Oh hi baby you smell so nice." Madison didn't realize all the natural herbs that were used to make her body scent smell so fresh.

"Thank you I feel so fresh it's almost like cleansing your spirit."

"That's nice; I take it that you and Jasmine had a nice time." Madison eyes brighten like a little girl.

"Yes, we had a wonderful time! I have to do this again. Not just the spa thing but the cruise as well this has been the best vacation ever!"

"You think so?"

"I know so."

We both sit up on the side of the bed as we talk to one another. I could see that Madison was all hyped up about this vacation and so I knew that she wouldn't mind doing this again not a bad idea for a honeymoon.

Raymond and I stood in the lobby dressed in our Michael

Jordan tux. Raymond hair was neatly trimmed in a fade. My hair was cut low, my facial hair was trimmed neatly and we both smelled good. Women passed by giving us that I want you look but of course I only had eyes for Madison. One woman stopped to ask me a question.

"Excuse me, but what is that you have on it smells so good?" I offered her a smile and said politely.

"Prada for Men"

"I have to say it fits you. You both look very handsome." We both smile while standing there with our hands in our pocket. We both answered in unison.

"Thank you"

The bright eyed woman smiled and walked over to her girlfriends that were standing in a corner laughing and giving each other high fives trying not to be loud and ghetto but couldn't help to be heard by Raymond and me as we play it cool. One lady said, "I m going to ask the brotha on the right is he married because he is fine_"

"Well they're both fine." Another lady said, "You ain't going to do a thang but what you doing right now looking and hoping and wishing." They all laugh.

In the meantime Jasmine and Madison take a last look in the mirror alone with fifty other women that stood in the bathroom. Jasmine wore a beaded white dress with spaghetti straps and a split that met her thigh. Her mane was short and sassy. She had on small diamond earrings that fit her round face perfect. Fitting her body like a glove, Madison sported her lovely royal blue, after five beaded attire. Her back was out and the split met her thigh her shoes looked like silver glass slippers that matched the stones in her dress. Her braids were pulled up in a bun with a bang that hung sideways, her makeup was polished and her body scent filled the air with a sweet soft fragrance.

"Girl, our men are standing out there so we better scoop them up before someone else does." Jasmine said.

Madison grinned as she raised one eye bra. "You're absolutely right about that!" They both walk out to see if they could locate their men, there stood groups of people in the lobby with Tux, evening gowns and the mixture of different scents that danced in the air. Madison stretched her neck to see if she could spot them from where she stands.

"I see them over there in the corner." Jasmine stretches her neck to see as well.

"Oh I see let's go." They both walk over, Jasmine puts her hand in Raymond's hand and Madison stands in front of me while everyone talk and admire how one another look. The fly jock walks into the lobby and speaks to everyone as he moves through the crowd. I said,

"I'll be right back."

"Alright but, don't be too long." Madison said with a smile. I walked over to the fly jock and was talking to him for a minute. Jasmine touched Madison on the shoulder.

"What is he talking to him about I wonder?"

"I really don't know they been chatting here and there since we been on the ship."

"Well the doors were open and the crowd started to move into the ball room. Madison, Raymond, and Jasmine started to move as well I caught up with my party.

"Sorry about that I had to chat with Tom for a minute."

As we were seated excitement filled the air. The music was playing; the room was lovely with blue and white balloons. Everyone looked so nice; it's amazing what a tux and a formal gown can do for a person. Tom stepped up to the microphone.

"Hello everyone I would like to welcome you to a night of food, fun and music for everyone. I would like to introduce to you all, the captain of this ship Mr. Marcus Pane." Everyone stood up as the captain walked towards the stage dressed in a white uniform. He was 5'9 light brown with a perfect set of white teeth.

"Good evening ladies and gentlemen, I would like to welcome you all to a night of pleasure. My staff and I have enjoyed serving each and every one of you; it is our duty to make your journey a pleasant one. Tonight I want you all to sit back, relax and enjoy the food, music and entertainment that we have prepared for you. But before we get started I would like for someone in the audience to step up to the microphone and give us blessings over our food."

Everyone looked around no one moved. I looked at Tom and nodded my head. Madison was holding my hand. I looked at her and kissed her hand as I stood up to walk towards the microphone. Madison looked at me with glazed eyes and smiled as I took a stand.

"Hello, my name is Cory Washington." A couple of women in the audience screamed when I said my name, I was a little nervous.

"I would like for everyone to bow their heads as we bless the food." Everyone bowed his or her heads.

"Lord I ask that you bless the food and the people that prepared it in Jesus name we pray amen."

Everyone raised their heads as the short prayer ended. Tom walked towards the stage and patted me on the shoulder.

"Everyone I would like to say that this is my friend Cory Washington for those who don't know who he is, he's actor/super model and have been on the cover of Essence, Ebony and Today's Black woman magazines. I have to say that he believes in education for our black youth and he also has a foundation fund set up for children with cancer. This man wears many hats not only do he set a positive example for our black youth I can say I am well pleased." Everyone clapped Tom asked, "Is there anything you would like to say?"

"Well, Tom since you put me on the spot like that I guess I have to say something." Everyone laughed

"I want to say that I am indeed blessed I come from a strong family background. Thanks to my mother who said to me every day of my life. *Baby you can do all things through Christ who gives you strength.*" "She keeps me in line by teaching me to be a strong black man with Christian values. My mother has been my backbone since I slipped into her womb. And I have to say to you ladies I have much respect for you because you put up with our egos our children our self pride and most of all our selfishness and so often we take you for granted. But remember this; all black men are not the same. As we know that all women are not the same, we must learn to love one another and be each other support through both good and bad. Now I would like to say one last thing and ask a question if I may." I looked over at Tom and smiled. Tom looked at the waiter that was standing in the left hand corner in the back of the room.

"Madison, will you please stand up for me?" She looked puzzled and nervous wondering what I was about to do as she stands at my request.

"Ladies and gentlemen this is a lady of substance, stability, and great strength. I love her for not her beauty but her inner peace she has going on inside, and this is why I know you're my soul mate so now I want to make this thing real between us. I walk down towards Madison and grab her hand and kneel down on my right knee. The room was quiet and all eyes were on us women whisper.

"How lucky she is."

"Madison, you have my rib, I love you with every fiber of my being will you, Madison Courtney do me the honor of being my wife?" Madison eyes met mine as our eyes fill with water. Not a dry eye in the room, both men and women were amazed at what was going on.

"Yes, Cory Washington I will be more than happy to be your wife." I stood up, smiled, and kissed my soon to be bride as the crowd gave us a standing ovation. Madison couldn't stop crying she was shaking all over. I grabbed her hand as we went to our table. The waiter brought us a glass of wine. As Tom raised his glass alone with the multitude of people in the ballroom he said.

"May peace be with you for the rest of your life now drink and be merry." Everyone tilt his or her glasses to drink up. Madison started to drink; she noticed something at the bottom of her glass.

"What is this? Cory looked alone with Jasmine and Raymond. Madison raised her glass to see what was going on in her white wine only to see a big beautiful shiny diamond that sit in the bottom of her glass.

"No you didn't have all this planned." Madison reached over to me and pulled my lips towards hers then she took a drink out of the glass so she could get to the ring. I took the silk napkin that was on the table to wipe off the ring that shined so beautiful and placed it on her beautiful hand.

"It's so beautiful girl."

"Thank you Jasmine."

"Man I wish you the best." Raymond said as he shook his new friend's hand.

"Thanks" Jasmine and Madison hugged and cried together as they look at the ring. I said with laughter.

"Man, I don't know about you two I guess women get all emotional over things like that."

"Man I know when I married this one she cried all the way down the aisle and back up I didn't know if someone was dead or alive_"

"Shut up Raymond you will never figure us out!" We all laugh.

Chapter 33 - - Madison

Cory checked his messages as soon as we got back to his condo.

"Hello Washington this is your agent Kimberly remember me? Give me a call when you get back ASAP call me on my cell if you can't reach me at home alright."

"Hello Cory this is Olivia I was just thinking about you and decided to give you a call when you get in holla at a sista I have so much to tell you."

"I have to get use to you and these women." Cory smiled.

"Baby that's not correct they have to get use to you." He then grabs me and places his arms around my waist and kisses me behind the neck. Then he walked back over to check more messages.

"Hey big bro give me a call ASAP love you I want to hear all about the trip alright, Julius and I are planning one." This next message was from Latisha she sounded as if she was crying.

"Hello Cory this Tisha I really need to talk to you. I had the baby it's a girl I named her Angel Marie I have to say she look just like you. My husband thinks she looks like me but I know better. I can't do this anymore I'm leaving him and I want to raise this child with you can you please call me I will be at my mother's house I'm getting a divorce this time please call me." Cory breathed deeply and hard. He always wanted to hear that. Now her timing was off.

He rubs his goatee as he looks at the phone. I walk over towards Cory and begin to rub his back.

"I will understand if you need some time to think about this." Cory eyes filled with water.

"I have a baby girl name Angel." I raised my right eye bra and shook my head as I cleared my throat.

"Yes, maybe_"

"Madison I need to call Tisha do you understand?" I walked over into the living room and sat down on the couch and picked up the remote to see what was on TV.

"No Cory I don't mind."

For the first time since we have been dating I felt insecure about this situation. He dealt with women all the time and why was this so hard for me now. I felt Tisha had advantage over me because she may have a baby by him and this may cause conflict in our relationship, which I didn't want to happen. I walk out the room because I didn't want to hear what he had to say. I decided to go out on the balcony; the moon was full, the stars were big and bright and the air gently blows across my face, as I sit in the lawn chair. I hear music coming from the condo next door I look over to the next balcony to see Kelly sitting there with a gentleman friend eating. Kelly looks over at me.

"Hi I see you guys made it back." I smiled at her.

"Yes, we did but I'm glad to be back."

"Girl, did you have fun?"

"Yes I had a blast it was wonderful I must go again."

"Where is Cory?"

"He's in the house."

"I'm sorry this is my friend Eric, and this is Madison." I offer him a smile, "it's nice to meet you Eric." Eric looked as if he was Indian and black with his smooth black hair and high cheek bones.

"It's nice to meet you as well." Eric smiled and picked up his plate and walked into the house. Kelly looked at me and winked at her and pointed in the house.

"Girl, this man is so sweet to me. We been dating for about three months and I tell you he keeps me on my toes."

"Girl, I'm so happy for you."

"Thanks, Ethan is not so happy. He wants me back but I won't give him the time of day because he will never have me again."

"I know that's right!"

"We'll tell Cory I said hello, Eric and I are about to go to the movies."

"Well, you two have fun."

"We will, we always do maybe we can do something together."

"Yeah that will be nice bye girl."

"Bye"

Cory continues to talk on the phone with Tisha about the baby.

"So when are you coming to see her?"

"I'm going to see what my schedule looks like in the next week or so I just got back off a cruise."

"Oh really was it nice?"

"Yes it was."

"Glad you had a nice time."

"Maybe we can take Angel on a Disney cruise when she's about two."

"That's not a bad idea but I will be taking her with my wife."

"What?"

"I'm getting married."

"Cory, please! I want to make things right between us."

"Girl there's no us. I will take care of Angel and I want joint custody of her if she's my baby."

"Cory I know you still love me and I still love you_"

"Latisha, listen to me good. I have someone else, and I want to spend the rest of my life with her, so understand that I will take care of my child and I will make sure that you have a decent place for her to live when she's with you but know that I don't want anything with you other than a friendship because of Angel. Is that understood?"

"No I don't understand how you can just cut me out of your life like that?"

"Girl, are you mad? I didn't cut you out you cut me out and it took God above to bring me out of this mess so you better get your life in order so you can be a mother to our daughter."

"Cory you don't have to talk to me like I'm a child I'm a full grown_"

"Well act like it."

"I have to go I don't care if you come or not Angel and I will be just fine."

"Oh you better believe I'm coming because I want blood test and I want to see my baby well I have to go you take care and give the baby a kiss for me, I will call_." Latisha slams the phone down as hard as she could in his ear. He looks at the phone and hangs up. He then walks into the bedroom.

"TV made for women I hope I'm not in trouble." I looked up with a halfhearted smile.

"Why would you be in trouble Guilty of something?" Cory lay across the bed.

"No I'm only guilty of loving you." I pulled the covers over my chest.

"Really?"

"Yes, really I told Latisha that we were getting married and she wasn't too happy about that."

"You told her that?"

"What? I wasn't supposed to tell her?"

"No, it's not that I was just thinking_"

"Honey look I have no secrets when it comes to you. I want you to be my wife and Tisha would have known sooner or later." I smiled.

"Well it feels good to know that." Cory then kissed me on the lips.

"Well since you took your shower before me I guess I'll do the same be right back."

"I guess I left you some hot water."

"You better or I'm coming to get you and make you take a cold one with me."

I rolled my eyes.

"Yeah right," Cory jumped out the bed; went into the bathroom. I started back watching Army wives on lifetime. The phone rings I pick up.

"Hello"

"Hello who is this?"

"Well, who would you like to talk to?"

"I want to know who this is." I started to get frustrated.

"And I said who would you like to talk to?"

"Cory, is he there?"

"Yes, but he is in the shower at the moment would you like to leave a message."

"Yes, you tell him Latisha called and I need him to call me back."

"Well Latisha I will be sure to give him the message."

"You do that!" Tisha hung up. I laughed it off but was concerned because I really don't want any baby mama drama. Seem as if she's going to be hell to deal with. Speaking of baby mamma I needed to call my baby. I pick up the phone to dial Collin's number the phone rings three times.

"Hello"

"Hello, how are you?"

"Hey girl what's up? You had a nice trip?"

"It was wonderful."

"Oh really,"

"Yes, really, where is my baby?"

"He's not a baby anymore he's a pimp."

"What did you say?"

"I'm just playing with you he went to the movies with a couple of his friends."

"Really, I wanted to talk with him but I guess I'll call him back later."

"Collin told me Cory was planning on asking you to marry him."

"How do you know all that?"

"Cory asked Collin first and said not to say anything to you about it. Madison, Cory is a good man and he's good with my son and you're a special woman I know, I will always love you."

"Thank you."

"Collin is having a blast he met so many little friends since he been here. He goes to the boy's club every day. The one thing I did notice he calls that little girl Deshay every day, oh he wants to stay a little longer."

"Collin I don't allow him to be on that phone all hours of the night."

"Woman I got this handled."

"Alright as long as he's okay with staying you know that's my baby."

"Oh woman he is ok."

"Well I will be here for two days tell Jr. to call me at Cory's."

"Will do tell Cory hello for me," We hang up, the phone rings again.

"Hello"

When the Honeymoon Is Over

"Did you tell him to call me or you forgot."

"Look girl I said I was going to tell him you don't have to act like that besides_"

"Look! I don't have to deal with you, but Cory I will deal with__"

"Why are you so ghetto?"

"Ghetto heffa I'm far from ghetto."

"I can't tell by the way your acting I'm trying to keep my cool but you're about to make me come of out a bag on your ass." Cory walks in the room and notice the expression upon my face.

"Baby who are you talking to?"

I looked at him and roll my eyes.

"Look you better get this phone because this girl is about to get a lashing from me." I roll my eyes again as I pass the phone to him.

"Hello Tisha?"

"Yes it's me and you tell your little hooker that____"

"Wait one minute! No need for name calling here that's childish_"

"Childish I'm far from being a child_"

"I can't tell you need to get your business straight life goes on."

"Whatever."

"Now you can make this easy or you can make this hard it's your choice. I think you're going to have it pretty easy if you just go with the flow."

"Maybe I don't want to go with the flow you ever thought about that?"

"It's up to you, now goodnight!" He slams the phone down.

"Baby, I'm sorry."

"Cory I'm sorry too."

"What are you sorry about?"

"Well I'm wondering if this is what our future holds day in and out dealing with her and her bitterness."

"Baby it's going to get better I promise you that."

"How you going to make a promise you know in your heart you can't keep, can you tell me that?" He rubs his chin.

"Maybe your right but we can't allow her to break us so please be patient things will get better."

"I know Cory I just like an easy and carefree life I don't like drama nor do I like confusion. This seems as if it's going to be a difficult__"

"Madison you always find some excuse to bail out when things seem to get hard or too damn difficult for your ass_"

"Wait one minute I know damn well you're not talking to me like that!" I stood up with tears in my eyes.

"Baby I'm sorry forgive me I'm upset because I don't want anything to come between us I am in love with you."

"Cory some time love isn't enough."

"Okay Madison what are you saying?"

"I'm saying that maybe we need time."

"Time for what?"

"Time to think about us," Cory throws his hands up.

"Whatever you want, you know what I'm tired of being tired. I have been played for the last time."

"Honey I haven't played you, Cory what is you talking about?"

"You want out because, you want out baby just say it_"

"That's not it Cory."

"Then what is it?"

"I'm scared!"

I begin to cry uncontrollable. I flop down on the bed and buried my face in the feather pillow." Cory begins to feel uneasy and didn't know what to do because he was feeling the same way.

"Honey please stop crying were suppose to be happy and were allowing this woman to come between us like this please stop."

I look up at Cory with my puffy eyes and red nose.

"I'm sorry but in the morning can you take me home?"

"Sure Madison I will take you home." Nothing was said for the rest of the night.

It's been the longest three weeks ever and missing Cory was a daily thing for me as I guess it was for him but I be damn if I let this break me. I want to call him but refuse to besides, he hasn't bothered to call me so what's the point!

"Hello"

"Hi big brotha I wanted to call and check on you and to see how your trip to California went?"

"It went well and Angel looks just like me. We had the DNA test and so I will know any day now."

"That's good have you heard from Madison?"

"No and I'm not trying to hear from her."

"Brother, look I know you're hurt and I have to say it's going to be _"

"Look Nina I don't want to be rude but I have work to do I have a photo shoot in an hour."

"Ok Cory it's like that? I love you anyway and mamma loves you too." Cory hangs up the phone he sits on the couch drinking a bottle of water when the phone rings again. "Now, who in the hell could this be I don't want to be bothered." So he lets the phone ring and the answering machine picks up.

"Hello Mr. Washington I hate talking into these things but I promised my daughter Solea___" And the woman started to cry. Cory picks up the phone.

"Hello"

"Hello Mr. Washington."

"It's Cory."

"Well I don't know if you remember me but I'm Solea Hampton mother Sharon we met____"

"Yes I remember you how are you?"

"I'm not good at all, Solea wanted me to call you and tell you that she wanted you to speak at her services."

"Services, Sharon I'm so sorry."

"I know my heart hurts I feel alone and broken. Her friends couldn't believe she met you and she wanted to prove to her little friend___" She started to cry all over again.

"Sure Sharon I will be there where?" While sniffing and trying to talk and keep from crying she said.

"At The Fathers House on Rapides you know where that is?"

"Yes, And Sharon you keep your head up ok."

"I will and you take care and Cory may God bless you." Cory hung the phone up this was not good he was stressed and not feeling this at all now this little girl who he thought of often wants him at her services. The doorbell rings.

He goes to the door there stood a woman dressed in a Fed Ex uniform. She was tall dark skin and healthy. Her hair was black and silk it dressed her shoulders. She looks at her clipboard as he stands there looking at her.

"I have a letter for Cory Washington."

"I'm Cory what you need?"

"I need you to sign for this letter." He looked at the woman and gave her a halfhearted smile as he looked at her hand only to see the big fat ring that decorated it. "Sure you have a pen?"

"I sure do sir sign right here." Cory signed and she gave him the letter.

"Thank you Mr. Washington you have a good day."

"You too," he closed the door opened the letter it was from the doctor's office out in California. The test results were in. Cory heart starts to pound as he read through the letter at the bottom the doctor signed the letter. *What this letter means is that you're the father of beautiful baby girl congratulations.*

Chapter 34 - - Jada

These doctor visits simply wear me out! I flop down on the couch and start pulling off my Nikes so I could relax. The house was quiet. Byron hasn't made it home yet and Jordan was with my mother, all I wanted to do was rest on the couch and catch the last of Days of our lives. I manage to get comfortable when the doorbell rings. I get up wondering who could this be holding the handle of the door I asks.

"Who is it?"

"Jada it's me Cole." I slightly open the door. Before I could say a word he holds up some beautiful flowers.

"These are for you."

"Cole I don't_"

"Look Jada I didn't come to make a mess of your life I come to let you know that you were on my mind and that I'm going to continue to pay you and hope you come back to work with me I miss you."

"Cole I don't think that's a good idea."

"Well may I come in at least for a minute I called and asked your husband could I come and see you so I know it's alright he didn't have a problem with that he told me about what time you would be home."

"Cole I can't believe you did that." I open the door wider and looked at the roses. I place them up to my nose as I close my eyes.

"They smell so fresh and they're so beautiful."

"I won't be here long I just wanted to come and see how you were doing."

"I'm doing just fine." I walk into the kitchen.

"Have a seat I'm going to put these in water. Cole looks around her home and admire how clean and well decorated it was, her house smelled fresh and looked as if she put a lot of love into it. He sits down. Jada walks back into the living area.

"So what brings you here?"

"I told you I wanted to see how you were doing everyone in the office miss you and so do I." I smiled "I miss them too but to be honest with you I don't think it's wise for me to come back." Cole looks at his feet as he folds his hands.

"I understand I just wanted you to know you still have a job and that you're welcome to come back at anytime."

"Thanks." Cole raised his head up to look at me with those deep bedroom eyes. "I want to say that I'm sorry for_"

"Look I just want to forget about that night because it caused so many problems I shouldn't have been there." Cole stood up.

"Well I better go I'm glad to see that you're doing okay and you still look good take care of yourself Jada and remember if you change your mind let me know."

I walk him to the door. He gives me a hug goodbye. I close my eyes as we embrace.

"Thank you Cole."

"For what?"

"For closure"

"No, thank you for allowing me to feel something again take care."

I close the door I find myself about to cry not because I felt bad but I felt forgiveness and Cole was a really wonderful man and he could have taken advantage of me that night.

When the Honeymoon Is Over

I wait at the coffee house in Books a Million to meet with Madison. I look at the two students in the corner they seem to be drinking coffee and studying with one another. I thought about my college days and was thinking about going back to school to get my masters. I look at my watch to see that it was six o'clock Madison should be coming any minute. I see someone I knew walk through the door. I walk over to greet her.

"Hello Reagan how are you doing?"

"I'm fine and you?" Reagan was dressed in a black Nike warm up suit with tennis to match she had her hair pulled up in a ponytail.

"Girl I'm blessed thank you."

"We all are blessed I have to say."

"So how you like being married?"

"I love it Jalen is wonderful. I hope he continues to be Mr. Wonderful."

"Well girl let me give you some sista advice. You will have good days and you will have bad days. Just pray that most of your days be good ones." Reagan looks at her watch.

"Yes girl I pray that we have more good ones then bad. I hate to rush but I have to pick up this book on baby development."

"What?"

"Yes, I'm pregnant Jalen wanted to start while we were on our honeymoon and girl I found out yesterday that I was having a baby. I'm so excited I'm planning a dinner for two tonight and I'm going to give him the book as a gift so I have to rush off it was nice seeing you again."

"Girl same here you take care and may God bless you honey."

"Bye"

"Bye" Reagan rushed off through the aisles. I see my best

friend pull up in her car as I look out the window. I stand at the door to greet her.

"Well it's about time it's five after six."

"Girl, don't start." We both walk over to the coffee house and grab a booth. Madison looked tired and sleepy she had on faded blue jeans and a Grambling tee shirt.

"What's going on with you?"

"I'm fine."

"Don't lie to me Madison I haven't talked with you in over a month girl and Cory been over to the house and he look the same way you're looking. What's going on it's obvious you two miss one another." Madison grabs a tissue out of her purse and wipes her eyes.

"I miss him so much_"

"Well what is your problem?"

"I'm scared."

"Scared of what?"

"I guess you can say I'm scared of commitment, more so of getting hurt."

"Girl you need to get real"

"I know but_"

"But what Madison you let Collin get away from you now you're going to let Cory do the same?"

"No"

"You think that being Miss Thang, miss independent is bringing you happiness."

"Jada no I miss Cory so much."

"Well I think you should call him because I know for a fact that he misses you a lot."

"Well he haven't_"

"I don't want to hear it Madison you left him remember I really think you need to contact him. You need to stop allowing things in your past control your future girl."

"What you mean?"

"You think I don't know about the little thing between you and that doctor friend of yours you had while you were in the Air force."

"How you know about him?"

"Well don't you worry about all that, don't allow him to control your future you hear me?"

"Madison looks down as tears fall from her eyes. I reach over to grab my friend's hand.

"Honey I know you put all your trust in that man but, I'm here to share with you that you have to put trust in God and God alone. Now he sent you a man who is wonderful and sweet and someone who loves you more than life itself."

"Thank you."

"Honey, you need to love you now and stop looking back at the past it's over and there's nothing you can do about that now alright?" Madison shakes her head as the tears fall from her eyes more so.

"Thank you Jada you are such a good friend. I been thinking about you so much lately and I didn't feel like calling or being bothered with anyone lately_"

"I know I been there remember. You were there for me so why shouldn't I be there for you; you're my best friend so you better go in the bathroom and get your stuff together because my husband and his friend are coming to meet us here."

"What?"

"I said_"

"I heard you; you mean Cory is coming here to meet us."

"Well not exactly." Madison looked confuse.

"What you mean?"

"Well Cory don't know you're here Byron told him that he wanted him to ride somewhere with him and this is somewhere and we happen to be here so dry your eyes it's your lucky day."

"No Jada I can't do this not today look at me girl I'm a mess and I don't know if he wants to see me."

"Stop the foolishness Madison and go to that bathroom now!" Madison walks to the ladies room to freshen up. Jada spots her husband coming through the crowd of people with Cory in tow. He greets his wife with a smile and hug.

"Hey baby what's up?" She whispers in his ear.

"She's in the bathroom getting herself together." Cory looks around the crowded room and spotted Madison coming towards them.

"Man no that's Madison I can't_"

"Well you can't go anywhere because your riding with me you two need to talk for real so don't be a jackass alright I'm tired of looking at your long face your beginning to depress me ok so talk!" Cory puts his hands in his pockets.

"Hello Cory"

"Hello"

"I didn't know that Jada was setting this up?"

"I didn't either." They both felt awkward.

"Well since we're here we should sit down." I said to Cory and Madison.

"Well were going to leave, Madison when you leave come to my house I have a bed there for you okay you're not going back tonight."

"Okay thanks." Cory look at Byron what about me I don't have my car here?" Madison looked at Byron and said.

"I can take him home."

"Thank you Madison for being so kind." Cory looked at Byron with the evil eye as if he was going to get him later for this. They both wave at their friends as they walk out the door hand in hand.

"I can kill Jada for this."

"I know what you mean." A lady walked over to the table and asks "what would you like to order? Madison looked at Cory.

"I would like to have a vanilla cappuccino." Cory said. "I'll have the same."

"Will this be on one ticket?" Cory answered.

"Yes she will pay for this." They both laughed. The lady walked off.

"So how you been doing?"

"You want an honest answer?"

"No tell me a lie." He smiles.

"Madison I miss you like crazy but I have to understand what it is you may be feeling and baby I have no other choice but to respect your decision that's why I haven't called." "I miss you too and Cory I want to make things right between us and I first have to start with cleaning up my house you know what I mean?"

"No tell me."

"Well I have been alone for so long I really don't know how to be in a relationship."

"I think we were doing okay until_"

"No listen I have some things I have to clear with myself before I can make things right with you and me." Cory relaxes in his seat.

"Oh I see."

"Can you give me some time?" Cory looks at his watch.

"How much time do you need?"

"I'm serious Cory."

"I'm serious too."

"Baby I love you and I want to marry you, not anyone else but you." We been together for a while and I don't want it to seem as if I'm pushing you but I want us to become as one."

"I understand that and I want the same thing and _"

" Well Madison I want you to know from me that I talked with my agent Kim and she wants me to move back to California and so I told her I will because she has some things lined up for me out there. I will be moving there in the next two months and I really don't want to go alone."

"Cory California?"

"Yes LA."

"What about Collin and his daddy? He will miss his daddy."

"Honey I will send Collin to his daddy anytime he wants to see him." Madison takes a deep breath.

"Yes, Cory I will marry you. Well tell me this is Angel your daughter?" The lady came back to the table and gives them there order.

Cory looked at the waitress and said. "Thanks"

"Well is Angel your daughter?"

"Yes she is my daughter I have the test results to prove it." Madison smiles,

"Well, I have to learn to deal with this because she is your flesh and blood." Cory smiles in agreement, "Yes she is and she is an Angel." He then reaches over to grab Madison's hand and gives her a kiss.

Chapter 35 - - Kelly

The doorbell rings Kelly gets up from the couch and answers.

"Who is it?"

"Your neighbor," She slowly opens the door.

"Hi girl what's up?"

"Come on in and have a seat."

"I don't have time to stay I just wanted to see you before we jet."

"You know I'm going to miss you boy."

"I know I'm going to miss you too, where's Eric?"

"He's at work he called me about an hour ago wanting me to meet him for dinner."

"You don't look too happy what's up?"

"I don't know Cory I'm not divorce yet and I'm not really ready to get all serious just yet."

"Who says you have to get serious all you have to do is have some fun."

"Eric is nice and all that but he's getting serious on a sista."

"I want to have fun and all that but this Negro wants to be under me all the time."

"Well take your time just hold on its all good."

"Cory I'm going to miss our little talks."

"Kelly look you can come to California anytime, besides you're a flight attendant you know this and I will be here because my mother and sister are here so you will see me at least twice a year."

"Gee thanks." I smile and give Cory a hug. We both walk to the door and across the hall where Madison and Collin sit in the empty apt.

"Hi Madison" She stood up and embrace me alone with a smile.

"Congratulations and girl I love that new hair cut I can't believe you cut all your hair off but it is so cute on you it goes with your sense of style black woman."

"Thank you I wanted to go natural so here I am you talking about me, I love your Mohawk not everyone can rock that style."

"Girl thanks, I was telling Cory I'm going to miss our talk time."

"I know I will make sure he keeps in contact with you. Besides we have to give you a party."

"A party for what?"

"A celebration of being single and truly loving you girl,"

"Oh I know what you mean. Ethan has been ringing my phone off the hook and wanting to talk. I have nothing for him. He met Eric when he came over without calling and it was nothing nice girl."

"I bet it wasn't"

"He was ugly for awhile called me all kinds of names. I care not to mention but it's all good."

"Well you just hang in there with Eric he seem to be a nice brotha."

"Yes he is I'm taking my time don't need to rush things I'm just loving myself right now!"

"I know exactly what you mean but take time for self but

remember sometimes Love won't let you wait and when the honeymoon is over just start over.

The End

Epilogue

Two Years later

Cory and Madison had a huge wedding in Belize with all their family and friends. Madison and Collin Jr. joined Cory in Beverly Hills California. Madison finally graduated from college with her English degree and started a business as a literary agent for new and unpublished authors while Cory work his way onto the silver screen in his first major role.

Jalen and Regan sold the house and moved back to Atlanta Georgia where they bought a new home not far from Reagan's parents, so they could have help with their new twin boys Caleb and Christian. Jalen still had his club in Alexandria but decided to let Byron run the show and he would fly in every other month to make sure things were good while he run another club in Atlanta called Over the Top.

Kelly is enjoying single life; the best thing that ever happened to her was the divorce because, if it wasn't for the bad she wouldn't know what good felt like. Eric, her new friend was a true gentleman however, she wanted to take time out to love self and see what the future holds. She often talks with Madison and Cory and sees them about every two or three months when she had a trip to California.

Jada finally broke down and told Byron what happened the

night she had her accident needless to say Byron was upset and they decided to get though their problems with prayer and counseling. Jada decided to help Byron out at the club and never went back to work for Cole Sinclair again. They closed the body shop and wanted to put the fire back into their marriage. They had a date night every week and promised to do something once a month just the two of them.

Kobe decided to leave the she devil and give her a divorce. She moved to Dallas and he and his daughter remained in their peaceful environment. Going home from a long day at work was a joy. He remained friends with Jewel and he really enjoyed his time with her. His business was on the rise and he couldn't ask for anything better.